ONCE COLD

(A RILEY PAIGE MYSTERY—BOOK 8)

BLAKE PIERCE

D1495661

BOOKS BY BLAKE PIERCE

RILEY PAIGE MYSTERY SERIES
ONCE GONE (Book #1)
ONCE TAKEN (Book #2)
ONCE CRAVED (Book #3)
ONCE LURED (Book #4)
ONCE HUNTED (Book #5)
ONCE PINED (Book #6)
ONCE FORSAKEN (Book #7)
ONCE COLD (Book #8)
ONCE STALKED (Book #9)

MACKENZIE WHITE MYSTERY SERIES
BEFORE HE KILLS (Book #1)
BEFORE HE SEES (Book #2)
BEFORE HE COVETS (Book #3)
BEFORE HE TAKES (Book #4)
BEFORE HE NEEDS (Book #5)
BEFORE HE FEELS (Book #6)

AVERY BLACK MYSTERY SERIES
CAUSE TO KILL (Book #1)
CAUSE TO RUN (Book #2)
CAUSE TO HIDE (Book #3)
CAUSE TO FEAR (Book #4)

KERI LOCKE MYSTERY SERIES
A TRACE OF DEATH (Book #1)
A TRACE OF MUDER (Book #2)
A TRACE OF VICE (Book #3)

PROLOGUE

The man walked into the Patom Lounge and found himself surrounded by a thick haze of cigarette smoke. The lights were dim, an old heavy metal tune blared over the speakers, and already he could feel his impatience.

The place was too hot, too crowded. He flinched as beside him a short cheer arose; he turned to see a dart game being played by five drunks. Beside them there was a lively pool game going on. The sooner he got out of here, the better.

He looked around the room for only a few seconds before his eyes lighted upon a young woman sitting at the bar.

She had a cute face and a boyish haircut. She was just a little too well dressed for a dive like this.

She'll do just fine, the man thought.

He walked over to the bar, sat on the stool beside her, and smiled.

"What's your name?" he asked.

He realized that he couldn't hear his own voice over the general din.

She looked at him, smiled back, pointed to her ears, and shook her head.

He repeated his question louder, moving his lips in an exaggerated manner.

She leaned close to him. Nearly yelling, she said, "Tilda. What's yours?"

"Michael," he said, not very loudly.

It wasn't his real name, of course, but that probably didn't even matter. He doubted that she could hear him. She didn't seem to care.

He looked at her drink, which was almost empty. It looked like a margarita. He pointed to the glass and said very loudly, "Care for another?"

Still smiling, the woman named Tilda shook her head no.

But she wasn't brushing him off. He felt sure of that. Was it time for a bold move?

He reached for a cocktail napkin and took a pen out of his shirt pocket.

He wrote on the cocktail napkin …

1

Care to go somewhere else?

She looked at the message. Her smile broadened. She hesitated for a moment, but he sensed that she was here looking for a thrill. And she seemed pleased to have found one.

Finally, to his delight, she nodded.

Before they left, he picked up a matchbook with the name of the bar.

He would need it later.

He helped her into her coat and they walked outside. The cool spring air and sudden quiet was startling after the noise and heat.

"Wow," she said as she walked along with him. "I almost went deaf in there."

"I take it you don't hang out there a lot," he said.

"No," she said.

She didn't elaborate, but he was sure that this was the first time she'd ever been to the Patom Lounge.

"Me neither," he said. "What a dive."

"You can say that again."

"What a dive," he said.

They both laughed.

"That's my car over there," he said, pointing. "Where would you like to go?"

She hesitated again.

Then, with an impish twinkle in her eye, she said, "Surprise me."

Now he knew that his earlier guess was correct. She really had come here looking for a thrill.

Well, so had he.

He opened the passenger door of his car, and she climbed inside. He got behind the wheel and started to drive.

"Where are we going?" she asked.

With a smile and a wink, he replied, "You said to surprise you."

She laughed. Her laughter sounded nervous but pleased.

"I take it you live here in Greybull," he said.

"Born and bred," she said. "I don't think I've seen you before. Do you live somewhere around here?"

"Not far away," he said.

She laughed again.

"What brings you to this boring little town?"

"Business."

2

She looked at him with a curious expression. But she didn't press the issue. Apparently she wasn't very interested in getting to know him. That suited his purposes just fine.

He pulled into the parking lot of a dingy little motel called the Maberly Inn. He parked in front of room 34.

"I've already rented this room," he said.

She said nothing.

Then, after a short silence, he asked, "Is this OK with you?"

She nodded a little nervously.

They went into the room together. She looked around. The room had a musty, disagreeable odor, and the walls were decorated with ugly paintings.

She walked to the bed and pressed her hand on the mattress, checking its firmness.

Was she displeased with the room?

He wasn't sure.

The gesture made him angry—furiously angry.

He didn't know why, but something inside him snapped.

Normally he wouldn't strike until he had her naked on the bed. But now he couldn't help himself.

As she turned around to head for the bathroom, he blocked her way.

Her eyes widened with alarm.

Before she could react further, he pushed her backward onto the bed.

She thrashed about, but he was much stronger than she was.

She tried to scream, but before she could, he grabbed a pillow and pressed it onto her face.

Soon, he knew, it would all be over.

CHAPTER ONE

Suddenly, the lights snapped on in the lecture hall, and Agent Lucy Vargas's eyes hurt from the glare.

The students sitting around her started murmuring softly. Lucy's mind had been focused deeply in the exercise—to imagine a real murder from the killer's point of view—and it was hard to snap back.

"OK, let's talk about what you saw," the instructor said.

The instructor was none other than Lucy's mentor, Special Agent Riley Paige.

Lucy wasn't actually a student in the class, which was for FBI Academy cadets. She was just sitting in today, as she did from time to time. She was still fairly new to the BAU, and she found Riley Paige to be a source of limitless inspiration and information. She took every opportunity she could to learn from her—and also to work with her.

Agent Paige had given the students details of a murder case that had gone cold some twenty-five years ago. Three young women had been killed in central Virginia. The killer had been nicknamed the "Matchbook Killer," because he left matchbooks with the victims' bodies. The matchbooks were from bars in a general area near Richmond. He'd also left napkins imprinted with the names of the motels where the women had been killed. Even so, investigating those places had not brought any breaks in the case.

Agent Paige had told the students to use their imaginations to recreate one of the murders.

"Let your imagination loose," Agent Paige had said before they started. *"Visualize lots of details. Don't worry about getting the little things right. But try to get the big picture right—the atmosphere, the mood, the setting."*

Then she'd turned out the lights for ten minutes.

Now that the lights were on again, Agent Paige walked back and forth in front of the lecture hall.

She said, "First of all, tell me a little about the Patom Lounge. What was it like?"

A hand shot up in the middle of the hall. Agent Paige called on the male student.

"The place wasn't exactly elegant, but it was trying to look more classy than it was," he said. "Dimly lit booths along the walls. Some kind of soft upholstery everywhere—suede, maybe."

Lucy felt puzzled. She hadn't pictured the bar as looking anything like this at all.

Agent Paige smiled a little. She didn't tell the student whether he was right or not.

"Anything else?" Agent Paige asked.

"There was music, playing low," another student said. "Jazz, maybe."

But Lucy distinctly remembered imagining the din of '70s and '80s hard rock tunes.

Had she gotten everything wrong?

Agent Paige asked, "What about the Maberly Inn? What was it like?"

A female student held up her hand, and Agent Paige picked her.

"Kind of quaint, and nice as motels go," the young woman said. "And pretty old. Dating to before most of the really commercial motel chain franchises came along."

Another student spoke up.

"That sounds right to me."

Other students voiced their agreement.

Again, Lucy was struck by how differently she'd pictured the place.

Agent Paige smiled a little.

"How many of you share these general impressions—both of the bar and the motel?"

Most of the students raised their hands.

Lucy was starting to feel a little awkward now.

"Try to get the big picture right," Agent Paige had told them.

Had Lucy blown the whole exercise?

Had everyone in the class gotten things right except her?

Then Agent Paige brought up some images on the screen in front of the classroom.

First came a cluster of photographs of the Patom Lounge—a night shot from outside with a neon sign glowing in the window, and several other photos from inside.

"This is the bar," Agent Paige said. "Or at least this is how it looked back around the time of the murders. I'm not sure what it looks like now—or if it's even there."

Lucy felt relieved. It looked much like she had imagined it—a rundown dive with cheaply paneled walls and fake leather upholstery. It even had a couple of pool tables and a dartboard, just like she'd supposed. And even in the pictures, one could see a thick haze of cigarette smoke.

The students gaped in surprise.

"Now let's take a look at the Maberly Inn," Agent Paige said.

More photos appeared. The motel looked every bit as sleazy as Lucy had imagined it—not very old, but nevertheless in bad repair.

Agent Paige chuckled a little.

"Something seems to be a little off here," she said.

The classroom laughed nervously in agreement.

"Why did you visualize the scenes like you did?" Agent Paige asked.

She called on a young woman who held up her hand.

"Well, you told us that the killer first approached the victim in a bar," she said. "That spells 'singles bar' for me. Kind of cheesy, but at least trying to look classy. I just didn't get an image of some working-class dive."

Another student said, "Same with the motel. Wouldn't the killer take her to a place that looked nicer, if only to trick her?"

Lucy was smiling broadly now.

Now I get it, she thought.

Agent Paige noticed her smile and smiled back.

She said, "Agent Vargas, where did so many of us go wrong?"

Lucy said, "Everybody forgot to take into account the victim's age. Tilda Steen was just twenty years old. Women who go to singles bars are typically older, in their thirties or middle-aged, often divorced. That's why you've visualized the bar wrong."

Agent Paige nodded in agreement.

"Go on," she said.

Lucy thought for a moment.

"You said she came from a fairly solid middle-class family in an ordinary little town. Judging from the picture you showed us earlier, she was attractive, and I doubt that she had trouble getting dates. So why did she let herself get picked up in a dive like the Patom Lounge? My guess is she was bored. She deliberately went someplace that might be a little dangerous."

And she found more danger than she'd bargained for, Lucy thought.

But she didn't say so aloud.

"What can we all learn from what just happened?" Agent Paige asked the class.

A male student raised his hand and said, "When you're mentally reconstructing a crime, be sure to factor in every bit of information you've got. Don't leave anything out."

6

Agent Paige looked pleased.

"That's right," she said. "A detective has to have a vivid imagination, has to be able to get into a killer's mind. But that's a tricky business. Just overlooking a single detail can throw you way off. It can make the difference between solving the case and not solving it at all."

Agent Paige paused, then added, "And this case never did get solved. Whether it ever will … well, it's doubtful. After twenty-five years, the trail's gone pretty cold. A man killed three young women—and there's a good chance he's still out there."

Agent Paige let her words sink in for a moment.

"That's all for today," she finally said. "You know what you're supposed to read for the next class."

The students left the lecture hall. Lucy decided to stay for a few moments and chat with her mentor.

Agent Paige smiled at her and said, "You did some pretty good detective work just now."

"Thanks," Lucy said.

She was very pleased. The slightest bit of praise from Riley Paige meant a great deal to her.

Then Agent Paige said, "But now I want you to try something a little more advanced. Shut your eyes."

Lucy did so. In a low, steady voice, Agent Paige gave her more details.

"After he killed Tilda Steen, the murderer buried her in a shallow grave. Can you describe for me how that happened?"

As she'd been doing during the exercise, Lucy tried to slip into the murderer's mind.

"He left the body lying on the bed, then stepped out of the motel room door," Lucy said aloud. "He looked carefully around. He didn't see anybody. So he took her body out to his car and dumped it in the back seat. Then he drove to a wooded area. Some place that he knew pretty well, but not very close to the crime scene."

"Go on," Agent Page said.

Her eyes still closed, Lucy could feel the killer's methodical coldness.

"He stopped the car where it wouldn't be easy to see. Then he got a shovel out of his trunk."

Lucy felt stumped for a moment.

It was night, so how would the killer find his way into the woods?

It wouldn't be easy to carry a flashlight, a shovel, and a corpse.

"Was it a moonlit night?" Lucy asked.

"It was," Agent Paige said.

Lucy felt encouraged.

"He picked up the shovel with one hand and slung the body over his shoulder with the other. He trudged off into the woods. He kept going until he found a faraway place where he was sure nobody ever went."

"A faraway place?" Agent Paige asked, interrupting Lucy's reverie.

"Definitely," Lucy said.

"Open your eyes."

Lucy did so. Agent Paige was packing up her briefcase to go.

She said, "Actually, the killer took the body to the woods right across the highway from the motel. He only carried Tilda's body a few yards into the thicket. He could easily have seen car lights from the highway, and he probably used the light from a street lamp to bury Tilda. And he buried her carelessly, covering her more with rocks than earth. A passing bicyclist noticed the smell a few days later and called the cops. The body was easy to find."

Lucy's mouth dropped open with surprise.

"Why didn't he go to more trouble to hide the murder?" she asked. "I don't understand."

Shutting her briefcase, Agent Paige frowned ruefully.

"I don't either," she said. "Nobody does."

Agent Paige picked up her briefcase and left the lecture hall.

As Lucy watched her leave, she detected an attitude of bitterness and disappointment in Agent Paige's stride.

Clearly, as detached as Agent Paige tried to seem, this cold case still was tormenting her.

CHAPTER TWO

Over dinner that evening, Riley Paige couldn't get the "Matchbook Killer" out of her mind. She had used that cold case as an example for her class because she knew she'd be hearing about it again soon.

Riley tried to concentrate on the delicious Guatemalan stew that Gabriela had prepared for them. Their live-in housekeeper and general helper was a wonderful cook. Riley hoped that Gabriela wouldn't notice that she was having trouble enjoying dinner tonight. But of course, the girls did notice.

"What's the matter, Mom?" asked April, Riley's fifteen-year-old daughter.

"Is something wrong?" asked Jilly, the thirteen-year-old girl that Riley was hoping to adopt.

From her seat on the other side of the table, Gabriela also gazed at Riley with concern.

Riley didn't know what to say. The truth was, she knew that she was going to get a fresh reminder of the Matchbook Killer tomorrow—a phone call that she got every year. There was no point in trying to put it out of her mind.

But she didn't like bringing her work home to the family. Sometimes, despite all her best efforts, she had even put her loved ones in terrible danger.

"It's nothing," she said.

The four of them ate quietly for a few moments.

Finally April said, "It's Dad, isn't it? It bothers you that he's not home again this evening."

The question took Riley a bit by surprise. Her husband's recent absences from the household had been troubling her lately. She and Ryan had gone to a lot of effort to reconcile, even after a painful divorce. Now their progress seemed to be crumbling, and Ryan had been spending more and more time at his own house.

But Ryan hadn't been on her mind at all right now.

What did that say about her?

Was she getting numb to her failing relationship?

Had she just given up?

Her three dinner companions were still looking at her, waiting for her to say something.

"It's a case," Riley said. "It always nags at me this time of year."

9

Jilly's eyes widened with excitement.

"Tell us about it!" she said.

Riley wondered how much she should tell the kids. She didn't want to describe the murder details to her family.

"It's a cold case," she said. "A series of murders that neither the local police nor the FBI were able to solve. I've been trying to crack it for years."

Jilly was bouncing in her chair.

"How are you going to solve it?"

The question stung Riley a little.

Of course, Jilly didn't mean to be hurtful—quite the opposite. The younger girl was proud to have a law enforcement agent for a parent. And she still had the idea that Riley was some kind of superhero who couldn't ever fail.

Riley held back a sigh.

Maybe it's time to tell her that I don't always catch the bad guys, she thought.

But Riley just said, "I don't know."

It was the simple, honest truth.

But there was one thing Riley did know.

The twenty-fifth anniversary of Tilda Steen's death was coming up tomorrow, and she wouldn't be able to get it out of her mind any time soon.

To Riley's relief, the conversation at the table turned to Gabriela's delicious dinner. The stout Guatemalan woman and the girls all started speaking in Spanish, and Riley had trouble following all that was said.

But that was OK. April and Jilly were both studying Spanish, and April was getting to be quite fluent. Jilly was still struggling with the language, but Gabriela and April were helping her to learn it.

Riley smiled as she watched and listened.

Jilly looks well, she thought.

She was a dark-skinned, skinny girl—but hardly the desperate waif Riley had rescued from the streets of Phoenix a few months ago. She was hearty and healthy, and she seemed to be adjusting well to her new life with Riley and her family.

And April was proving to be a perfect big sister. She was recovering well from the traumas she had been through.

Sometimes when she looked at April, Riley felt that she was looking in a mirror—a mirror that showed her own teenage self from many years ago. April had Riley's hazel eyes and dark hair, though none of Riley's touches of gray.

Riley felt a warm glow of reassurance.

Maybe I'm doing a pretty good job as a parent, she thought.

But the glow faded quickly.

The mysterious Matchbook Killer was still lurking around the edges of her mind.

*

After dinner, Riley went up to her bedroom and office. She sat down at her computer and took a few deep breaths, trying to relax. But the task that awaited her was somehow unnerving.

It seemed ridiculous for her to feel this way. After all, she had hunted and fought dozens of dangerous killers over the years. Her own life had been threatened more times than she could count.

Just talking to my sister shouldn't get to me like this, she thought.

But she hadn't seen Wendy in … how many years had it been?

Not since Riley had been a little girl, anyway. Wendy had gotten back in touch after their father had died. They had talked on the phone, mulling over the possibility of getting together in person. But Wendy lived far away in Des Moines, Iowa, and they hadn't been able to work out the details. So they'd finally agreed on this time for a video chat.

To prepare herself, Riley looked at a framed picture that was sitting on her desk. She had found it among her father's belongings after his death. It showed Riley, Wendy, and their mother. Riley looked like she was about four, and Wendy must have been in her teens.

Both girls and their mother looked happy.

Riley couldn't remember when or where the picture had been taken.

And she certainly couldn't remember her family ever being happy.

Her hands cold and shaking, she typed Wendy's video address on her keyboard.

The woman who appeared on the screen might as well have been a perfect stranger.

"Hi, Wendy," Riley said shyly.

"Hi," Wendy replied.

They sat staring at each other dumbly for a few awkward moments.

Riley knew that Wendy was about fifty, some ten years older than her. She seemed to wear her years pretty well. She was a bit heavyset and looked thoroughly conventional. Her hair didn't appear to be graying like Riley's. But Riley doubted that it was her natural color.

Riley glanced back and forth between the picture and Wendy's face. She noticed that Wendy looked a little like their mother. Riley knew that she looked more like their father. She wasn't especially proud of the resemblance.

"Well," Wendy finally said to break the silence. "What have you been up to ... during the last few decades?"

Riley and Wendy both laughed a little. Even their laughter felt strained and awkward.

Wendy asked, "Are you married?"

Riley sighed aloud. How could she explain what was going on between her and Ryan when she didn't even know herself?

She said, "Well, as the kids say these days, 'It's complicated.' And I do mean *really* complicated."

There was a bit more nervous laughter.

"And you?" Riley asked.

Wendy seemed to be starting to relax a little.

"Loren and I are coming up on our twenty-fifth anniversary. We're both pharmacists, and we own our own drugstore. Loren inherited it from his father. We've got three kids. The youngest, Barton, is away at college. Thora and Parish are both married and on their own. I guess that makes Loren and me your classic empty-nesters."

Riley felt a strange pang of melancholy.

Wendy's life had been nothing at all like hers. In fact, Wendy's life had apparently been completely normal.

Just as she had with April over dinner, she again had the feeling of looking in the mirror.

Except this mirror wasn't of her past.

It was of a future self—someone she once might have become, but now would never, ever be.

"What about you?" Wendy asked. "Any kids?"

Again, Riley felt tempted to say ...

"It's complicated."

Instead, she said, "Two. I've got a fifteen-year-old, April. And I'm in the process of adopting another—Jilly, who's thirteen."

"Adoption! More people should do that. Good for you."

Riley didn't feel like she deserved to be congratulated at the moment. She might feel better if she could be sure that Jilly would grow up in a two-parent family. Right now, that issue was in doubt. But Riley decided not to go into all that with Wendy.

Instead, there was some business she needed to discuss with her sister.

And she was afraid it might be awkward.

"Wendy, you know that Daddy left me his cabin in his will," she said.

Wendy nodded.

"I know," she said. "You sent me some pictures. It looks like a nice place."

The words were a bit jarring …

"… a nice place."

Riley had been there a few times—most recently after her father died. But her memories of it were far from pleasant. Her father had bought it when he retired as a US Marine colonel. Riley remembered it as the home of a lonely, mean old man who hated just about everybody—and a man that just about everybody hated in return. The last time Riley had seen him alive, they had actually come to blows.

"I think it was a mistake," she said.

"What was?"

"Leaving the cabin to me. It was wrong for him to do that. It should have gone to you."

Wendy looked genuinely surprised.

"Why?" she asked.

Riley felt all kinds of ugly emotions welling up inside her. She cleared her throat.

"Because you were with him at the end, when he was in hospice. You took care of him. You even took care of everything afterwards—his funeral and all the legal stuff. I wasn't there. I—"

She almost choked on her next words.

"I don't think I could have done that. Things weren't good between us."

Wendy smiled sadly.

"Things weren't good between him and me either."

Riley knew it was true. Poor Wendy—Daddy had beaten her regularly until at last she ran away for good at the age of fifteen. And yet Wendy had shown the decency to take care of Daddy at the end.

Riley had done no such thing, and she couldn't help feeling guilty about it.

Riley said, "I don't know what the cabin is worth. It must be worth something. I want you to have it."

Wendy's eyes widened. She looked alarmed.

"No," she said.

The bluntness of her reply startled Riley.

"Why not?" Riley asked.

"I just can't. I don't want it. I want to forget all about him."

Riley knew just how she felt. She felt the same way.

Wendy added, "You should just sell it. Keep the money. I want you to."

Riley didn't know what to say.

Fortunately, Wendy changed the subject.

"Before he died, Dad told me you were a BAU agent. How long have you been doing that kind of work?"

"About twenty years," Riley said.

"Well. I think Dad was proud of you."

A bitter chuckle rose up in Riley's throat.

"No, he wasn't," she said.

"How do you know?"

"Oh, he let me know. He had his own way of communicating things like that."

Wendy sighed.

"I suppose he did," Wendy said.

An awkward silence fell. Riley wondered what they should talk about. After all, they'd barely spoken for many years. Should they try again to figure out how to get together in person? Riley couldn't imagine traveling to Des Moines just to see this stranger named Wendy. And she was sure Wendy felt the same way about coming to Fredericksburg.

After all, what could they possibly have in common?

At that moment, Riley's desk phone rang. She was grateful for the interruption.

"I'd better get that," Riley said.

"I understand," Wendy said. "Thanks for getting in touch."

"Thank *you*," Riley said.

They ended the call and Riley answered her phone. Riley said hello, then heard a confused-sounding woman's voice.

"Hello … who's speaking?"

"Who's calling?" Riley asked.

A silence fell.

"Is … is Ryan at home?" the woman asked.

Her words sounded slurred now. Riley felt pretty sure the

woman was drunk.

"No," Riley said. She hesitated for a moment. After all, she told herself, it could be a client of Ryan's. But she knew it wasn't. The situation was all too familiar.

Riley said, "Don't call this number again."

She hung up.

She bristled with anger.

It's starting all over again, she thought.

She dialed up Ryan's home phone number.

CHAPTER THREE

When Ryan answered the phone, Riley wasted no time getting to the point.

"Are you seeing someone else, Ryan?" she asked.

"Why?"

"A woman called here asking for you."

Ryan hesitated before asking, "Did you get her name?"

"No. I hung up."

"I wish you hadn't. She might have been a client."

"She was drunk, Ryan. And it was personal. I could hear it in her voice."

Ryan didn't seem to know what to say.

Riley repeated her question, "Are you seeing someone else?"

"I—I'm sorry," Ryan stammered. "I don't know how she got your number. It must have been some kind of mistake."

Oh, there's been a mistake, all right, Riley thought.

"You're not answering my question," she said.

Ryan was starting to sound angry now.

"What if I *am* seeing someone else? Riley, we never made any agreement to be exclusive."

Riley was stunned. No, she couldn't remember them making any such agreement. But even so ...

"I just assumed—" she began.

"Maybe you assumed too much," Ryan interrupted.

Riley tried to fight down her temper.

"What's her name?" she asked.

"Lina."

"Is it serious?"

"I don't know."

The phone was shaking in Riley's hand.

She said, "Don't you think it's about time you made up your mind?"

A silence fell.

Finally, Ryan said, "Riley, I've been meaning to talk to you about this. I need some space. This whole family thing—I thought I was ready for it, but I wasn't. I want to enjoy my life. You should take some time to enjoy your life too."

Riley could hear an all-too-familiar tone in his voice.

He's back in playboy mode again, she thought.

He was relishing his new liaison, pulling away from Riley and his family. He'd seemed like a changed man recently—more committed and responsible. She should have realized all along that it wouldn't last. He hadn't changed at all.

"What are you going to do now?" she asked.

Ryan sounded relieved to be getting his feelings out at last.

"Look, this whole thing of going back and forth between your house and mine—it's not really working for me. It feels too temporary. I think I'd better leave."

"April's going to be upset," Riley said.

"I know. But we'll work something out. I'll keep spending time with her. And she'll be OK. She's been through worse."

Ryan's glibness was making Riley angrier by the second. She felt ready to explode.

"And what about Jilly?" Riley said. "She's become very fond of you. She's come to count on you. You help her with lots of things, like her homework. She needs you. She's going through so many changes, and it's hard for her."

There was another pause. Riley knew that Ryan was getting ready to say something she really wasn't going to like.

"Riley, Jilly was your decision. I admire you for it. But I never signed up for it. Somebody else's troubled teenager is too much for me. It's not fair."

For a moment, Riley was too furious to speak.

Ryan was back to thinking about no one's feelings but his own. The whole thing was hopeless.

"Come over here and get your things," she said through clenched teeth. "Be sure to come when the girls are in school. I want everything of yours out of here as soon as possible."

She hung up the phone.

She got up from her desk and paced the room, seething with anger.

She wished she had some outlet for her rage, but there wasn't a thing she could do right now. She was in for a sleepless night of it.

But tomorrow, she could do something to let off steam.

CHAPTER FOUR

Riley knew that an attack was coming, and it was going be up close and sudden. And it could come from anywhere in these labyrinthine spaces. She worked her way carefully along a narrow hallway of the abandoned building.

But memories from last night kept intruding …

"I need some space," Ryan had said.

"This whole family thing—I thought I was ready for it, but I wasn't."

"I want to enjoy my life."

Riley was angry—not just with Ryan, but with herself for letting such thoughts distract her.

Stay focused, she told herself. *You've got a bad guy to take down.*

And the situation was grim. Riley's younger colleague Lucy Vargas had already been wounded. Riley's longtime partner Bill Jeffreys had stayed with Lucy. They were both around a corner behind Riley, holding off approaching shooters. Riley heard a three-round burst from Bill's rifle.

With danger lurking ahead of her, she couldn't look back to see what was happening.

"What's your situation, Bill?" she called out.

Now she heard a series of semiautomatic shots.

"One down, two more to go," Bill called to her. "I'll take these guys out, no problem. And I've got Lucy covered, she'll be OK. You keep your eyes forward. That guy in front is good. Real good."

Bill was right. Riley couldn't see the shooter up ahead, but he'd already hit Lucy, who was an excellent markswoman herself. If Riley didn't take him out, he was likely to kill all three of them.

She kept her M4 carbine raised and ready. She hadn't handled an assault weapon in a long time, so she was still getting used to its bulk and weight.

Before her lay the hallway with all its doors standing open. The shooter could be in any one of those rooms. She was determined to find him, to blow him away before he could do any more damage.

Riley crept along near the wall, moving toward the first doorway. Hoping he was in there, she stood clear of the opening, reached out with the weapon, and fired a three-round burst inside. The gun jerked sharply in her hands. Then she stepped in front of the doorway and fired another three-round burst. This time she pressed the stock against her shoulder, which absorbed the recoil.

She lowered her weapon and saw that the room was empty. She whirled to make sure the hallway was still clear, then stood there for a moment considering her next move. Aside from being dangerous, checking from room to room like this was going to cost precious ammo. But right now, she seemed to have no choice. If the shooter was in one of those rooms, he was poised to kill whoever tried to pass the open doorway.

She paused for a moment to monitor her own physical reactions.

She was agitated, nervous.

Her pulse was pounding.

She was breathing hard and fast.

But was it from adrenaline or anger from last night?

Again she remembered …

"What if I am *seeing someone else?"* Ryan had said.

"Riley, we never made any agreement to be exclusive."

He'd told her the woman's name was Lina.

Riley wondered how old she was.

Probably too young.

Ryan's women were always too young.

Damn it, stop thinking about him! She was reacting like some stupid rookie.

She had to remind herself of who she was. She was Riley Paige, and she was respected and admired.

She had years of training and fieldwork under her belt.

She'd been to hell and back over and over again. She'd taken lives and she'd saved lives. She was always cool in the face of danger.

So how could she let Ryan get to her like this?

She physically shook herself, trying to push the distractions out of her head.

She crept toward the next room, fired a burst around the doorframe, then stepped directly into the doorway and pulled the trigger again.

At that very moment, her rifle jammed.

"Damn," Riley grumbled aloud.

By a stroke of luck, the shooter wasn't in this room either. But she knew that her luck might run out at any second. She put down the M4 and drew her Glock pistol.

Just then, a flash of motion caught her eye. He was there, in that doorway just ahead, his rifle aimed directly at her. Instinctively,

Riley hit the floor and rolled, avoiding his gunfire. Then she came up to a kneeling position and fired three times, bracing herself against the recoil with every round. All three bullets hit the shooter, who fell backward to the floor.

"Got him!" she yelled back at Bill. She watched the figure carefully and saw no sign of life. It was over.

Then Riley stood up and removed her VR helmet with its goggles, headphones, and microphone. The fallen shooter disappeared, along with the maze of hallways. She found herself in a room about the size of a basketball court. Bill was standing nearby, and Lucy was getting to her feet. Bill and Lucy were also taking off their helmets. Like Riley, they were wearing lots of other gear, including straps around their wrists, elbows, knees, and ankles that tracked their movements in the simulation.

Now that her companions weren't simulated puppets, Riley paused for a moment to appreciate their real-life presence. They seemed like an odd pair—one of them mature and solid, the other young and impulsive.

But they were both among her favorite people in the world.

Riley had already worked with Lucy in the field more than once, and she knew that she could count on her. The dark-skinned, dark-eyed young agent always seemed to sparkle from inside, radiating energy and enthusiasm.

By contrast, Bill was Riley's age, and although his forty years were slowing him a little, he was still a topnotch field agent.

He's also still pretty good-looking, she reminded herself.

For a moment she wondered—now that things were tanking between her and Ryan, maybe she and Bill might … ?

But no, she knew that was a terrible idea. In the past, she and Bill had both made clumsy efforts to start something serious, and the results had always been a disaster. Bill was a great partner and an even greater friend. It would be stupid to spoil all that.

"Good work," Bill said to Riley. He was grinning broadly.

"Yeah, you saved my life, Agent Paige," Lucy said, laughing. "I can't believe I let myself get shot, though. I missed that guy when he was right in front of me!"

"That's part of what this system is for," Bill told Lucy, patting her on the back. "Even very experienced agents tend to miss their targets at close range, within ten feet. VR helps you deal with those kinds of problems."

Lucy said, "Well, there's nothing like taking a virtual bullet in the shoulder to teach you that lesson." She rubbed her shoulder, where the equipment had delivered a slight sting to let her know she was hit.

"It's better than a real one," Riley said. "Anyway, I wish you a speedy recovery."

"Thanks!" Lucy said, laughing again. "I'm feeling better already."

Riley holstered the model pistol and picked up the fake assault rifle. She remembered the sharp recoil that she'd felt firing both weapons. And the nonexistent abandoned building had been detailed and vivid.

Even so, Riley felt strangely empty and unsatisfied.

But that certainly wasn't the fault of either Bill or Lucy. And she was grateful that they'd taken some time this morning to join her in this exercise.

"Thanks for agreeing to do this with me," she said. "I guess I needed to blow off some steam."

"Feel better?" Lucy asked.

"Yeah," Riley said.

It wasn't true, but she figured a little lie wouldn't hurt.

"How about the three of us go get a cup of coffee?" Bill asked.

"Sounds great!" Lucy said.

Riley shook her head.

"Not today, thanks. Some other time. You two go ahead."

Bill and Lucy left the huge VR room. For a moment, Riley wondered whether maybe she should go with them after all.

No, I'd be lousy company, she thought.

Ryan's words kept echoing through her mind …

"Riley, Jilly was your decision."

Ryan really had some nerve, turning his back on poor Jilly.

But Riley wasn't angry now. Instead, she felt achingly sad.

But why?

Slowly she realized …

None of it's real.

My whole life, everything's fake.

Her hopes for becoming a family again with Ryan and the kids had just been an illusion.

Just like this damned simulation.

She fell to her knees and started to sob.

It took a few minutes for Riley to pull herself together. Grateful that no one had spotted her collapse, she got to her feet and headed back to her office. As soon as she stepped inside, her desk phone started ringing.

She knew who was calling.
She was expecting it.
And she knew that the conversation wasn't going to be easy.

CHAPTER FIVE

"Hello, Riley," a woman's voice said when Riley picked up the phone.

It was a sweet voice—quavering and feeble with age, but friendly.

"Hello, Paula," Riley said. "How are you?"

The caller sighed.

"Well, you know—today's always hard."

Riley understood. Paula's daughter, Tilda, had been killed on this day twenty-five years ago.

"I hope you don't mind my calling," Paula said.

"Of course not, Paula," Riley assured her.

After all, Riley had initiated their rather peculiar relationship years ago. Riley had never actually worked on the case that included Tilda's murder. She had gotten in touch with the victim's mother long after the case had gone cold.

This annual call between them had been a ritual for years.

Riley still found it strange, having these conversations with someone she'd never met. She didn't even know what Paula looked like. She knew that Paula was sixty-eight now. She had been forty-three, just three years older than Riley, when her daughter was murdered. Riley imagined her as a kindly, gray-haired, grandmotherly figure.

"How is Justin?" Riley asked.

Riley had talked to Paula's husband a couple of times, but had never gotten to know him.

Paula sighed again.

"He passed away last summer."

"I'm sorry," Riley said. "How did it happen?"

"It was sudden, completely out of the blue. It was an aneurysm—or maybe a heart attack. They offered to do an autopsy to determine which it was. I said, 'Why bother?' It wasn't going to bring him back."

Riley felt terrible for the woman. She knew that Tilda had been her only daughter. The loss of her husband couldn't be easy.

"How are you coping?" Riley asked.

"One day at a time," Paula said. "It's lonely here now."

There was a note of almost unbearable sadness in her voice, as if she felt ready to join her husband in death.

Riley found such loneliness hard to imagine. She felt a burst of gratitude to have caring people in her life—April, Gabriela, and now Jilly. Riley had endured fears of losing all of them. April had been seriously endangered more than once.

And of course, there were wonderful old friends, like Bill. He had also faced more than his share of risks.

I won't ever take them for granted, she thought.

"And how about you, dear?" Paula asked.

Maybe that was why Riley felt as though she could talk with Paula about things that she couldn't with most people.

"Well, I'm in the process of adopting a thirteen-year-old girl. That's been an adventure. Oh, and Ryan came back for a while. Then he took off again. Another sweet young thing caught his eye."

"How awful for you!" Paula said. "I was lucky with Justin. He never strayed. And I suppose in the long run he was lucky too. He went quickly, no lingering pain or suffering. I hope when my time comes …"

Paula's voice trailed off.

Riley shuddered.

Paula had lost a daughter to a killer who had never been brought to justice.

Riley had also lost someone to a killer who was never found.

She spoke slowly.

"Paula … I still have flashbacks about it. Nightmares too."

Paula replied in a kindly, caring voice.

"I don't suppose that's surprising. You were little. And you were there when it happened. I was spared what you went through."

That word *spared* startled Riley.

It didn't seem to her that Paula had been *spared* in any way.

True, Paula hadn't been forced to watch her daughter die.

But surely losing one's only child was even worse than what Riley had suffered.

Paula's capacity for selfless empathy always astonished Riley.

Paula kept on speaking in a soothing voice.

"Grief never goes away, I don't suppose. Maybe we shouldn't want it to. What would we become if I forgot Justin or you forgot your mother? I don't ever want to become that hard. As long as I still hurt and grieve, I feel human … and alive. It's a part of who we both are, Riley."

Riley blinked back a tear.

As always, Paula was telling her exactly what she needed to hear.

But as always, it wasn't easy.

Paula continued, "And look at what you've done with your life—protecting others, pursuing justice. Your loss has helped make you who you are—a champion, a good and caring person."

A single sob broke out of Riley's throat.

"Oh, Paula. I wish things didn't have to be like this—for either of us. I wish I could have—"

Paula interrupted.

"Riley, we talk about this every year. My daughter's killer will never be brought to justice. It's nobody's fault, and I don't blame anybody. Least of all you. It was never your case to begin with. It's not your responsibility. Everybody else did the best they could. The best thing you can do is just talk to me. And that makes my life ever so much better."

"I'm sorry about Justin," Riley said.

"Thank you. It means a lot to me."

Riley and Paula agreed to talk again next year, then ended the call.

Riley sat quietly alone in her office.

Talking with Paula was always emotionally difficult, but most of the time it made Riley feel better.

Today Riley only felt worse.

Why was that?

Too much is going wrong, Riley realized.

Today, all the troubles in her life seemed to be linked together.

And somehow, she couldn't help blaming herself for all the loss, for all the pain.

At least she didn't feel like crying anymore. Crying certainly didn't help. Besides, Riley had some routine paperwork to do today. She settled down at her desk and tried to work.

*

Later that afternoon, Riley drove straight from Quantico to Brody Middle School. Jilly was already waiting on the sidewalk when Riley pulled up to the curb.

Jilly jumped into the passenger seat.

"I've been waiting here for fifteen minutes!" she said. "Hurry! We'll be late for the game!"

Riley chuckled a little.

"We're not going to be late," she said. "We're going to be just in time."

Riley drove on toward April's high school.

As she drove, Riley began to worry again.

Had Ryan come to the house during the day to pick up his things?

And when and how was she going to break the news to the girls that he was gone?

"What's the matter?" Jilly asked.

Riley hadn't realized that her face had betrayed her feelings.

"Nothing," she said.

"It's not nothing," Jilly said. "I can tell."

Riley held back a sigh. Like April and Riley herself, Jilly was nothing if not observant.

Should I tell her now? Riley wondered.

No, this wasn't the time. They were on their way to watch April play in a soccer game. She didn't want to ruin the afternoon with bad news.

"It's really nothing," she said.

Riley parked at April's school minutes before the game was to start. She and Jilly headed toward the viewer stands, which were already pretty crowded. Riley realized that maybe Jilly was right— maybe they should have arrived sooner.

"Where can we sit?" Riley asked.

"Up there!" Jilly said, pointing to the top level, where some space was still available. "I'll be able to stand up against the back railing and see everything."

They climbed up the bleachers and took their seats. In a matter of minutes, the game started. April was playing midfield, obviously having a great time. Riley noticed right away that she was an aggressive player.

As they watched, Jilly commented, "April says she wants to really develop her game skills during the next couple of years. Is it true that soccer might get her a college scholarship?"

"If she really works at it," Riley said.

"Wow. That's cool. Maybe I can do that too."

Riley smiled. It was wonderful that Jilly was taking such a positive view of the future. In the life she'd left behind, Jilly had had little to hope for. Her prospects had been grim. She almost certainly wouldn't have finished high school, let alone think about college. A whole world of possibilities was opening up for her.

I guess I do some things right, Riley thought.

As Riley watched, April got inside her defender's position and made a beautiful corner kick that slammed past the opposing goalkeeper. She'd scored the first goal of the game.

Riley leaped to her feet, cheering and clapping.

As she cheered, Riley recognized another girl on the team. It was April's friend Crystal Hildreth. Riley hadn't seen Crystal in quite some time. The sight of the girl stirred up some complicated emotions.

Crystal and her father, Blaine, used to live right next door to Riley and her family.

Blaine was a charming man. Riley had gotten romantically interested in him, and he in her.

But all that ended a few months ago when something terrible happened. Then Blaine and his daughter had moved away.

Riley really, really didn't want to be reminded of those awful events.

She looked around the crowd. Since Crystal was playing, Blaine was surely here somewhere. But at the moment, she couldn't see him.

She hoped she wouldn't have to meet him.

*

Halftime arrived and Jilly ran off to talk to some friends she had spotted.

Riley noticed that she had a text message. It was from Shirley Redding, the real estate agent she had contacted about selling her father's cabin.

It read …

Good news! Call me right away!

Riley made her way out of the stands and dialed the agent's number.

"I've looked into the sale," the woman said. "The property should bring in well over a hundred thousand dollars. Perhaps twice that."

Riley felt a tingle of excitement. That kind of money would be a huge help for the girls' college plans.

Shirley continued, "We need to talk over details. Is now a good time?"

It wasn't, of course, so Riley made arrangements to talk to her tomorrow. Just as she ended the call, she saw someone making his way through the crowd toward her.

Riley recognized him right away. It was Blaine, her former neighbor.

She noticed that the good-looking, smiling man still had a scar on his right cheek.

Riley's heart sank.

Did he blame Riley for that scar?

She couldn't help blaming herself.

CHAPTER SIX

Blaine Hildreth felt a rush of conflicting emotions as he made his way through the crowd. He had spotted Riley Paige when she stood up to cheer. She looked as vital and striking as ever, and he found himself automatically going toward her at the halftime break. Now she was looking back at him as he approached, but he couldn't tell much from her expression.

How did she feel about seeing him?

And how did he feel about seeing her?

Blaine couldn't help flashing back to a traumatic day more than two months ago …

He was sitting in his own living room when he heard a terrible racket next door.

He rushed over to Riley's townhouse and found the front door partially open.

He charged inside and saw what was going on.

A man was attacking April, Riley's daughter. The man had thrown April on the floor, and she was squirming and twisting, beating him with her fists.

Blaine rushed toward them and pulled the attacker off April. He struggled with the man, trying to subdue him.

Blaine was taller than the attacker, but not stronger, and not nearly as agile.

He kept swinging his fists at the man, but most of his blows missed, and the ones that connected made no apparent impact.

Suddenly, the man landed a crashing punch to Blaine's abdomen. The wind exploded out of Blaine's lungs. He buckled over and couldn't breathe.

Then the attacker delivered a swift kick to his face …

… and the world went black.

The next thing Blaine knew, he was in the hospital.

And now, as he was approaching Riley, Blaine was shaking a little from the memory.

He tried to steady himself.

When he reached Riley, he didn't know what to do. Shaking hands seemed a bit ridiculous. Should he give her a hug?

He saw that Riley's face was red with embarrassment. She didn't seem to know what to do either.

"Hi, Blaine," Riley said.

"Hi."

They stood there staring at each other for a moment, then laughed a little at their own awkwardness.

"Both of our girls are playing well today," Riley said.

"Yours especially," Blaine said.

April's goal early in the game had really impressed him.

"Are you here with anybody?" Riley asked.

"No. And you?"

"Just Jilly," Riley said. "You don't know her, I guess. Jilly is … well, it's a long story."

Blaine nodded.

"I've heard about Jilly from my daughter," he said. "Adopting her is really a great thing to do."

Blaine remembered something else Crystal had told him. Riley was trying to get back together with Ryan. Blaine wondered how that was going. Ryan wasn't here at the game, anyway.

Rather shyly, Riley said, "Listen, we're sitting up in the back of the stands. We've got some extra room. Would you like to watch the rest of the game with us?"

Blaine smiled.

"I'd like that," he said.

They made their way to the bleachers and climbed up to the back. A thin young girl smiled as she saw Riley approach. But she didn't look happy when she noticed that Blaine was with her.

"Jilly, this is my friend Blaine," Riley said.

Without saying a word, Jilly got up from the bench and started to walk away.

"Sit with us, Jilly," Riley said.

"I'm going to sit with my friends," Jilly said, pushing past them and continuing down the stairs. "They can squeeze me in."

Riley looked shocked and dismayed.

"I'm sorry," she said to Blaine. "That was very rude."

"It's OK," Blaine said.

Riley sighed as they both sat down.

"No, it's not OK," she said. "A whole lot of things aren't OK. Jilly's mad because I'm sitting with someone who's not Ryan. He had moved back in with us, and she'd gotten very attached to him."

Riley shook her head.

"Now Ryan's moving out again," she said. "I haven't had a chance to tell the girls yet. Or maybe I just haven't found the nerve. They're both going to be crushed."

Blaine felt a little relieved that Ryan wasn't in the picture. He had met Riley's handsome ex-husband a couple of times, and the man's arrogance had put him off. Besides that, he had to admit, he was hoping that Riley was free of romantic relationships.

But he felt also guilty for reacting that way.

The game quickly started again. Both April and Crystal were playing well, and Blaine and Riley cheered from time to time.

But through it all, Blaine kept thinking about the last time he'd seen Riley. It was soon after he returned home from the hospital. He'd knocked on her door to tell her that he and Crystal were moving away. Blaine had given Riley a lame excuse. He'd said that the townhouse was too far from the restaurant that he owned and managed.

He'd also tried to make it sound like the move was no big deal.

"It'll be like nothing has changed," he'd told her.

It wasn't true, of course, and Riley hadn't bought it.

She'd been visibly displeased.

This seemed like as good a time as any to broach the subject.

In a hesitant voice, he said, "Listen, Riley, I'm sorry about how things were the last time I saw you. When I told you we were moving, I mean. I wasn't at my best."

"No need to explain anything," Riley said.

But Blaine felt very differently.

He said, "Look, I think we both know the reason Crystal and I moved."

Riley shrugged.

"Yeah," Riley said. "You were scared for your daughter's safety. I don't blame you, Blaine. I really don't. You were only being sensible."

Blaine didn't know what to say. Riley was right, of course. He'd been scared for Crystal's safety, not his own. He was also scared for Crystal's mental well-being. Blaine's ex-wife, Phoebe, was an abusive alcoholic, and Crystal was still dealing with the emotional scars of that relationship. She didn't need any new traumas in her life.

Riley knew all about Phoebe. She'd actually rescued Crystal from one of Phoebe's drunken rages.

Maybe she really does understand, he thought.

But he couldn't tell how she really felt.

Just then, their daughters' team scored another goal. Blaine and Riley clapped and cheered. They watched the game in silence for a few moments.

Then Riley said, "Blaine, I admit I was disappointed with you when you moved. Maybe even a little angry. I was wrong. It wasn't fair of me. I'm sorry about what happened."

She paused, then continued.

"I felt terrible about what happened to you. And guilty. I still do. Blaine, I—"

For a moment, she seemed to struggle with her thoughts and feelings.

"I can't help but feel that I bring danger to everyone who crosses my path. I hate that about my job. I hate that about myself."

Blaine started to object.

"Riley, you mustn't—"

Riley stopped him.

"It's true, and we both know it. If I were my neighbor, I'd want to move too. At least, as long as I had a teenager in the house."

At that moment, a play went wrong for their daughters' team. Blaine and Riley groaned along with the rest of the home crowd.

Blaine was starting to feel somewhat reassured. Riley sincerely didn't seem to hold his moving against him—at least not anymore.

Could they reawaken the interest they once had for each other?

Blaine gathered up his nerve and said, "Riley, I'd love to treat you and your kids to a dinner at my restaurant. You can bring Gabriela too. She and I could swap Central American recipes."

Riley sat quietly for a moment. She looked almost as if she hadn't heard.

Finally she said, "I don't think so, Blaine. Things are just too complicated right now. Thanks for asking, though."

Blaine felt a pang of disappointment. Not only was Riley turning him down, but she didn't seem to be leaving any future possibilities open.

But there was nothing to be done about it.

He watched the rest of the game with Riley in silence.

*

Riley was still thinking about Blaine over dinner that evening. She wondered if maybe she'd made a mistake. Maybe she should have accepted his invitation. She liked him and missed him.

He'd even invited Gabriela, which was sweet. As a restaurateur, he had appreciated Gabriela's cooking in the past.

And Gabriela had made a typically delicious Guatemalan meal tonight—chicken in onion sauce. The girls were enjoying it and chattering about this afternoon's soccer victory.

"Why didn't you come to the game, Gabriela?" April asked.

"You'd have enjoyed it," Jilly said.

"*Sí*, I enjoy the *futbol*," Gabriela said. "Next time I will come."

This seemed to Riley like a good time to mention something.

"I've got good news," she said. "I talked to my Realtor today, and she thinks that selling your grandfather's cabin should bring in quite a bit of money. It should really help with college plans—for both of you."

The girls were pleased and talked about that for a while. But soon Jilly's mood seemed to darken.

Finally Jilly asked Riley, "Who was that guy at the game with you?"

April said, "Oh, that was Blaine. He used to be our neighbor. He's Crystal's dad. You've met her."

Jilly ate in sullen silence for a few moments.

Then she said, "Where's Ryan? Why wasn't he at the game?"

Riley gulped anxiously. She'd noticed earlier that Ryan had come to the house during the day to take his things. It was time to tell the girls the truth.

"There's something I've been meaning to tell everybody," she began.

But she had trouble finding the right words.

"Ryan ... says he needs some space. He's—"

She couldn't bring herself to say more. She could see by the girls' faces that she didn't need to. They understood all too well what she meant.

After a few seconds of silence, Jilly burst into tears and fled the room, hurrying upstairs. April quickly followed to console her.

Riley realized that April was accustomed to Ryan's on and off attentions. These disappointments must still hurt, but she could handle them better than Jilly could.

Sitting at the table with only Gabriela, Riley started feeling guilty. Was she completely incapable of maintaining a serious relationship with a man?

As if reading her thoughts, Gabriela said, "Stop blaming yourself. It is not your fault. Ryan is a fool."

Riley smiled sadly.

"Thanks, Gabriela," she said.

It was exactly what she needed to hear.

Then Gabriela added, "The girls need a father figure. But not someone who will come and go like that."

"I know," Riley said.

*

Later that evening, Riley looked in on the girls. Jilly was in April's room, silently doing homework.

April looked up and said, "We're OK, Mom."

Riley felt a flood of relief. As sad as she felt for both girls, she was proud that April was comforting Jilly.

"Thank you, sweetheart," she said, and quietly closed the door.

She thought that April would talk to her about Ryan whenever she felt ready. But Jilly might have a harder time of it.

As she went back downstairs, Riley found herself thinking about what Gabriela had said.

"The girls need a father figure."

She looked at the phone. Blaine had made it clear that he would like to get their relationship going again.

But what would he actually expect of her? Her life was packed full with kids and work. Could she really include anyone else in it right now? Would she just disappoint him?

But, she admitted, *I do like him.*

And he clearly liked her. Surely there had to be room in life for…

She picked up the phone and dialed Blaine's home number. She was disappointed to get his answering machine, but not surprised. She knew that his work at the restaurant often kept him away from home at nights.

At the sound of the beep, Riley left a message.

"Hi, Blaine. This is Riley. Listen, I'm sorry if I acted a little distant at the game this afternoon. I hope I didn't seem rude. I just want to say, if your dinner offer still stands, count us in. Give me a call whenever you can to let me know."

Riley immediately felt better. She went to the kitchen and poured herself a drink. As she sat sipping it on the living room couch, she found herself remembering her conversation with Paula Steen.

Paula had seemed at peace with the fact that her daughter's killer would never be brought to justice.

"It's nobody's fault, and I don't blame anybody," Paula had said.

Those words now troubled Riley.

It just seemed so unfair.

Riley finished her drink, took a shower, and went to bed. She'd barely fallen asleep when the nightmares started.

*

Riley was just a little girl.

She was walking through some woods at night. She was scared, but she wasn't sure why.

After all, she wasn't really lost in the woods.

The woods were close to a highway, and she could see cars going back and forth. The glow from a streetlight and a full moon both lit her way among the trees.

Then her eyes fell on a row of three shallow graves.

The dirt and stones that covered the graves were shifting and heaving.

Women's hands clawed their way out of the graves.

She could hear their muffled voices say ...

"Help us! Please!"

"I'm just a little girl!" Riley answered tearfully.

Riley snapped awake in bed. She was trembling.

It's just a nightmare, she told herself.

And it wasn't especially surprising that she'd dream about the Matchbook Killer's victims the night after she'd talked to Paula Steen.

She took several long, deep breaths. Soon she felt relaxed again, and her consciousness started to fade into sleep.

But then ...

She was still just a little girl.

She was in a candy store with Mommy, and Mommy was buying her lots of candy.

A scary man wearing a stocking over his head came toward her.

He pointed a gun at Mommy.

"Give me your money," he told Mommy.

But Mommy was too scared to move.

The man shot Mommy in the chest, and she fell down right in front of Riley.

Riley started screaming. She whirled around looking for someone to help.

But suddenly, she was in the woods again.

35

The women's hands were still groping out of the three graves. The voices were still calling ...

"Help us! Please!"

Then Riley heard another voice beside her. This one sounded familiar ...

"You heard them, Riley. They need your help."

Riley turned and saw Mommy. She was standing right there, her chest bleeding from her bullet wound. Her face was deathly pale.

"I can't help them, Mommy!" Riley cried. "I'm just a little girl!"

Mommy smiled.

"No, you're not just a little girl, Riley. You're all grown up. Turn around and look."

Riley turned and found herself looking into a full-length mirror. It was true.

She was a woman now.

And the voices were still calling out ...

"Help us! Please!"

Riley's eyes snapped open again.

She was shaking even more than before, and gasping for breath.

She remembered something that Paula Steen had said to her.

"My daughter's killer will never be brought to justice."

Paula had also said ...

"It was never your case to begin with."

Riley felt a new sense of determination.

It was true—the Matchbook Killer hadn't been her case before.

But she could no longer leave it to the past.

At long last, the Matchbook Killer had to be brought to justice.

It's my case now, she thought.

CHAPTER SEVEN

Riley had no more nightmares that night, but even so her sleep was restless. Surprisingly, she felt wide awake and energized when she got up the next morning.

She had work to do that day.

She got dressed and went downstairs. April and Jilly were in the kitchen eating a breakfast that Gabriela had made for them. The girls both looked sad, but not as devastated as they'd been yesterday.

Riley saw that a place had been set at the table for her, so she sat down and said, "Those pancakes look wonderful. Pass them over, please."

As she ate her breakfast and drank coffee, the girls began to look more cheerful. They didn't mention Ryan's absence, instead chatting about other kids at school.

They're tough, Riley thought.

And they'd both gotten through their share of tough times before now.

She was sure that they'd pull through this crisis about Ryan as well.

Riley finished her coffee and said, "I do have to get to the office."

She stood up and kissed April on the cheek, and then Jilly.

"Go catch some bad guys, Mom," Jilly said.

Riley smiled.

"I'll be sure to do that, dear," she replied.

*

As soon as she got to her office, Riley opened up computerized files on the twenty-five-year-old case. As she scanned old newspaper stories, she remembered reading some of them when they had first appeared. She'd been a teenager at the time, and the Matchbook Killer had seemed like the stuff that nightmares were made of.

The murders had happened here in Virginia near Richmond, with just three weeks in between each death.

Riley opened up a map and found Greybull, a small town off of Interstate 64. Tilda Steen, the last victim, had lived and died in Greybull. The other two murders had taken place in the towns of

Brinkley and Denison. Riley could see that all the towns lay within about a hundred miles of each other.

Riley closed the map and looked at the newspaper stories again.

One banner headline screamed …

MATCHBOOK KILLER CLAIMS THIRD VICTIM!

She shuddered a little.

Yes, she remembered seeing that headline from many years ago.

The article went on to describe the panic that the murders had struck throughout the area—especially among young women.

According to the article, the public and the police were both asking the same questions:

When and where was the killer going to strike next?

Who was going to be his next victim?

But there had been no fourth victim.

Why? Riley wondered.

It was a question that law enforcement had failed to answer.

The murderer had seemed like a ruthlessly motivated serial killer—the type who was likely to keep right on killing until he was caught. Instead, he had simply disappeared. And his disappearance had been as mysterious as the killings themselves.

Riley began to pore over old police records to refresh her memory.

The victims didn't seem to be connected in any way. The killer had used much the same MO for all three murders. He'd picked up young women in bars, driven them to motels, and killed them. Then he'd buried their bodies in shallow graves not far from the murder scenes.

The local police had had no trouble locating the bars where the victims had been picked up and the motels where they had been killed.

As some serial killers do, he had left clues for the police.

With all of the bodies, he had left matchbooks from the bars and notepaper from the motels.

Witnesses at the bars and motels were even able to give fairly good descriptions of the suspect.

Riley pulled up the composite sketch that had been created years ago.

She saw that the man looked fairly ordinary, with dark brown hair and hazel eyes. As she read witness descriptions, she noticed a few more details. Witnesses had mentioned that he looked strikingly pale, as if he worked at a job that kept him indoors and out of the sun.

The descriptions hadn't been very detailed. Even so, it seemed to Riley as though the case shouldn't have been all that tough to crack. But somehow it had been. The local police never found the killer. The BAU took over the case, only to conclude that the killer had either died or left the area. Continuing the search nationwide would be like looking for a needle in a haystack—a needle that might not even exist.

But there had been one agent, a master at cracking cold cases, who had disagreed.

"He's still in the area," he had told everybody. *"We can find him if we just keep looking."*

But his bosses hadn't believed him, and they wouldn't back him up. The BAU had let the case go cold.

That agent retired from the BAU years ago and moved to Florida. But Riley knew how to get in touch with him.

She reached for her desk phone and dialed his number.

A moment later, she heard a familiar rumbling voice. Jake Crivaro had been her partner and mentor back when she joined the BAU.

"Hello, stranger," Jake said. "Where the hell have you been? What have you been doing with yourself? You don't call, you don't write. Is that any way to treat the lonely, forgotten old buzzard who taught you everything you know?"

Riley smiled. She knew he didn't mean it. After all, they'd seen each other fairly recently. Jake had even come out of retirement to help her with a case just a couple of months ago.

She didn't ask, *"How have you been?"*

She remembered his litany the last time she'd asked.

"I'm seventy-five years old. I've had both knees and a hip replaced. My eyes are shot. I've got a hearing aid and a pacemaker. And all my friends except you have croaked. How do you think I've been?"

Asking him would only get him started complaining all over again.

The truth was, he was still physically spry, and his mind was as sharp as ever.

"I need your help, Jake," Riley said.

"Music to my ears. Retirement stinks. What can I do for you?"

"I'm looking into a cold case."

Jake chuckled a little.

"My favorite kind. You know, cold cases were a specialty of mine back in the day. They still are, as a kind of hobby. Even in retirement, I can collect and review stuff that nobody solved. I'm a regular packrat that way. Do you remember that 'Angel Face' killer in Ohio? I solved that one a couple of years ago. It had been cold for more than a decade."

"I remember," Riley said. "That was some good work for an over-the-hill old codger."

"Flattery will get you everywhere. So what have you got for me?"

Riley hesitated. She knew that she was about to stir up unpleasant memories.

"This case was one of yours, Jake," she said.

Jake fell silent for a moment.

"Don't tell me," he finally said. "The Matchbook Killer case."

Riley almost asked, *"How do you know?"*

But it was easy to guess the answer.

Jake was obsessed with past failures, especially his own. Doubtless he was keenly aware of the anniversary of Tilda Steen's death. He'd probably also noted the anniversaries of the other victims' deaths. Riley guessed that they probably haunted him every year.

"That was before your time," Jake said. "Why do you want to dredge up all that ancient history?"

She heard bitterness in his voice—the same bitterness she remembered hearing from him when she was still a young rookie. He'd been furious with the powers-that-be for shutting the case down. He'd still been bitter when he retired a few years later.

"You know I've been in touch with Tilda Steen's mother over the years," Riley said. "I talked to her just yesterday. This time ..."

She paused. How could she put it into words?

"It hit me harder than usual, I guess. If nobody does anything, the poor woman will die without her daughter's killer getting brought to justice. I don't have any other cases going and I ..."

Her voice trailed off.

"I know just how you feel," Jake said, his voice suddenly sympathetic. "Those three dead women deserved better. Their families deserved better."

Riley felt relieved that Jake shared her feelings.

"I can't do much without BAU support," Riley said. "Do you think there's any way I could reopen the case?"

"I don't know. Maybe. Let's get right to work."

Riley could hear Jake's fingers rattling on his computer keyboard as he brought up his own files.

"What went wrong when you worked on it?" Riley asked.

"What *didn't* go wrong? My theories didn't fit with anybody else's at the BAU. The area was fairly rural back then, just three little small towns. Even so, along an interstate that close to Richmond, there were plenty of transients. The Bureau just decided it must have been some drifter who moved along. My gut told me something different—that he lived in the area and might live there still. But nobody cared what my gut had to say."

While he was typing, he grumbled, "I might have cracked this thing years ago if it weren't for my shit-for-brains partner."

Riley had heard about Jake's incompetent partner, who had been fired before Riley joined the BAU.

She said, "I hear he screwed up almost everything he touched."

"Yeah, literally. In one of the bars, he handled a drinking glass the killer had touched, smeared up the fingerprints but good."

"Weren't there any fingerprints on the napkins or the matchbooks?"

"Not after being covered with dirt in a shallow grave. The guy screwed up royally. He should've been fired right then and there. He didn't last long, though. Last I heard he was working in a convenience store. Good riddance."

Riley heard a pause in Jake's typing. She guessed that he now had all his materials ready at hand.

"OK, now close your eyes," Jake said.

Riley shut her eyes and smiled. He was going to put her through much the same exercise she had taught to her students. She had learned it from him in the first place.

Jake said, "You're the killer, but you haven't killed anybody yet. You just walked into McLaughlin's Pub in Brinkley, and you've just introduced yourself to a girl named Melody Yanovich. You've put some moves on her, and things seem to be going pretty smoothly."

She began to see things from the killer's point of view. The scene playing out clearly in her mind.

Jake said, "There's a little bowl of matchbooks on the bar. In the middle of your pickup, you grab one and pocket it. Why?"

Riley could practically feel the little matchbook between her fingers. She imagined herself tucking it into her shirt pocket.

But why? she wondered.

When the case had been open, there had been a fairly

41

commonsensical theory about that. The killer had left matchbooks from the bars and notepaper from the motels on the victims' bodies to taunt the police.

But now she realized—Jake didn't think so.

And now she didn't either.

She said, "He didn't even know he was going to kill her—at least not when he was in McLaughlin's Pub, not that first time. He picked up the matchbook as a souvenir of his impending conquest, a trophy for the good time he expected to have."

"Good," Jake said. "Then what?"

Riley could clearly visualize the killer helping Melody Yanovich out of his car and escorting her into the motel room.

"Melody was willing, and he was feeling confident. As soon as they got into the room, she went to the bathroom to get ready. Meanwhile, he picked up a piece of notebook paper with the motel logo—for the same reason he'd picked up the matchbook, as a souvenir. Then he took off his clothes and got under the covers. Soon Melody came out of the bathroom ..."

Riley paused to get a clearer picture.

Had the woman been naked right then?

No, not exactly, Riley thought.

"Melody came out with a towel wrapped around her. Right then he started to get uneasy. He'd had trouble performing in the past. Was he going to have that problem again this time? She climbed into bed with him and pulled off the towel and ..."

"And?" Jake coaxed.

"And he knew then and there—he couldn't do it. He was ashamed and humiliated. He couldn't let the woman get away knowing that he'd failed. A burning rage took him over completely. His fury wiped away his humanity. He grabbed her by the throat and strangled her in the bed. She died very quickly. His rage ebbed away, and he realized what he'd done, and he was seized by guilt. And ..."

Riley's mind hurried through the rest of the crime. The killer had not only buried the victims in shallow graves, but he'd put the graves close to streets and highways. He knew perfectly well that the bodies would be found. In fact, he'd made sure of it.

Riley's eyes snapped open.

"I get it, Jake. When he first picked up the matchbooks and pieces of notepaper, he was only collecting souvenirs. But after the murders, he used them for something different. He left them with the bodies to *help* the police, not to taunt them. He wanted to be caught. He didn't have the nerve to turn himself in, so leaving clues was the best he could do."

"You're catching on," Jake said. "My guess is, both of the first two murders played out pretty much exactly that way. Now take a look at the local police summary of the murders."

Riley looked at the report on her computer screen.

"How was the last murder different?" Jake asked.

Riley scanned the text. She didn't notice anything she hadn't known already.

"Tilda Steen was fully clothed when he buried her. It seemed that he hadn't tried to have sex with her at all."

Jake said, "Now tell me what it says about the cause of death for all three victims."

Riley quickly found it in the text.

"Strangulation," she said. "The same for all of them."

Jake grunted with dismay.

"That's where the locals went wrong," he said. "The first two, Melody Yanovich and Portia Quinn, were both definitely strangled. But I found out from the medical examiner—there weren't any bruises on Tilda Steen's neck. She'd been suffocated but not strangled. What does that tell you?"

Riley's brain clicked along, processing this new information.

She closed her eyes again, trying to imagine the scene.

"Something happened when he got Tilda into that motel room," Riley said. "She confided something to him, maybe something she'd never told anybody else. Or maybe she told him something about himself he wanted to hear. She suddenly became …"

Riley paused.

Jake said, "Go ahead. Say it."

"*Human* to him. He felt guilty for what he was *going* to do. And in a twisted way …"

It took Riley a moment to put her thoughts together.

"He decided to kill her as an act of mercy. He didn't strangle her with his hands. He did it more gently. He overpowered her on the bed and suffocated her with a pillow. He felt so remorseful that …"

Riley opened her eyes.

"… he didn't ever kill again."

Jake let out a grunt of approval.

He said, "That was the same conclusion I came to back in the day. I still think it. I believe he's still in that general area, and he's still haunted by what he did all those years ago."

A word started echoing through Riley's mind …

Remorse.

Something suddenly seemed crystal clear to her.

Without stopping to think, she said, "He's still remorseful, Jake. And I'll bet anything he leaves flowers on the women's graves."

Jake chuckled with satisfaction.

"Good thinking," he said. "That's what I always liked about you, Riley. You get the psychology, and you know how to turn it into action."

Riley smiled.

"I learned from the best," she said.

Jake grumbled his thanks for the compliment. She thanked him and ended the call. She sat in her office thinking.

It's up to me.

She had to hunt down the killer and bring him to justice once and for all.

But she knew she couldn't do it alone.

She needed help just getting the BAU to reopen the case.

She rushed out into the hall and headed for Bill Jeffreys' office.

CHAPTER EIGHT

Bill Jeffreys was enjoying an unusually quiet morning at BAU when his partner burst into his office. He immediately recognized the expression on her face. This was how Riley Paige looked when she was excited about a new case.

He gestured toward the chair on the other side of his desk, and Riley sat down. But as he listened attentively to her description of the murders, Bill grew puzzled about her enthusiasm. Even so, he made no comment while she gave him the complete rundown of her phone conversation with Jake.

"So what do you think?" she asked Bill when she finished.

"About what?" Bill asked.

"Do you want to work the case with me?"

Bill squinted with uncertainty.

"Sure, I'd like to, but … well, the case isn't even open. It's out of our hands."

Riley took a deep breath and said cautiously, "I was hoping you and I could fix that."

It took Bill a moment to catch her meaning. Then his eyes widened and he shook his head.

"Oh, no, Riley," he said. "This one is long gone. Meredith isn't going to be interested in opening it up again."

He could see that she also had doubts, but she was trying to hide them.

"We've got to try," she said. "We can solve this case. I know it. Times have changed, Bill. We've got new tools at our disposal. For instance, DNA testing was in its infancy back then. Now things are different. You're not working another case right now, are you?"

"No."

"Neither am I. Why not give it a shot?"

Bill gazed at Riley with concern. In less than a year his partner had been reprimanded, suspended, and even fired. He knew that her career had sometimes hung by a thread. The only thing that had saved her was her uncanny ability to find her prey, sometimes in unorthodox ways. That skill and his occasional covering for her had kept her in the BAU.

"Riley, you're asking for trouble," he said. "Don't rock the boat."

He could see her bristle at that and immediately regretted his choice of words.

"OK, if you don't want to do it," she said, getting up from her chair, turning, and heading for his office door.

*

Riley hated that phrase. *"Don't rock the boat."*

After all, she was a boat-rocker to the core. And she knew perfectly well that it was one of the things that made her a good agent.

She was on her way out of Bill's office when he called, "Wait a minute. Where are you going?"

"Where do you think I'm going?" she called back.

"OK, OK! I'm coming!"

She and Bill hurried down the hall toward the office of Team Chief Brent Meredith. Riley knocked on their boss's door and heard a gruff voice call out, "Come in."

Riley and Bill stepped inside Meredith's spacious office. As always, the team chief cut a daunting presence with his large physique and his black, angular features. He was hunched over his desk poring over reports.

"Make it quick," Meredith said without looking up from his work. "I'm busy."

Riley ignored Bill's worried glance and boldly sat down beside Meredith's desk.

She said, "Chief, Agent Jeffreys and I want to reopen a cold case, and we wondered if—"

Still focused on his papers, Meredith interrupted.

"Nope."

"Huh?" Riley said.

"Request denied. Now if you don't mind, I've got work to do."

Riley stayed seated. She felt momentarily stymied.

Then she said, "I just got off the phone with Jake Crivaro."

Meredith slowly lifted his head and looked at her. A smile formed on his lips.

"How is old Jake?" he asked.

Riley smiled too. She knew that Jake and Meredith had been close friends back during their early days at the BAU.

"He's grouchy," Riley said.

"He always was," Meredith said. "You know, that old bastard could be downright intimidating."

Riley suppressed a chuckle. The very idea that Meredith would find anybody intimidating was rather funny. Riley herself had never

46

been intimidated by Jake at all.

She said, "Yesterday was the twenty-fifth anniversary of the Matchbook Killer's last murder."

Meredith swiveled toward her in his chair, starting to look interested.

"I remember that one," he said. "Jake and I were both field agents back then. He never got over not being able to solve it. We talked about it over drinks a lot."

Meredith folded his hands together and looked at Riley intently.

"So Jake gave you a call about it, eh? He wants to reopen the case, come out of retirement?"

Riley felt a fleeting impulse to lie. Meredith would surely be more open to the idea if he thought it came from Jake. But she just couldn't do it.

"I called him, sir," she said. "But it was already on his mind. It always is this time of year. And we talked through some possibilities."

Meredith leaned back in his chair.

"Tell me what you've got," he said.

She quickly collected her thoughts.

"Jake thinks the killer is still in the general area of the killings," she said. "And I trust Jake's hunches. We think he was consumed by guilt—probably still is. And I had this idea that he might regularly leave flowers on the grave of the last victim, Tilda Steen. So that's something new to check out."

Riley could tell by Meredith's face that he was getting interested.

"That could be a really good lead," he said. "What else have you got?"

"Not much," she said. "Except Jake mentioned a glass that had been picked up as evidence."

Meredith nodded.

"I remember. His idiot rookie partner ruined the fingerprints."

Riley said, "It's probably still in the evidence locker. Maybe we can get some DNA off of it. That wasn't much of an option twenty-five years ago."

"Good," Meredith said. "What else?"

Riley thought for a moment.

"We've got an old composite sketch of the killer," she said. "It's not all that good. But maybe our tech guys could age the picture, come up with some ideas about what he might look like now. I could turn it over to Sam Flores."

Meredith didn't say anything right away.

Then he looked at Bill, who was still standing near the doorway.

"Have you got any cases going, Agent Jeffreys?"

"No."

"Good. I want you to work this case with Paige."

Without another word, Meredith turned his attention back to his reports.

Riley looked at Bill. Like her, he was gaping with surprise.

"When do we start?" Bill asked Meredith

"Five minutes ago," Meredith said, waving them away. "What's the matter with you two? Quite wasting time. Get to work."

Riley and Bill hurried out of the office, excitedly talking about how to get things underway.

CHAPTER NINE

A little while later, Riley was relaxing as Bill drove the FBI car to the town of Greybull, where Tilda Steen had been killed. Riley felt good to be working on a new case, especially one of her own choosing.

It was a warm, sunny day. She felt as though her troubles and anxieties were fading behind her. Now that she had time to clear her head, Riley was beginning to feel quite differently about Ryan's departure.

Why would she want him to stay, anyway?

She certainly didn't want him sleeping over now that he was seeing somebody else.

And it was wrong to let the girls keep living with an illusion that he was truly part of their family.

Things could be worse, she thought.

Ryan might have hung around for a much longer time, only to eventually crush the girls' hopes and expectations even more hurtfully.

Good riddance, she thought.

Just then, Riley's phone buzzed. She saw that the call was from Blaine. It took her a second to remember that she'd left a message with him just last night, belatedly accepting his dinner offer. So much had happened this morning, it felt like much more time had passed since she'd made that call.

She answered the phone. Blaine sounded upbeat and cheerful.

"Hi, Riley. I got your message. Yeah, the offer still stands."

"Thanks," Riley said. "I'm glad."

"So when do you and your family want to come over to the restaurant? Tonight, maybe?"

Riley hated to put the whole thing on hold. But what else could she do?

"Blaine, I'm out of town right now, working on a case. I'll be back later today, but I might have to keep working."

"How about tomorrow, then?" Blaine asked.

Riley suppressed a sigh. Things had gotten awkward fast. The last thing she wanted was for Blaine to think she was pushing him away again. But with a new case underway, she simply didn't know when she would be able to accept his invitation.

The awkwardness was compounded by Bill's glances at her from behind the wheel. It was obvious from his mischievous grin that he'd heard who she was talking to.

Riley felt herself blush.

She said, "Blaine, I'm so sorry. I just don't know right now when it'll be possible."

Blaine didn't reply. Riley knew that he must feel a bit puzzled. After all, she had sounded so eager in her message. She figured that honesty was the best approach.

"I'm not being coy, Blaine. I'm really not. I promise, when this case gets settled, we'll come to your restaurant the first chance we get. And we'll return the invitation. Gabriela will cook up something wonderful for you and Crystal."

Now she could hear a smile in Blaine's voice.

"Great. I'll let you get back to work, then."

They ended the call. Bill's grin widened, and Riley's blush deepened.

"So who was that?" Bill asked.

"Mind your own business," Riley said with a slight giggle.

Bill let out a peal of laughter.

"No, I don't think I will, Riley. I think I still qualify as your best friend. I'm supposed to be nosy. That was Blaine, wasn't it? Your nice handsome neighbor."

Riley silently nodded.

Bill said, "So are you going to tell me what's going on, or what? The last I heard, Blaine had moved across town and you were trying to fix things up with Ryan."

Riley remembered how hotly Bill had protested when she told him that she and Ryan were getting back together.

"Do I need to remind you of everything that guy did to hurt you?" Bill had said. *"Because I can remember every detail."*

"Whatever you do, don't say 'I told you so.'"

"Why not?" Bill asked.

Riley sighed aloud now.

There's no use fighting it, she thought.

There was nothing she could do except swallow her pride.

"Because you did. Tell me so. And you were right. Ryan's the same old insufferable, unreliable Ryan."

"He bailed on you, huh? I'm sorry to hear that." He sounded genuinely sympathetic. "It must be tough on the kids."

Riley couldn't bring herself to tell him how true that was.

"Anyway," Bill said, "I'm glad you're finally giving 'Mr. Right' a chance."

Riley groaned with exasperation. She wanted to throw

something at him. Instead, she joined in his laughter.

Her phone buzzed again. She saw that it was a message from Sam Flores.

Riley was glad to have her attention snapped back to the job at hand. Before they'd left Quantico, she and Bill had talked to Sam Flores, the head of the lab team. They asked him to get right to work looking for DNA on the glass and aging the old composite sketch.

Riley checked her tablet computer. Sure enough, Sam had sent her some new sketches of the suspect.

"He sent the new pics," Riley said.

"How do they look?"

"They're not much to look at, but they'll do," Riley said.

Riley compared the sketches Sam and his team had put together to the old sketch. The original hadn't been very lifelike. The artist had been too careful. In Riley's experience, a little imagination and creativity sometimes helped capture a suspect's personality.

Still, Riley could see that Sam and his tech people had done a good job with what they had to work with. They'd tried to cover a range of possibilities. In one of the sketches, the man looked much as he had in the old sketch, except with more lines and wrinkles and graying hair. In another, he had put on more weight, and his jowls drooped. A third showed him with a beard and mustache.

Riley knew better than to show all three new sketches to potential witnesses at the same time. They'd only get confused. She had to choose just one of them.

She had a hunch that the sketch that most closely resembled the original would be the best one to work with. She didn't know exactly why. Something about the original's expression suggested someone who might not deliberately change his appearance over the years. Also, the man seemed to have a distinctly thin body type. Riley guessed that he wouldn't have put on much weight.

Of course, she could be completely wrong. But she knew that it was best to trust her instincts.

Just then they pulled into the sleepy little town of Greybull. Riley figured that it had a population of less than a thousand people.

"Where's our first stop?" Bill asked.

"The cemetery," Riley said.

She gave Bill directions, and they arrived at the cemetery within minutes. Riley brought up a map of the cemetery on her tablet. She and Bill got out of the car and wended their way among the tombstones.

Soon they found the grave that they were looking for. It was marked by a modest, average-sized stone with the inscription ...

TILDA ANN STEEN
beloved friend and daughter
1972–1992

The dates startled Riley. Of course she already knew that Tilda had been twenty when she'd been killed. But Riley hadn't really stopped to think that Tilda would be forty-five if she were still alive. What might her life have been like? Would she have stayed in this little town and raised a family, or would she have gone far away and pursued an altogether different kind of life? Riley had no idea. And the truth was, nobody would ever know.

Riley suddenly felt more determined than ever.

I've just got to solve this case.

Riley saw that two sets of flowers decorated the grave. One was a little bucket of daffodils in cheerfully mixed shades of yellow, orange, and white.

"Those are pretty," Bill said, pointing to the daffodils. "Do you think they're what we're looking for?"

Riley didn't think so. The flowers didn't look store bought.

She leaned down and opened a little note that was tied to the bucket handle. The message was short, simple, and heartfelt.

Dear Tilda,
Honey, I still miss you. I'll always miss you. I'll always love you.
Mother

"They're from Tilda's mother," Riley told Bill. "I'm sure the flowers are from Paula's own garden." She could imagine Paula carefully cultivating a bed of bulbs she'd planted in a sunny area for early blooms.

"Does Paula live here in Greybull?" Bill asked.

"No. Tilda's parents moved away soon after the murder. Paula still lives in Virginia, though, over on the other side of Richmond. Her husband died last year."

Riley felt a pang of sympathy as she remembered Paula telling her on the telephone ...

"What would we become if I forgot Justin or you forgot your mother? I don't ever want to become that hard."

Paula had always struck Riley as a brave person. But she knew that Paula was also intensely private.

How lonely she must be! Riley thought.

The other flowers were a more formal bouquet with gladiolas and carnations—an arrangement that might come from a florist. They were held in a plastic cone that had been stuck into the ground.

Obviously thinking about fingerprints, Bill put on plastic gloves and picked up the cone of flowers, then emptied out the water. He put the arrangement in a plastic bag that he'd brought along for this very purpose.

A voice called out. "What are you folks doing there?"

Riley and Bill turned around and saw an anxious-looking man in a security guard uniform walking toward them. He looked as though he might be in his late fifties.

Riley and Bill produced their badges and introduced themselves. The guard's eyes widened with interest.

"Has this got something to do with what happened to Tilda?" the guard asked. "That was a long time ago."

"We're reopening the case," Bill said.

"Did you see whoever it was that brought these flowers?" Riley asked.

The guard shook his head.

"They were put here late last night. I don't know who it was. The others are from Paula Steen—I've known her for ages. She comes around every year and we talk a bit. I always get rid of her flowers for her when they fade."

Pointing to the bouquet in Bill's hand, Riley asked, "Does somebody else bring flowers every year?"

"Yeah," the guard said. "Always at night. I've seen him a few times."

Riley showed the guard the composite sketch.

"Does he look anything like this?" Riley asked.

The guard shrugged.

"I couldn't say. I never get a good look at him at night, and he always wears a broad-rimmed hat that shadows his face. He's pretty tall, though. And thin."

Riley mentally seized on these details. They fitted her hunch that the killer would still be as thin as he'd always been.

"What was he driving?" Bill asked.

The guard thought for a moment. "Just a regular sedan. Light-colored, I think. But I'm not sure."

"Can you remember anything else at all about him?" Riley asked.

The guard just slowly shook his head no.

Bill asked, "Do you have any idea where he might have bought this arrangement?"

"Probably Corley's Flowers," the guard said. "It's the only florist in town." He pointed beyond the cemetery and added, "It's right over yonder, just a block along Bowers Street. You can't miss it."

Riley and Bill thanked the guard and left the cemetery. There was no point in driving such a short distance, so they walked. Riley looked around at the town, which seemed eerily peaceful. She and Bill passed a few others out walking who politely waved and smiled at the strangers.

Of course, the people had no idea who Bill and Riley were, or why they were here.

Some of them probably hadn't even been born when Tilda Steen had died.

It made Riley feel strange, knowing that she and her partner were here to stir up ghosts that the townspeople would surely rather forget.

She and Bill arrived at the corner flower shop, an old brick building with a slightly faded sign that looked weathered with age. Riley could see right away that Corley's Flowers had been here for a long time—probably for decades before the murder.

Riley and Bill went inside. The interior had an old-fashioned look with wooden counters and walls. There were lots of flowers sitting around, with posters advertising various arrangements. There were also a couple of framed photographs of the shop from many years ago—one of the exterior and the other taken in this same room.

Riley could see that the owner had gone to some pains to keep the shop looking much as it always had. Little had changed, except that the arrangements on the counters were all artificial flowers. The live blooms were now stored in a glass-door cooler that took up most of one wall.

A smiling young woman approached Bill and Riley. She told them her name was Loretta and asked if she could help them.

Bill and Riley took out their badges and introduced themselves.

Riley said, "We're investigating three murders that took place in this area twenty-five years ago."

Loretta looked puzzled.

"I'm afraid that was before my time," she said.

A kindly looking elderly woman stepped out of a back room.

"Why, does this have something to do with what happened to Tilda Steen?" she asked.

When Riley said yes, the woman introduced herself.

"I'm Gloria Corley, and this store has been in my family for years. I remember that awful murder like it was yesterday. Poor Tilda, she was so trusting of everyone. Of course, growing up in a town like this, why wouldn't she be? And there were two other victims too, weren't there? One over in Brinkley, and another in Denison. So terrible."

A worried look crossed Gloria's face.

"But has there been another murder? After all this time, I can't imagine."

"No," Riley said. "We're reopening it as a cold case."

Gloria looked a bit puzzled. Riley could understand why. After twenty-five years, reopening the case must seem to her like a strange thing to do. And the truth was, Riley knew that it *was* rather strange. Nothing about the case itself had actually changed, after all. No new evidence had come to light.

So how could Riley explain why the case was being reopened—to this woman or to anybody else?

Because I had a nightmare?

That would sound absurd.

Riley found it strange to realize that she couldn't think of a rational reason. That made her feel all the more grateful to Meredith for allowing her to proceed with it.

Bill took the flower arrangement out of the bag and showed it to both women.

"We're wondering if this bouquet might have come from your store," he said.

Gloria put on a pair of glasses that she had hanging around her neck and peered closely at the flowers.

"It's a pretty ordinary arrangement," she said. "Wasn't there a sticker or a card on it?"

"No," Bill said.

"Where did you find it?" Gloria asked.

"On Tilda's grave," Riley said.

The woman's eyes widened. Riley could see that she understood that whoever had left flowers at the grave was possibly the killer.

Loretta, too, examined the flowers.

"We've only sold one that was anything like this in the past week or two," she said.

Riley pulled up the aged composite sketch on her tablet and showed it to Loretta.

"The buyer might have looked like this," she said.

Loretta shrugged.

"I'm afraid I'm not very observant," she said. "And I didn't think it was important to really look—not at the time."

She squinted, trying to remember.

"I do remember him wearing a nice overcoat," she said. "And a hat. A fedora, maybe."

Riley's attention quickened as she remembered—the cemetery guard had said the man wore a broad-rimmed hat.

"Did anything else strike you about him?" Bill asked.

"He was tall, I think. Yes, I remember looking up at him."

Riley and Bill glanced at each other.

"How did he pay for the flowers?" Bill asked.

"With a credit card, I think," Loretta said. "I'll go check."

Riley and Bill followed Loretta over to the front counter. She clicked through her computer records.

She nodded when she found what she was looking for.

"Yes, I think this was him," she said. "He was here the day before yesterday. His name is Lemuel Cort."

"Do you have an address for him?" Bill asked.

"Sorry, I don't."

Riley and Bill thanked both women and left the store.

"We've got a name!" Riley said.

"And Lemuel Cort's a pretty distinctive name," Bill added. "If it's his real name, it shouldn't be too hard to track him down."

Riley agreed. She took out her cell phone and called Sam Flores at the BAU.

"Sam, we might have a suspect," she told the technician. "His name is Lemuel Cort, and we're hoping he lives in the area where the Matchbook Killings took place."

"I'll check," Sam said.

Riley could hear Sam's fingers dancing on his keyboard.

"He sure does," Sam said. "He lives in Glidden."

Riley remembered seeing signs on the road pointing to Glidden. She felt pretty sure it was close by.

"Can you check and see if he's got any kind of criminal record?" she asked.

"Already done," Flores said. "Yeah, he did some jail time for domestic violence. That was ten years ago."

Riley felt a tingle of excitement.

"Thanks, Sam," she said. "Send me whatever you can find on him, OK?"

"I'll do that."

Riley ended the call just as she and Bill got back to the car.

Bill said, "Sounds like we might have a suspect."

"Could be," Riley said. "Let's go."

Bill started the car, and Riley started giving him directions to Glidden.

She felt a tingle of anticipation. Maybe they were actually getting somewhere with this old case.

CHAPTER TEN

During the drive to Glidden, Riley pored over her tablet looking at materials that Sam Flores sent along. Many of them were articles from the local newspaper.

"What have we got?" Bill said as he drove.

"It looks like Lemuel Cort is a pretty prominent citizen," Riley said. "He owns the local lumberyard, belongs to the local Rotary Club, and is very active in public service. He's got a couple of grown children, but he's been divorced for years. Soon after his stint in jail, his wife Janet left him."

Bill looked intrigued.

"Sounds like maybe we should try talking to his ex-wife," he said.

Riley kept perusing the information on her tablet.

"I wish we could," she said. "But she left town, and Flores can't seem to find any record of where she wound up."

Some of the articles had pictures of Lemuel Cort. He was always presented as smiling, handsome, and elegant.

Riley tried to determine whether he resembled the composite sketch. She couldn't be sure one way or the other. In any case, he didn't look *unlike* the drawing.

Riley finished reading the materials and looked up to see that they were driving past upscale farms and horse properties. When they entered Glidden, Riley saw that the town was definitely higher class than Greybull. It was a suburban neighborhood with large lots and impressive homes. Checking it out on her tablet, she could see that many of the homes included elaborate gardens and swimming pools.

They arrived at the address and parked in the driveway. It was a good-sized brick house that overlooked a golf course. They walked among exquisitely groomed hedges to the front door and rang the doorbell.

They were quickly greeted by a tall, smiling, stylishly dressed man.

"May I help you?" he asked.

"Are you Lemuel Cort?" Riley asked.

"I am," he replied in a voice that sounded almost too smooth to be pleasant.

Riley and Bill got out their badges and introduced themselves.

Bill showed him the flower arrangement and said, "We'd like

to know if you're the person who bought these."

Lemuel Cort tilted his head curiously.

"No," he said. "But this is odd ... where did they come from?"

"Possibly from Corley Flowers in Greybull, Mr. Cort," Riley said. "Two days ago."

He smiled with mild surprise.

"Good Lord," he said quietly. "This *is* very odd."

Riley studied his face carefully. Was this the man portrayed in the composite sketch? Riley still couldn't be sure either way.

"But where are my manners?" the man said. "Do come in. And please—call me Lemuel."

He led them through the entry hallway into a light and airy dining area with a chandelier hanging above a well-polished table. Sitting on the table was a bouquet of flowers that looked very much like the ones Bill was holding, except that it also had a bit of greenery.

Lemuel gestured toward the flowers.

"As a matter of fact, I *did* buy these in Greybull the day before yesterday. Do sit down. I'd love to know why you've come here asking about them."

Riley wasn't sure what to think. Did the flowers prove that he wasn't their suspect? There remained a possibility that he'd bought the extra bouquet as a ruse for just this sort of situation.

Riley and Bill sat down at the table. From the moment she'd set eyes on him, Cort had somehow rubbed her the wrong way. Now she was starting to understand why.

He's a regular Southern gentleman, she realized.

Everything about his bearing and demeanor was perfectly studied and rehearsed. His accent was as flawlessly tailored as his suit, which was obviously expensive but also slightly out of date. His bow tie gave him an air of calculated but likeable eccentricity.

He was charm personified. But his charm didn't work on Riley. She knew his type too well—not so much from DC and Fredericksburg, but from her younger days in less populated parts of Virginia. Every well-to-do town had at least one gentleman like him. All her life, Riley had found their pretensions to be quite annoying—as well as their obsession with small talk. Riley knew that Lemuel would want to chat aimlessly before getting down to serious business.

He opened up a cabinet and took out a bottle of whiskey.

"Would you care for a sip of bourbon?" he said. "Blanton Single Barrel—my personal favorite these days." He winked slyly.

"But I can still be tempted by a spot of Kentucky Tavern now and again."

"No, thank you," Riley said.

He poured himself a glass and said, "But of course not. You're on duty after all. Some coffee or tea, perhaps?"

"We're good," Bill said.

Lemuel sat down and swished the whiskey around in his glass and sniffed it.

"You're from the FBI, you say? What division?"

"The BAU," Riley said.

Lemuel's eyebrows lifted.

"My goodness! Aren't you the folks who specialize in profiling? That must be fascinating work."

He leaned forward with an air of mock drama.

"But tell me. Are you here to investigate a murder?"

"As a matter of fact, we are," Bill said.

Lemuel drew back a little in a posture of slight surprise. Riley wondered—was the surprise feigned or real? She couldn't see through his veneer of refinement.

Before he could speak, Riley heard approaching footsteps.

A voice called out, "Darling, do we have company?"

A woman stepped into the dining room. She was well dressed and not much younger than Lemuel Cort. Like him, she projected an air of elegance and Southern gentility.

Lemuel rose from his chair, and so did Bill. Riley was silently amused. She understood that Bill was hastily adapting his manners to the present circumstances. After all, according to the anachronistic customs of the household, a gentleman must always stand when a lady entered the room.

"May I introduce you to my lovely wife, Thea?"

Thea lowered her head shyly. Riley suspected that there was a blush behind her layers of makeup.

She said, "I'm still getting used to him calling me that."

Lemuel chuckled a little. He sat back down, and so did Bill.

"We're newlyweds, you see. Just coming up on our one-month anniversary. Thea, these are Agents Jeffreys and Paige from the FBI—the BAU, to be exact."

Thea sat close to Riley and said, "Oh, my! This sounds quite serious! But would you care for some tea or coffee?"

"I've already offered, dearest," Lemuel said. "They courteously declined."

"Well, then," Thea said, folding her hands in her lap and

60

smiling.

Riley sensed right away that Thea's pretensions didn't come as easily as they did to Lemuel. Even her accent was not as perfectly honed. She was new to this lifestyle and its affectations.

Lemuel took a small sip of whiskey and said, "My dearest, our guests seem to be here on rather unpleasant business. They say there's been a murder."

Thea gasped aloud.

Riley said, "Actually, there hasn't been a murder, at least not recently. We're reopening an old case. Are either of you familiar with the so-called Matchbook Killings?"

"I'm afraid not," Thea said.

"My wife is new to the vicinity, you see," Lemuel said. "She arrived in town to start teaching in the elementary school just this year."

Lemuel pursed his lips thoughtfully.

"The Matchbook Killings, you said? It does ring a bell. Yes, I think I do remember. Three young women were murdered in these parts, weren't they? Such a pity. But wasn't that an awfully long time ago? Why are you investigating now, after all these years? I would think that the case would be cold indeed."

Neither Riley nor Bill said anything for a moment.

Riley's instincts were telling her that something was very wrong here.

Perhaps Lemuel really was the murderer.

Riley looked carefully at the flowers.

Finally she said, "Tell me, Lemuel. Why did you go all the way to Greybull to buy these?"

Lemuel let out an abrupt, single-syllable chuckle.

"Well, it's not so far, after all," he said.

"But surely there are florists right here in Glidden. Besides, these flowers are perfectly ordinary—the kind you might find in a grocery store. Why drive out of your way to get them? It seems like a lot of trouble."

He nodded toward Thea, still smiling.

"No trouble at all for my lovely wife."

Riley sensed that something was about to become clear. She looked at Thea until something caught her eye.

"That's a lovely ring, Thea," Riley said. "May I see it?"

"Why, certainly."

With a proud smile, the woman lifted her hand toward Riley. The engagement ring was simple but attractive, with a single tasteful diamond. But that wasn't what Riley wanted to see.

Thea's sleeve pulled back from her wrist, revealing something that had been only partly visible—a large, red bruise.

"How did this happen?" Riley asked.

The woman drew her hand back, looking more offended than alarmed.

"I don't see how that's any of your business," Thea said.

"Nor do I," Lemuel said.

Now Riley understood. Lemuel had physically abused her. Her clothing might well cover other bruises.

Riley knew that Lemuel had apologized, of course. Abusive husbands usually did—and he had more charm at his disposal than most. He'd also bought her these flowers as penance. But as concerned as he was about appearances, he'd bought the flowers in another town. It was easier than answering questions from some nosy local.

Her suspicions were now growing.

The so-called gentleman who could do this to his wife was capable of anything.

Riley briefly wondered what to do next.

She decided to confront the situation directly.

"Tell me, Thea," Riley said in a disarmingly pleasant tone. "Did you know that your husband did jail time for domestic violence some years back?"

"Now see here!" Lemuel said.

Thea's eyes widened.

No, she doesn't know, Riley realized.

After all, she'd only moved here recently. And in a town like this, dark secrets were jealously guarded—especially when they pertained to a fine, reputable gentleman like Lemuel Cort.

"I don't know what you mean," the woman said, her lips trembling. "And I don't want to know."

Lemuel rose from his chair.

"I'm afraid I must ask you both to leave," he said.

Bill stood up also. Riley knew that they had no choice but to go. But she didn't budge for a moment. She reached into her shirt pocket and took out a card with her BAU contact information.

"Contact me," she said to Thea. "Whenever you're ready."

It was something Riley sometimes did when faced with abuse victims. She'd offered her help to several such women in the past—ranging from a prostitute brutalized by her pimp husband to the trophy wife of a heartless millionaire. Some had taken her up on her offer. Others hadn't, at least not yet.

But Thea wouldn't take the card.

And it wasn't fear that Riley saw in her eyes.

It was simple indignation.

"Keep it," the woman said in a tight, angry voice.

Riley was stunned. The woman's righteous sense of propriety outweighed any fear she had of her husband. What could Riley do?

She felt Bill's hand on her shoulder.

"Come on, we've got to go," Bill said.

*

Bill could feel Riley's anger as they walked down the hallway on the way out of the house. He knew from experience how strongly she reacted to this kind of situation.

When they stepped out the front door, Bill heard Lemuel's voice behind him.

"You, sir ..."

Bill turned to look at Lemuel as Riley continued on her way to the car. Lemuel stood glaring at him with an expression of self-righteous haughtiness.

"In a more civilized time, sir, you and I ..."

Lemuel let the words trail off.

Bill stared back at him, trying to understand what he meant.

In a more civilized time—we'd what? Bill asked himself.

When it dawned on him, Bill almost laughed.

This faux-gentleman was talking about a duel.

Bill smiled and pointed at Riley.

"She's a better shot than I am," he said.

Without another word, Bill turned away and followed Riley to the car. They both got in and Bill started the engine.

Before Bill could start driving, Riley said through clenched teeth, "Let's nail that prick."

Bill looked at her. She was staring straight ahead, her face red with anger.

"What are you talking about?" Bill said. "We can't do anything. The woman doesn't even want help. Riley, I understand how you feel, but you can't save everybody."

Riley stared at him as if she couldn't believe what he was saying.

Bill said, "Don't tell me you still think he's our killer."

"Don't you?" Riley said.

Bill could see that Riley was letting her rage get the better of her judgment. This happened from time to time. And the truth was, Bill admired her capacity for moral outrage. She had the keenest sense of right and wrong of anybody he'd ever known. But at times like this, it was up to him to make her see reason.

"Riley, think about this. Do you seriously think Lemuel bought both bouquets—one bouquet at Corley's Flowers for his wife, and the other for the grave at some other store? It doesn't make sense. Let's face it, he's not our man. We're back at square one."

Riley's face softened, looking more sad than angry.

Bill said, "You can't help Thea, Riley. She wouldn't even take your card."

In a quiet voice, Riley said, "I know."

Bill looked at her sympathetically for a moment.

"So what do we do next?" he asked.

"Drive back to Greybull," Riley said. "There's a cop there who worked the case years ago. We need to talk to him."

Just as Bill started to drive, Riley's phone rang. She answered it.

He heard her saying in an alarmed voice, "What? ... What? ... OK ... I'll get there as soon as I can."

She ended the call.

"You've got to drive me back to Fredericksburg," she said. "Jilly's in trouble."

CHAPTER ELEVEN

Riley brooded silently during most of the drive back to Fredericksburg. The guidance counselor hadn't told her much over the phone. The only thing Riley knew right now was that Jilly had hit another kid in school. Riley was expected at the counselor's office to help sort things out.

As they neared the school, Bill broke the silence.

"Stop beating yourself up about this, Riley."

Riley continued to stare out the window.

"What makes you think that's what I'm doing?" she said.

"Come on, Riley. This is Bill you're talking to."

Riley hesitated, then said, "I'm afraid I'm really screwing things up."

Bill let out a grunt of disapproval.

"So what? Who isn't screwing up? Do you think I'm such a perfect parent? Hell, I only see my boys on weekends. What kind of dad does that make me?"

But Bill's situation was different from hers, and Riley knew it.

"I know I'm doing the best I can," she said. "That's not the point. The point is my best isn't good enough. I'm way out of my depth. The girl is troubled, Bill. She's had an awful life. The social workers back in Phoenix had a hard time handling her. So did would-be foster parents. Why did I ever think I could do a better job?"

"You *can* do it, Riley. You probably saved the girl's life. Give yourself some credit."

Bill parked in the school visitors' lot.

"Do you want me to come in with you?" he asked.

Riley shook her head.

"No. I'm sorry to drag you all the way here. If you want to go on back to work, I can get a cab home."

"We can get back to work tomorrow. I'll wait for you right here, then drive you to Quantico so you can get your car."

Riley sighed.

"OK," she said. "But if you see any troublemaking kids, don't arrest them. One of them might be mine."

Riley walked into the school building. She checked in with the school receptionist and made her way to the guidance counselors' offices. In the small room next to the offices, she found Jilly sitting quietly in a chair reading a school textbook.

On the other side of the room sat a large, tough-looking boy with a bandage on his nose. A woman was sitting right next to him. From the way the woman glared at her, Riley guessed that she was the boy's mother.

Riley sat down beside Jilly, who closed her book and looked at her.

"I'm sorry," she whispered.

"You should be," Riley whispered back. "You've got no business hitting people."

"Oh, I'm not sorry about that," Jilly said. "I'm just sorry you had to come. They told me to sit here until you showed up."

Jilly's guidance counselor, Joyce Uderman, stepped out of the office. Riley had met her several times. Riley always got the feeling that she didn't like Jilly very much. The woman's smile also sometimes struck Riley as rather insincere.

Right now was one of those moments.

"Ms. Paige, Jilly, please come in," she said.

Riley and Jilly went into the office and sat down. Ms. Uderman sat behind her desk.

Still smiling rather emptily, the counselor said, "Thank you for coming, Ms. Paige."

"Please tell me what happened," Riley said.

"I will in a moment. I just called Assistant Principal Morlan. He'll join us."

An awkward, silent moment passed. Ms. Uderman managed to keep smiling the whole time. Jilly's arms were crossed, and Riley could see that she was angry. Riley mentally compared this rather skinny girl to the considerably bigger boy outside.

What happened exactly? Riley wondered.

Mark Morlan, the assistant principal, came into the office. Riley had also met him once or twice. He was about Riley's age, a large and imposing man. He, too, thanked Riley for coming. But his expression was dour and serious.

Still smiling, Ms. Uderman said, "Ms. Paige, Jilly hit her classmate Mark Hinkle. She bloodied his nose and he had to go to the nurse's office. His mother is very upset. She wants your daughter suspended from school. I thought it would be best if we talked with the students separately and with their parents before taking any action."

Mr. Morlan didn't sit down.

He said, "Jilly, could you please explain your behavior?"

Jilly spoke in a loud, angry voice.

"It was Mark's fault. He had it coming."

"Now Jilly," Ms. Uderman said, "violence is never acceptable."

"He's a bully," Jilly said. "He picks on girls. He says gross things to them. He grabs them in nasty ways."

Ms. Uderman folded her hands on the desk.

"Does he do that to you, Jilly?" she asked.

"Not so much. I'm not scared of him. The other girls are. Today he made fun of Hayley Crow for her weight. He made her cry. But even then he wouldn't leave her alone. He got a bunch of boys together and they all kept making fun of her. She cried and cried, and they pushed and shoved her, and Mark kept goading them on. And that was when I ..."

Jilly paused, then added, "He deserved it."

Riley was playing the scene out in her mind—a tough, mean boy teasing a fat little girl and getting all his pals in on the action. It must have taken Jilly some courage to defy them all and punch Mark Hinkle. But after all that Jilly had dealt with in life, Riley knew that a school bully wasn't likely to intimidate her.

Of course, Riley also knew that the other two adults in the room probably didn't see it that way.

Tread carefully, she told herself.

"I'm not defending Jilly's actions," Riley said. "But it sounds to me as though Mark has some explaining to do. His behavior might well be described as harassment."

Ms. Uderman's smile faded.

"I think you should let Mr. Morlan and I be the judges of that, Ms. Paige," she said.

Then Ms. Uderman turned to Jilly.

"I'm going to bring Mark in here. And you're going to apologize."

"What?" Jilly snapped.

"You're going to tell him you're sorry and you won't do it again."

"I will not!"

Riley felt thoroughly nonplussed. She knew what Jilly did was wrong and that she had to apologize. But she also knew exactly how Jilly felt.

She said, "Ms. Uderman, I think the situation's pretty complicated."

But the counselor kept staring at Jilly.

"You won't apologize?" she asked.

"No."

Ms. Uderman leaned back in her chair.

"Well then, it seems to me that you give us no choice. This *will* go on your permanent record. Mr. Morlan, what further action do you recommend?"

Riley dreaded whatever was going to come next. Suspension would be a terrible setback for Jilly.

But Mr. Morlan didn't say anything for a moment. He looked straight at Riley. She could see that his mood had changed. He was almost smiling.

He gets it, Riley thought. *He understands why Jilly did what she did.*

Finally, he said, "Jilly, I promise that we'll get to the bottom of whatever Mark did. But you really need to tell him you're sorry. Will you do that?"

Jilly stubbornly shook her head.

"Wait outside the office for a moment, Jilly," Ms. Uderman said. "We need to talk to your mother in private."

Jilly got up from her chair and walked out. Mr. Morlan shut the door.

Ms. Uderman said, "Ms. Paige, your daughter really gives us no choice. I think suspension is in order. If it happens again, it could lead to expulsion."

"Not so fast, Ms. Uderman," Mr. Morlan said. "I think we should give the girl's mother a chance to deal with this."

Looking at Riley, he said, "We've had trouble with Mark Hinkle before. We'll check out your daughter's side of the story. And if it's true ..."

He didn't finish the sentence. Riley sensed by his tone that Mark was surely going to be in a lot more trouble than Jilly.

Then he added, "Jilly does need to write a note of apology and bring it here tomorrow. I leave it up to you to encourage her to do that."

Ms. Uderman was staring at him with her mouth hanging open. Riley could see that she didn't like this approach at all.

"Does this sound fair?"

"Yes," Riley said.

"Good," Mr. Morlan said. "That will be all for now."

Riley left the office and found Jilly standing right outside the door. The boy and his mother were still seated. Mr. Morlan called for them and they went into the office. Riley and Jilly walked on down the hallway.

"Where are we going?" Jilly asked.

"Home," Riley said.

"Am I in trouble?"

"It depends."

And a lot depends on me, Riley thought.

Could she get Jilly to write that letter?

CHAPTER TWELVE

As Riley and Jilly walked out of the school and toward the parked car, Jilly stopped dead in her tracks. Riley looked down and saw a puzzled look on the girl's face.

"What's wrong?" Riley asked.

"Is that the car you're using today?" Jilly replied.

"Sure," Riley said. "It's an FBI car."

"Who's that guy in it?" Jilly demanded. "I've seen him somewhere before."

"My partner, Bill. You met him once in Phoenix."

"OK then," Jilly mumbled and started walking again.

Riley climbed into the front seat and Jilly got in the back. Riley quickly reintroduced Jilly to Bill. The girl still had a look of annoyance on her face as she fastened her seat belt.

When Bill headed the car toward the highway to Quantico, Jilly snapped, "I thought you said we were going home."

"We are. My car's at Quantico. Bill's taking us there to get it."

Jilly fell silent then and nobody else said anything during the drive. Riley knew that Bill was too considerate to ask how things had gone at the school. She also knew that now was not the time to sort things out with her new daughter.

The silence was anything but comfortable, and the ride seemed longer than the half hour it really was. They arrived at Quantico, where a security guard waved them through the gate. Riley glanced back and saw Jilly watching the guard with interest. Then the girl's eyes widened at the sight of the huge building they drove by as Bill took them straight to Riley's car in the parking lot.

"Thanks, Bill," Riley said as she and Jilly got out. "We'll get back on track tomorrow."

Bill drove away and Riley unlocked the door of her car.

"Wait a minute!" Jilly cried out. "Don't I get to see where you work? I mean, it's got to be cool! You've told me there's a shooting range. And a virtual reality room. I want to see everything!"

"Not this time," Riley said. "You and I have got to talk."

They got into the car and Riley started to drive home.

"What kind of trouble am I in?" Jilly asked.

"It depends. Suspension, maybe. Unless—"

"Unless what?"

"You've got to write a note to Mark. You've got to say you're sorry."

Jilly let out a yelp of protest.

"Huh-uh! It wasn't my fault!"

Riley stifled a groan of frustration.

This isn't going to be easy, she thought.

"Jilly, you *chose* to hit Mark."

"Yeah, well, isn't it what you would do? You beat up bad guys all the time. You even kill them when you have to."

Riley winced at the word "kill." The last thing she wanted was for Jilly to think that her job was glamorous—especially the parts that involved violence.

"Jilly, I'm trained and licensed for my job. And I don't use violence unless it's absolutely necessary."

Jilly crossed her arms and glared forward.

"I thought it was necessary," she said.

"Well, it wasn't."

"How do you mean?"

"Well, maybe you should tell me. He's a bully, you say. He does gross things to girls. He made your friend cry. He got all his friends to make her feel worse. I know how terrible that is. But what else could you have done besides hitting him?"

Jilly sulked silently for a moment.

Then she said, "I could have gone to my counselor and reported him. But it wouldn't have done any good."

"Yes, it would have, Jilly. Your school has a zero tolerance policy toward bullying. And if nobody had done anything, you could have told me, and I'd have complained. I'd have made sure something got done about it."

They drove on in silence for a little while.

Finally Jilly muttered, "Just once I wanted to be in charge."

Riley was puzzled.

"In charge of what?" she asked.

"Everything. School, family, home, life. Ryan left us, there wasn't anything I could do about it. I'm tired of things always happening *to me.* Just once I wanted to be the one who made things happen."

Riley stopped to think about what Jilly meant. Little by little, she was starting to understand. All her life, Jilly had been on her own, fending for herself, trying to solve problems that were beyond her control. Nobody had been there for her, least of all the adults in her life.

For a while, Riley had thought that Jilly was feeling that things in her life were changing for the better.

71

But Ryan leaving had been a huge setback.

Ryan had proven to be just like all the other grown-ups Jilly had ever known.

Riley felt a surge of guilt.

How could I have ever trusted that bastard again?

But she put such thoughts out of her mind. Right now she had to focus on Jilly.

"Jilly, maybe we all need to make some changes. Me especially. I'm not home enough. I don't see enough of you or April. I've been thinking for a long time ... maybe it's time for me to quit at the BAU. There are lots of other kinds of work I could do—work that would let me spend more time with you and April."

Now Jilly sounded alarmed.

"You can't quit! You've got to keep catching bad guys! If you don't do it, who will?"

Riley was surprised by the passion in Jilly's voice.

It was obvious that nothing would disappoint Jilly more than Riley quitting the BAU.

Well, I guess that's settled, Riley thought.

"Jilly, you're not alone," she said. "I'm here. I'm not running away. I promise. April's here too, and Gabriela. You've got to learn to lean on us. You don't *have* to be in charge all the time."

Jilly didn't reply, but Riley sensed that she was listening.

Riley said, "You're doing so well in school. Don't blow it for yourself. You do want to pass eighth grade, don't you? And go on to high school?"

"Yeah," Jilly said. "A whole lot."

"Then don't you think you should write that letter?"

Jilly was quiet for a moment.

"I should," she said. "But how can I apologize? I don't feel sorry, I don't feel bad. I wouldn't really mean it."

She has a point, Riley thought.

Riley certainly didn't want to encourage Jilly to be hypocritical.

Finally Riley said, "Even if you don't feel bad about hurting Mark, you know it was the wrong thing to do, right?"

"Yeah."

"Well, you can say just that. That you're sorry you did it because it was the wrong thing to do."

Riley thought for a moment, then added, "And you can say other things too."

"Like what?"

"I'll let you figure it out for yourself. Do you think you can do it?"

"I'll try."

Riley hoped that Jilly meant it.

She said, "Anyway, a punk like Mark isn't worth getting kicked out of school over. And for what it's worth, Mr. Morlan gave me the distinct impression that Mark is going to be in a lot worse trouble than you are."

Now Riley could hear a smile in Jilly's voice.

"Really?" she said.

"Really."

Riley and Jilly didn't say much during the rest of the ride home. But Riley, at least, felt a whole lot better.

Maybe I'm doing some things right after all, she thought.

*

When Riley woke up the next morning, she quickly noticed an envelope that had been slipped under the door. She knew right away that it was Jilly's note to Mark. Jilly must have put it there late last night for Riley's approval.

Riley opened up the note and read ...

Hi Mark—

I'm sorry I hit you. It was the wrong thing to do. Violence is never good, and I know that now, and I won't do anything like that again. I hope your nose feels better.

But I hope you understand that you hurt people too. The way you mistreat girls hurts them badly. And it hurts me to see you act that way. It makes me angry, but more than that, it makes me sad. Please stop.

Sincerely,
Jilly

Riley smiled. She got dressed and went downstairs, where Gabriela and the girls were already eating breakfast. She handed the note back to Jilly and kissed her on the cheek.

"This is perfect," she said. "I'm proud of you."

A smile exploded across Jilly's face. But then she looked a little worried.

"Are you sure Mr. Morlan will think it's OK?" Jilly asked.

"If he doesn't, he'll definitely hear from me," Riley said.

Jilly's smile came back in full force.

Riley sat down and ate breakfast with her family.

*

A little while later, Riley was relieved to be finally driving to the BAU to go back to work with Bill. She had delivered both Jilly and her note to school, and hoped that would settle at least one issue in her life.

She felt eager to get back to work. There was plenty to do today, such as talking to the cop in Greybull who had worked the case years ago. She and Bill also needed to visit the bars where the victims had last been seen alive.

When Riley pulled onto the interstate, her cell phone rang. She put the call on speakerphone.

"Hi, Riley. This is Shirley Redding, your real estate agent."

Riley was happy to hear from her. She hadn't had time to check in with her yesterday as she'd hoped.

"Hi, Shirley. What's going on?"

"Great news! It turns out that the property is prime hunting land. I've got more than one potential buyer on the hook. The best offer is close to two hundred thousand dollars."

"Wow!" Riley said. "Should we take it or hold off for more?"

"That's up to you," Shirley said. "But I've got a hunch that's as high as we'll get."

Riley knew better than to hesitate.

"Then let's accept it."

"Great! I'll get right back to the buyer!"

Riley felt a warm rush of happiness as she ended the call.

Two hundred thousand dollars!

It was going to be wonderful security, knowing that she had that kind of money for the girls' college years.

Riley had started to hum a happy tune when the phone rang again.

She answered, figuring that Shirley was calling back about some kind of detail.

Instead, she heard a man's voice.

"Don't accept that offer."

Riley shuddered so hard that she almost lost control of her car.

She knew that voice all too well.

It was possibly the last person in the world she wanted to hear from right now.

CHAPTER THIRTEEN

As Riley struggled to control her car, the voice on the phone repeated, "Don't accept that offer."

There was no doubt in Riley's mind.

The caller was Shane Hatcher.

The criminal genius had come to Riley's aid on more than one case—but always at a terrible cost, both personal and professional.

"Do you hear me?" Hatcher asked.

"I hear you. Don't accept the offer or what?"

"Or—you'll miss a great opportunity."

Then came a sinister chuckle.

He said, "Maybe you'd better get off the highway before we discuss it. You'll be safer that way."

Riley groaned aloud. Hatcher was right. She was badly shaken and driving erratically.

Hatcher's knowledge of her every move, of the most intimate details of her life, often seemed uncanny.

Riley swerved onto an exit ramp that led her to a side street. She pulled over to the curb and stopped her car.

"Why should I talk to you?" Riley asked.

"Because you're still wearing my bracelet."

Riley's flesh crawled as she felt the weight of the gold bracelet on her wrist. Hatcher had given it to her back in January as a symbol of what he called their "bond." The bracelet was also engraved with a number she had used for contacting him.

Every day, she tried to tell herself not to wear it.

But Hatcher's hold on her was too strong.

"You just got an offer on your father's cabin," Hatcher said. "For a whole lot of money. Don't accept it. Don't sell it."

Riley's mind boggled.

Did he know that she'd just gotten off the phone with Shirley?

Was he tapping her phone?

"Why shouldn't I sell it?" she asked.

"Because I want it. I like it there. It agrees with me. I'd like to spend some time there." Then with another laugh he added, "With your permission, of course."

Riley remembered the last time she'd seen Hatcher. She'd gone to the cabin shortly after her father's death. Hatcher had tracked her down there, and their encounter had been as disturbing as usual. The last image she had of him was walking away from the cabin, his back turned toward her.

Why didn't I shoot him when I had the chance? Riley wondered.

But now was no time to second-guess herself.

She had to figure out what Hatcher was driving at here and now.

Riley knew that Hatcher had both money and criminal connections. He'd flaunted his power and wealth ever since his escape from Sing Sing.

Riley said, "If you want the cabin so bad, why don't you just buy it yourself?"

Hatcher didn't reply. He simply let out a long, rumbling chuckle.

Then Riley understood.

The "buyer" who had offered Shirley $200,000 had been Shane himself.

He'd been using a fake identity, surely.

But if he wanted it so much, why hadn't he bought it?

It would be tricky, of course. After all, he ranked high on the FBI's most wanted list. But Riley knew that Hatcher wouldn't have let a little problem like that get in his way. If he really wanted to buy the property, he'd figure out a way to handle the transaction.

But he didn't want to buy it.

That would be too simple, Riley realized.

He found it much more interesting for Riley to keep on owning it.

He loved playing mind games with her.

"I'm not asking for the title," Hatcher said. "I'm just asking you to look the other way while I live there."

Riley didn't reply. She was still struggling to understand what this was really all about.

Hatcher said, "I know you've got reasons to want to sell it. The money would be a great help, with two girls on their way to college. You want them to have a good education. But they're getting that already, living with you. By the way, I admire that little Jilly. She's got some spunk, taking down a school bully like that. She really takes after her mom."

Riley's stomach sank. He even knew about Jilly's altercation!

He added, "You won't need to worry about college funds. Trust me, that won't be a problem, not in the long run."

Riley's head reeled with confusion. Was he seriously promising to put her kids through college?

If so, how could she possibly accept that kind of help?

Worse yet, how could she turn it down?

She'd never known Hatcher to take no for an answer.

She sat there staring at the phone.

She didn't dare ask the obvious question—*why* should she agree not to sell the cabin?

The answer might be too horrible to imagine. Might he put the kids in danger? Perhaps he had them in his clutches already.

But no, that wouldn't be his style.

He'd actually saved April's life once—and Ryan's life as well.

Finally Hatcher said, "I can make it worth your while."

"How?"

"Like I always do. Give you information."

Riley almost scoffed aloud. Had he overplayed his hand for once?

"You haven't got any information I need," she said. "I'm working on a cold case. I'm in no hurry. I've got plenty of time. I can solve it on my own."

A chilling silence fell.

"There's another cold case you haven't solved," Hatcher finally said. "You've got no hope of solving it—without my help."

"I don't know what you're talking about," Riley said.

"I'm talking about something that's been on your mind most of your life."

Riley gasped. She didn't want to ask. But he said nothing more until she whispered, "What?"

"Your mother's death. I can give you her killer."

CHAPTER FOURTEEN

Riley felt her whole body shake with shock at Hatcher's words. She closed her eyes, trying to pull herself together.

For a moment, memories came flooding back …

She was right there all over again, a little girl in a candy store with Mommy, when a bad man with a stocking over his head and a gun walked toward them, and the bad man said to Mommy, "Give me your money," but Mommy was too scared to move, and then …

"Did you hear me?" Hatcher asked.

Her eyes snapped open again.

"I heard you," she said.

"Is it a deal?"

Riley's throat was so tight with anxiety that she could barely speak.

"I don't believe you," she managed to say.

Hatcher let out a peal of laughter.

"Oh, you believe me. Why wouldn't you believe me? Haven't I always been true to my word? Haven't I always come through for you?"

Although Riley couldn't bring herself to say so, it was true. Hatcher had never let her down, not during the whole time she'd known him.

And now she felt an abyss opening up beneath her feet.

It was an abyss of hope—hope that she'd denied to herself all her life. Suddenly that abyss was real and gaping.

She'd spent years telling herself that she could never find justice for her mother.

But now she could do it at long last. She could find her mother's killer and bring him to justice …

… or make and choose her own justice, terrible though it might be.

Riley tingled all over. Deep inside, she was at war with herself.

What about April and Jilly?

What about their college money?

She remembered what Hatcher had said just now.

"You won't need to worry about college funds. Trust me, that won't be a problem, not in the long run."

It was true.

Hatcher was going to be their benefactor—if she made the right choice now. Of course, that could also depend on his remaining free and wealthy.

And what would be the cost to Riley?

Favors from Hatcher always came at a price. Ever since she'd known him, he'd never been content with anything less than part of her soul.

She felt like she'd been losing her soul to him little by little, piece by piece. Was she now going to hand over the largest piece of her soul yet?

And how much soul would she have left?

How long before her soul was gone?

The temptation was terrible—and irresistible.

"Yes," she said in a choked voice.

"Yes what?"

"You've got a deal."

Silence followed. Was he still on the line?

"Tell me now," she said. "Tell me what you know. Tell me how I can find him."

"Not so fast. You know what you've got to do next. And you've got to do it right now. Right this minute."

Riley heard a click.

The phone call had ended.

Riley was shaking almost uncontrollably. Tears were pouring down her face. Were they tears of frustration at Hatcher's viselike hold on her, or tears of pain from the memory of her mother's death? It all seemed to be hopelessly mixed together.

But she'd made her choice, and now she had to follow through on it.

It's now or never, she thought.

She dialed up her Realtor's number. When she got Shirley on the line, she had trouble breathing.

"Shirley, I've thought it over. I've decided to turn down that offer."

"What?" Shirley asked.

Riley gulped hard, then forced a cheerful tone.

"I can't explain it, Shirley. I know it sounds ridiculous. But when it finally came to giving it up, I somehow just couldn't. I guess I want to keep the place after all, at least for now. Maybe I'll sell it later."

Shirley sounded both shocked and angry.

"Riley, you're crazy to let this go. We might never get this kind of offer again. The market is unpredictable. Especially if interest rates go up."

"I understand. But I've changed my mind. I want to take it off the market."

Shirley was sputtering now.

"I—I don't get it. When we first talked, you were so emphatic. You said you really didn't want the place, and you had bad memories of it. You said you could use the money to send your girls to college. I took you at your word. I worked hard to make this deal happen."

"I know. I'm sorry."

"I just don't understand what could have changed your mind in just a few minutes."

Riley knew that she simply couldn't give a reasonable explanation.

There was no point in even trying.

"It just happened, Shirley. I realized I couldn't sell it. So turn down the offer. Right now. And take it off the market."

"But—"

"That's my final word."

They ended the call. Riley sat in the car mulling over what was going to happen next. If Riley's hunch had been right and the "buyer" had actually been Hatcher, Shirley would be calling him right now to tell him of Riley's decision.

Then what would Hatcher do?

She'd find out soon enough.

She looked at her watch and saw that it was almost time to meet Bill at the BAU. She started the car and got back on the interstate.

*

When Riley parked in the BAU parking lot, she noticed that she'd received a text message during the drive. It was marked from an "unknown sender"—but of course, Riley knew who had really sent it.

She picked up her phone and saw that the message was very short:

Deny thy father and refuse thy name.

She recognized the words at once. It was a line from *Romeo and Juliet*. It followed Juliet's melancholy outcry, "O Romeo, Romeo! Wherefore art thou Romeo?"

She'd read the play in high school and had seen movies of it, so she remembered the scene clearly. Juliet was standing on her bedroom balcony one night, sighing over her newly awakened infatuation for a kid named Montague. The trouble was, Juliet was a Capulet, and the Montagues were her family's sworn enemies. That was why she wanted Romeo to "deny" his father and "refuse" his name.

But what did this have to do with Riley—much less her mother's death?

Riley groaned aloud.

She should have known that Hatcher wasn't going to offer any clear and simple information. As usual, he was going to speak in riddles.

But what did this riddle mean? His cryptic messages always meant something, no matter how silly they seemed.

She said the line aloud.

"Deny thy father and refuse thy name."

One thing seemed obvious. Hatcher was referring to Riley's own father, and her troubled relationship with him. Also, the line seemed to be some kind of instruction or order.

But how was she supposed to comply?

Her father was dead. How could she "deny" him or "refuse" his name?

Perhaps she was doing that right now—by turning the cabin over to Hatcher.

But what did that have to do with her mother's death?

Again, Riley felt the weight of the bracelet on her wrist. She looked at it and saw the tiny inscription on one of its links:

"face8ecaf"

It, too, had been a riddle, and it meant "face to face."

It had been Hatcher's way of telling her that he was her mirror—a mirror that showed her the darkest parts of herself.

But the inscription was more than that. It was a video address, a means of getting in touch with Hatcher.

Should she do that now? Should she ask him what his message meant?

Riley's heart sank.

Of course he wouldn't tell her.

And besides, maybe this time the message meant nothing at all.

Maybe Hatcher was only teasing her.

Sooner or later, surely he'd give her a real clue of some sort.

Meanwhile, how much teasing was she going to have to

endure?

She had no choice but to put it out of her mind for the time being. Bill was expecting her, and they needed to get back to work.

As she got out of her car and walked toward the building, her phone buzzed again. This time the text was from Brent Meredith. And it was as terse and blunt as could be.

Get in my office. Now.

CHAPTER FIFTEEN

Riley felt a burst of panic. The chief's text sounded angry and she didn't like to even think of all the reasons why he might be mad at her. One big question pushed its way into her mind. Had Meredith found out about her communications with Hatcher?

She continued into the BAU building, wondering what she was on her way to. If Meredith knew that she had just been exchanging messages with a dangerous criminal on the FBI's most wanted list, he would be much, much more than just angry.

Riley had already been officially reprimanded for her relationship with Hatcher. She had failed to apprehend him more than once, and she knew that her failure was due to her own reluctance even more than to Hatcher's cunning.

Nobody at the BAU—not even Bill—knew that Hatcher had helped her with her last case in Seattle. Surely no one knew that he had contacted her today about her father's cabin.

Or maybe she was wrong.

Maybe Meredith had found out.

Maybe Meredith even knew about her phone contact with Hatcher just now.

Steady, Riley told herself. *Don't get paranoid.*

But it was less a feeling of paranoia than of guilt.

She knew it was wrong to maintain her contact with Hatcher, let alone get deeper and deeper into whatever this relationship was turning into. The criminal had said that he wanted to work with her. She found the idea mystifying.

It was also wrong to conceal it from the colleagues who most trusted her.

And maybe it was right if she got into trouble for it.

She approached Meredith's office with bated breath. But as she got nearer, she was surprised to hear laughter pouring out of the open door.

When Riley reached the doorway and looked inside, she saw Bill and Meredith standing there and laughing. Another man stood with his back toward her. But she recognized the short, sturdy physique at a glance.

"Jake!" she shouted.

Jake Crivaro turned toward her with a wide grin. They hugged each other.

Riley felt both relieved and guilty at escaping trouble one more time.

So this was what Meredith's message was about, she realized.

"What the hell are you doing here?" Riley asked Jake.

"What do you think I'm doing here?" Jake said in his gravelly voice. "I'm testing this joint's security. Boy, does it ever suck. Some maniac could come right in here and kill you all."

Still laughing, Brent Meredith said, "This wily old bastard talked his way straight through security. Got in without a badge or any clearance at all. He's the same sly dog he always was. You could have knocked me over with a feather when he walked into my office."

"But I just talked to you yesterday," Riley said. "You were at home. Did you fly all the way from Miami?"

"Yeah, and are my arms tired!" Jake said, flapping his arms like a bird.

Riley and the others laughed at Jake's familiar corny joke.

Riley said, "Seriously, what brings you here?"

"What do you think brings me here?" Jake growled at Riley. "It's your own damned fault, getting me thinking about the Matchbook Killer again. I couldn't sleep last night. Caught a flight early this morning. If you're going to nail him at long last, I want a piece of that action."

Riley looked at Meredith.

"What do you say, chief?" she said. "Can we bring this guy out of retirement?"

"Absolutely," Meredith said. "He can be an official consultant assigned to this case. But what are you hanging around here for? Hit the road, all three of you. Get back to work."

*

A little while later, Bill was driving Riley and Jake to Greybull. Jake was sitting in the front seat, where he and Bill kept up a running conversation.

In the back seat, Riley relaxed against the headrest. She felt as if a load had been lifted from her mind, at least for now. It was great to be working with Jake again. It was also great to have something to think about other than Shane Hatcher.

Bill was obviously enjoying Jake's company. The two had met back in January when they'd all worked on a case in Florida. Bill and Jake had hit it off famously.

When they started going over the case, she paid closer

attention.

"Let me make sure I understand this," Bill said. "These were considered sexual murders, even though no semen was found."

"That's right," Jake said. "He *intended* to have sex with those women. Even fantasies count."

Riley added, "The women seem to have gone to the motels with him willingly. But he apparently couldn't perform."

Riley could tell by Bill's expression that he was getting interested.

"So the murders were acts of rage," he said.

"The first one definitely was," Jake said. "Probably the first two."

"The last one was different," Riley said. "Her body was found fully clothed, so it seems that he didn't really try to have sex with her, even if that had been his original intention. And she wasn't strangled like the other two. She was smothered, probably with a pillow."

"At the time we thought that was really odd," Jake said. "It flew in the face of the assumption that serial killers always increase their violence with each victim."

He grinned and nodded when Riley added, "Which was one of those old notions that BAU research has found was wrong."

"It also suggests an element of remorse," Bill added.

"That's what Jake and I think," Riley said. "We also think he's still in the area somewhere."

"Is there a reason why?" Bill asked.

After a moment, Jake replied, "Just call it a strong hunch."

"Well, both of you are famous for your hunches," Bill said. "And if he's there, we'll find him,"

I sure hope so, Riley thought, remembering her last sad conversation with Paula Steen.

Justice was much too long overdue.

*

When they pulled into Greybull, Riley watched Jake as he gazed around at the sleepy little town.

"I guess it's been a while since you were here," she said.

"Doesn't look like this place has changed all that much over the years," Jake replied. "I don't figure they've had any more unsolved murder sprees since I was last here. What's our first order of business?"

"We're going to talk to the former sheriff, Woody Grinnell," Riley said.

"Good old Woody," Jake said. "Hell of a nice guy. Not much of a cop, though. He wasn't ready to handle a case like that, but I liked him. What's he doing these days?"

"He retired as sheriff a long time ago," Riley said. "Now he owns a local diner."

Within minutes, they parked in front of Woody's Diner. It was a long, retro-looking diner with a stainless steel exterior. They walked inside and introduced themselves to the hostess, who went back to the kitchen. A moment later, a tall, smiling man came out through the swinging doors, wiping his hands on his apron. Riley knew he was about Jake's age, but Grinnell looked older and softer.

He hurried to Jake and eagerly shook his hand.

"Why, Jake Crivaro, as I live and breathe. How the hell are you?"

"Still living and breathing," Jake said with a hearty laugh.

"I got a call that somebody from the BAU was going to come by today," Grinnell said to Jake. "But I sure wasn't expecting you. Last I'd heard, you'd retired down to Florida."

"You heard right," Jake said. "I got bored finally. Decided to come back and see what's been going on in the bustling metropolis of Greybull."

Both men laughed some more. Riley and Bill introduced themselves, and Grinnell escorted them to an oversized empty booth. A waitress brought coffee for all of them.

Grinnell said, "I don't know if you folks have had breakfast, but as long as you're here, you've got to try my famous omelets. On the house, of course."

The group agreed, and Grinnell gave the waitress the order. "One for me too," he added. "And tell the cook to make 'em good."

Grinnell slid into the booth beside Jake, and the two of them chatted, catching each other up on their lives and what their grown children were doing. The omelets soon arrived and the group started eating.

"So what brings the BAU here?" Grinnell asked. "Things have been quiet, as far as I know."

Riley sensed that Jake was hesitating.

Finally Jake said, "Woody, these folks are reopening the Matchbook Killer case."

The man's perpetual smile disappeared. Riley sensed that this was about the last news he wanted to hear.

86

"I thought that was all in the past," he said. "After all these years, I figured the killer would be long gone and probably dead. He didn't kill again, after all. That's pretty rare for serial killers, isn't it? As I understand it, they usually don't stop until they're caught or dead."

Bill said, "Actually, that's something of a myth. Some serials actually do stop altogether."

Riley added, "We think the Matchbook Killer might have been that type of serial. And we've got a hunch that he's still in this area."

"A hunch, huh?" Grinnell said.

His voice now sounded sad and grim.

"That was an awful thing. Hell, a sheriff of a town like this doesn't expect something like that. Law enforcement here is all about expired fishing licenses, hunting out of season, parking tickets, the occasional rowdy drunk. Premeditated murder was a whole lot more than I signed up for."

Riley remembered what Jake had said.

"Hell of a nice guy. Not much of a cop, though."

Now she understood that Jake hadn't meant to be critical. The poor man had simply been out of his depth, grappling with a terrifying case that even a seasoned pro like Jake Crivaro hadn't been able to crack.

Riley spoke in a gentle tone.

"Mr. Grinnell, we're hoping to revisit some places and witnesses here in Greybull. What about Patom Lounge, where the killer picked up Tilda Steen?"

Grinnell shook his head.

"That place closed years ago. Got turned into a video rental store until that went out of business, what with streaming and all. The building's standing empty now. The guy who owned the bar left the area, and so did the bartender who was working that night."

Riley asked, "What about the motel where the murder took place?"

"It got bulldozed, it's now a parking lot. The man who owned it and was working the front desk that night was Nolden Rich. He died just two years ago. No, there's not a trace of that whole business left here in Greybull. Good riddance, as far as I'm concerned."

Grinnell thought for a moment.

"If you want to check out places and witnesses, you need to go over to Brinkley. McLaughlin's Pub is still there, although I don't know who owns it now. So is the Baylord Inn, where Melody Yanovich was killed."

Grinnell's finger drew an invisible map on the tabletop.

"You'll want to go to Denison, too, way across the interstate. Let me tell you, that town's seen better days. But nobody comes or goes there, so you should find everything pretty much like it was back then. The motel where the body was found is gone, but the bar where he picked the woman up is still there."

He added with a dark laugh, "Who knows? You might even be able to track down old Roger Duffy in Denison."

Jake chuckled.

"Roger Duffy! I haven't thought about him in years!"

Riley didn't remember that name from the police reports.

"Who is he?" she asked.

Jake said, "Oh, only the least reliable witness in the whole history of law enforcement. He was drinking in the Waveland Tap when Portia Quinn got picked up there. Gave a rather colorful description of the killer. Said he was an alien from outer space."

Grinnell shook his head with a smile.

"The last I heard, he was still hanging out at the Waveland—and as certifiably nuts as ever. Still harmless, though."

Grinnell thought for a moment, then said, "Hey, have you still got that old composite sketch?"

"Better than that," Riley said. "We've got a sketch that might show how the killer looks now."

She brought up the image she'd chosen on her tablet. Grinnell looked at it and shook his head.

"I don't recognize the face any more than I ever did. But somebody else might. Send it to me attached to an email and I'll print it out. I'll put on the bulletin board, distribute it as a flyer."

Riley and her companions agreed that it was a good idea. She sent him the image then and there.

Riley, Jake, and Bill finished eating. They thanked Grinnell for the omelets and the advice. As they left the diner, Riley turned and saw Grinnell waving in the doorway. He was still smiling—but it wasn't the same hearty smile as when they'd arrived.

Now he looked sad and somehow broken.

It was the same expression she'd seen in Gloria Corley's eyes at the flower shop yesterday.

As she got into the car with Jake and Bill, Riley felt a pang of sorrow at having reawakened such ugly memories for Woody Grinnell and Gloria Corley.

She knew that they would soon stir up the same memories in others.

Was it the right thing to do?

Only if we catch the killer, Riley thought.

Now she felt as though they had no choice.

CHAPTER SIXTEEN

Riley felt a flash of discouragement as Bill drove the FBI car into Brinkley. She and Jake and Bill were all here to follow up on the cold case. But Brinkley didn't look like she had expected it to.

Can this really be the right town? she wondered.

It hardly seemed possible that Melody Yanovich had actually been murdered here so many years ago. Everything was so different from sleepy little Greybull. Brinkley was all bustling and new, with strip malls and apartment complexes and office buildings. Even the older buildings were heavily remodeled and held what looked like new, thriving businesses.

She said to Bill and Jake, "I don't think I see anything here that could possibly be twenty-five years old."

Jake said, "Yeah, it sure looks different from when I was last here. But it's a college town, you know. Brinkley College was a women's school back then, and now it's coed and much larger than it used to be. Brinkley's seen a lot of changes. It's grown in all directions. But don't worry, there's still some trace of that old crime around here somewhere. We'll find it."

Riley hoped Jake was right. But nothing she saw seemed very encouraging, least of all the sight of McLaughlin's Pub when they pulled into its parking lot. It, too, looked like it had been put here very recently.

Still, a matchbook from this pub had been found with Melody Yanovich's body—a matchbook most likely picked up as a souvenir of a good time but then left in anger and remorse.

Riley and her companions walked inside and looked around. Everything looked shiny and polished, with huge mirrors and simple but tasteful furniture.

"Wow, this place is completely different," Jake said. "I hardly recognize anything. It used to be a lot smaller, but they've added on a lot. This used to be a simple neighborhood bar—nothing fancy but pleasant. Now it's as much a restaurant as a bar, and a pretty high-class joint at that."

Riley looked all around. The place was starting to fill up with lunchtime business. All the customers and staff looked alarmingly young. McLaughlin's Pub had obviously become a hangout for well-to-do college students.

She and her companions walked over to the bar with its huge bank of TV screens, some playing sports and others with news channels. A tall young man wearing a white shirt and a black necktie stood cleaning glasses. Riley thought he looked too good-looking by half, like a male fashion model.

"What can I get for you folks?" the bartender asked with a perfect smile.

Riley and Bill showed their badges and introduced themselves, then introduced Jake.

"I'm Terence Oster," the bartender said. "But everybody calls me Terry."

Jake asked him, "Does the owner of this place still work here—Bill McLaughlin?"

Terry shook his head.

"I never even met him. I don't think anyone else here did either. He sold this place a long time ago. I hear he died a few years back."

Riley pulled up the composite sketch on her tablet.

"Do you remember ever seeing this man?" she asked.

Terry looked at the sketch carefully.

"No, I'm pretty sure I don't."

"He's wanted in connection with a murder," she said.

When Terry looked alarmed, Bill added, "An old cold case. But we want to find him if he's still around."

"If I send it to you with an email, could you print it out?" Riley asked. "Post it up somewhere where people can see it? Maybe make copies and pass them around?"

"Be glad to help in any way I can," Terry said.

Riley took down his email address right away and sent him the image. As she and her companions walked out of the bar, Riley felt a different kind of strangeness surrounding her. Elsewhere she had had to stir up dark memories among people who would rather have forgotten the murders. But coming into McLaughlin's pub was like entering a more innocent world where the murders had never happened.

Either way, she felt like an unwelcome intruder bringing darkness into people's lives.

"That was a bust," Riley said as they walked toward the car.

"We'll get lucky," Jake said. "You'll see."

Riley knew that in some ways Jake's gut instincts were better than her own. Even so, she was beginning to doubt his optimism.

Maybe his instincts have gotten rusty, she thought.

They got into the car and Bill asked, "Where to next?"

"Let's check out the motel," Riley said.

As they drove across town to the Baylord Inn, Riley was struck by the change in their surroundings. The motel was in a pleasant wooded area. There was a three-story main house that appeared to be a bed-and-breakfast-style inn, with a number of quaint little cabins nestled alongside of it. They got out of the car and walked up the steps onto a broad porch with a white wooden railing and white wooden columns.

In the cozy lobby they found an elderly couple. The man was sitting at a table reading a newspaper and the woman was standing at the counter. They both looked up as the group entered. They were pudgy and cheerful and greeted Riley and her companions with broad smiles.

Riley could tell at a glance that they'd been happily married for many years. They probably had children and grandchildren, perhaps even great-grandchildren. She felt a tingle of envy. What would it be like to be in a blissful relationship for so many years? She couldn't begin to imagine.

"Can we help you?" the woman asked.

Riley and Bill took out their badges and introduced themselves. The couple's smiles faded a little.

"Are you the owners?" Riley asked.

"We are," the man said in a charming Southern drawl. "I'm Ronald Baylord, and this is my wife, Donna."

Riley gulped a little as she prepared to explain the purpose of their visit. She was relieved when Jake stepped forward.

"I don't know if you remember me," he said. "I'm Jake Crivaro, and I was with the BAU some years back."

Ronald Baylord's eyes widened.

"Why, I think I *do* remember you. You came around her way back when …"

His voice trailed off. Riley could see a painful realization in his eyes.

"We're looking into a murder that happened here many years ago," Riley said.

The couple wasn't smiling anymore.

"Oh, dear," Ronald said.

"We thought we'd put all that behind us," Donna said. "The police and you other folks kept coming here again and again back in those days, asking all sorts of questions."

Riley felt truly sorry now. But there was nothing she could say to make this easier. She showed them the composite sketch on her tablet.

"We think that the suspect might look like this now," she said. "Do you think you might have seen him?"

"No," Donna said. "I'm sure of it."

"Me too," Ronald said. "If we ever saw the man who came here that night again, I'm sure we'd recognize him. Not that there was anything special about him. He came in here alone and paid in cash. We didn't see the poor woman at all until we found her ..."

His voice faded again.

Riley said, "I wonder if we could get a look at the room where it happened."

"Of course," the man said.

The woman took a key from behind the counter and handed it to Riley.

"It's cabin three. You'll come right to it if you follow the path."

Riley thanked the couple, and she and her companions walked out of the house. As they headed down the path among the trees, Riley was again struck by how different this place was from the rest of Brinkley.

Like it's frozen in time, she thought.

She felt a familiar chill—the kind of feeling she got when she was about to get a true sense of how a murder had happened.

Jake was right, she realized.

There still was a trace of the crime here in Brinkley.

In fact, it was more than a trace.

It was beginning to feel like a palpable reality.

CHAPTER SEVENTEEN

As Riley walked toward the cabin along with Bill and Jake, she felt a sharp tingle up her spine. It was connected with a flash of déjà vu.

Just yesterday on the phone with Jake, she had tried to visualize the murder of Melody Yanovich from the killer's point of view. But her impressions then had been sketchy and possibly inaccurate.

Now she was going to try it again—here where it had happened.

And with Jake here to help her, her impressions were going to be much more reliable, much more vivid.

And much more terrifying, she thought.

With Bill and Jake behind her, Riley turned the key in the door and opened it.

She flipped on the wall light switch and stepped into the room. Jake stayed close to her, while Bill remained standing in the doorway.

Riley saw that the room was clean and cheerful, with elegant drapes, antique-looking furniture, Japanese prints on the walls, and one big bed with tall carved wooden posts at each corner.

"What's the first thing he notices?" Jake asked.

"He notices how bright the room is with the light on," Riley said.

"How does that make him feel?" Jake asked.

Riley paused for a moment.

"Uneasy. Unsafe somehow. He's afraid of the light at times like this. It reveals too much. He knows that it's crazy, but he's afraid she'll see inside him."

"Afraid that she'll see the heart of a murderer?" Jake asked.

Riley's hands grew cold and her palms dampened.

"No. He's never killed anybody. He's never even imagined killing anybody. He's afraid she'll see his uncertainty, his insecurity. He feels like his whole body is emitting cold waves of self-doubt, a visible aura."

A chest of drawers stood just inside the door to the room. There was a pad of paper there with the motel's logo on it.

"He takes a sheet of notebook paper," she said, carrying out the same action. "He puts it in his pocket with the matchbook he picked up at the bar."

"As a souvenir?" Jake asked.

Riley paused.

She remembered playing out these moments with Jake over the phone. She'd figured then that the killer had picked up both the matchbook and the notepaper as souvenirs.

But now she was getting a different impression.

"Maybe partly as a souvenir," she said. "But it's mostly just a nervous gesture. A distraction from his insecurity."

Then Riley reminded herself that the man hadn't been alone in the room.

There was also the girl, Melody Yanovich.

She'd been a college freshman.

Riley said, "He notices how nervous the girl is—but how eager too. After all, she's away from home for the first time in her life. And this is the first real adventure she's had out in the world. Her eagerness makes him uneasy. She's got high expectations. He doesn't know if he can fulfill them."

"Who makes the first move when they're in the room together?" Jake asks.

For a moment, Riley wasn't sure.

Does the man grab her and kiss her?

No, she thought. *He's too shaky and uncertain.*

"She makes the first move," Riley said. "She's jumpy and excited and in a hurry to get things underway. She throws her arms around him and kisses him. It's a clumsy, sloppy kiss that takes him off guard. She pulls away and giggles a little. Is she laughing at him? He's not sure."

Riley tried to relax, to breathe more slowly. But she couldn't. Her breath came in short pants. That was a good thing. She wasn't just seeing things from the killer's point of view. She was viscerally *feeling* his experience.

"What does she do next?" Jake asked.

Riley paused again. When she'd played out this scenario with Jake on the phone, she'd been sure that the girl had gone to the bathroom right away and undressed, then had come back out with a towel wrapped around her.

But now that Riley was here in the actual room, events were playing out differently in her mind.

She remembered something in the police report.

When the girl's clothes were found buried next to her body, a single button had been missing from her blouse. The button had turned up on the floor right beside the bed.

Riley sat down on the bed.

"She pulls him onto the bed. She grabs his hands and tries to get him to undress her. His hands are shaking all over the place. One of her blouse buttons is already loose and it falls off. He apologizes and reaches down to get it. She tells him never mind, it doesn't matter. She undresses herself and he does the same."

Riley pulled back the covers on the bed. She ran her hand over the crisp, clean sheet on the mattress.

"The girl scampers under the covers, still giggling. He gets under the covers too. But the sheets are cold all over his skin. He and the girl try to grope each other, but her body is cold, and her hands are cold too, and everything is …"

Riley gulped hard on the terror that was rising up inside her.

"Everything is wrong, nothing is right. He just … can't. He apologizes. He's ashamed."

Riley tried to imagine the girl's reaction to the killer's impotence.

Does she tell him it's all right, that she knows this happens, and maybe they should just wait for a few minutes and try again?

No, she's too young and inexperienced.

She has no idea how to react.

She just lies there staring at him.

Riley said, "He's wondering—why doesn't she do or say something helpful? Doesn't she understand how painful this is for him? Doesn't she care how he feels? No, she doesn't care, and he's shocked at how shallow and self-centered she is, and suddenly he's not cold anymore, his body is hot with rage, and without even thinking about what he's doing he—"

Riley couldn't say aloud what came next.

But she could feel the man's hard fingers burrow into the girl's soft throat.

She could see the girl's eyes bulging, hear the weird croaking sounds coming out of her mouth.

She could feel the girl's life ebbing away.

"In just minutes it's over," Riley said. "She's lying there with her eyes open. She's not breathing. He can't believe what just happened. He wants to think it's a nightmare that he'll wake up from any second. But the horrible truth closes in around him like a dark fog."

Jake nodded and said, "He knows he's killed a human being."

Riley was feeling lightheaded, a little dizzy.

She was gasping, almost in tears now.

"He's thinking no, no, no, this is impossible! This isn't him, he's not a killer, surely he can make it right, but how?"

She closed her eyes, and the scene became still more vivid. She was the murderer, sitting upright on the bed, looking down at the naked body.

"Does he try CPR?" Jake asked.

Riley struggled to keep her panic under control.

"He thinks he should, but he's not sure how. He remembers something about pressing down on the chest with both hands. He tries it once or twice."

Riley could feel the woman's sternum cracking beneath the killer's outstretched arms.

"But then he stops and thinks. *What if I do bring her back? What then?* She'd contact the authorities. She'd tell them what he did."

"So he can't let her live," Jake said.

"No," Riley said. "Not now."

She stopped to collect her thoughts—or rather the killer's thoughts.

"He's got to get rid of the body. He doesn't know where, but that doesn't matter yet. He clumsily pulls his clothes back on. And as he does ..."

Riley reached into her own pocket, where she had put the piece of notepaper.

"The first things he thinks of are the matchbook and the piece of paper. How differently they feel to him now! They're like tangible pieces of guilt and self-hatred. He knows that he'll leave them with the body. Maybe someone will find them. Maybe someone will find *him*."

Riley had reached into the killer's consciousness as far as she needed to for now—and as far as she dared.

She opened her eyes and almost collapsed onto the bed.

She felt Jake's comforting hand on her shoulder.

"Good work," he said. "Now you own him. He's yours. You'll get him in the end."

Riley pulled herself together, and she and her companions left the cabin.

"You scare me sometimes," Bill said as they headed back to the main house.

Sometimes I scare myself, Riley thought.

But she knew that she had to learn more if they were going to catch this killer.

CHAPTER EIGHTEEN

The next stop for Riley, Bill, and Jake was the town of Denison. Riley took her turn driving there. She felt charged up and energized after her experience back at the Baylord Inn.

Jake's right, she thought. *I own this killer now.*

And she was going to bring him to justice.

Or maybe not.

How could she be sure?

A case this cold presented challenges that Riley wasn't used to. Fortunately, the criminal's mind still seemed to be accessible after all these years. At least, if she wasn't just misleading herself about her insight into him. She would keep going until she found out one way or the other.

Anyway, she and her colleagues weren't going to finish solving it today. It was getting late in the day, and they had to drive back to Quantico after finishing their work in Denison.

As she drove, Bill and Jake were hitting it off really well, telling each other stories about old cases.

After a lull in the conversation, Bill said to Jake, "Hey, my older son Kevin's got a swim meet tomorrow. Want to come?"

"Sure!" Jake said.

Riley found it odd to hear them making weekend plans. When was the last time she'd worked on a case that she and her team been able to take a break away from? There was usually a sense of urgency, a threat of impending disaster in the air, the grim possibility of a murder about to happen.

But not this time.

Not with a case that had almost been forgotten.

Riley was having trouble getting used to this unfamiliar situation.

Interrupting Riley's thoughts, Bill said, "How about you, Riley? Do you want to join us tomorrow?"

Riley hesitated, then said, "Not this time, thanks. You guys have a good time."

She knew that her mind wouldn't be on the swim meet. Something else was going to be dogging her—Shane Hatcher's mysterious promise to help her find her mother's killer.

She remembered again his cryptic message.

"Deny thy father and refuse thy name."

What could it possibly mean?

Did it mean anything that mattered?

She tried to push it out of her mind.

Keep your mind on your work, she told herself.

After all, she'd have a whole weekend to drive herself crazy trying to figure out Shane Hatcher's riddle.

As they approached Denison, Riley sensed that this was going to be a very different town from the others. Denison was some fifty miles from the interstate. The countryside was markedly less plush than it had been around Greybull or Brinkley—and positively poor in comparison to Glidden's surroundings.

This impression grew as she drove across the town line into Denison. Greybull had seemed suspended in time, and Brinkley had been alarmingly new. By contrast, Denison seemed sadly abandoned. There was shabbiness every way she looked—buildings, businesses, and houses in disrepair and near-ruin.

She drove past the Cozy Rest Motel, where Portia Quinn had been murdered. Riley saw that it was closed and boarded up. She'd learned that the motel's owner had long since died. That part of the trail had definitely gone cold.

Was that going to be true everywhere in Denison?

She hoped not.

Soon they arrived at their destination—the Waveland Tap, where the murderer had picked up his second victim. As they pulled into the parking lot, Riley saw that the place looked especially rundown. For a moment she was afraid that it had closed like so many other local businesses. But then she saw the faint glow of a neon sign through the dirty front window.

Riley, Bill, and Jake got out of the car and walked inside. Riley saw that what had once been a flourishing working-class bar was now nothing more than a dimly lit, gloomy dive. Only a handful of customers were sitting at tables and the bar.

A gaunt-looking old bartender was listlessly wiping the bar with a cloth. He looked up at the sight of the new arrivals. Riley and Bill showed him their badges and introduced themselves and Jake.

"FBI, huh?" the man said in a bored tone. "Well, I'm Pete Burridge, and I own this place."

Then he looked at Jake and said, "Hey, haven't I met you before? Yeah, you were here years ago, about that girl who got killed—Portia Quinn was her name. Did you ever catch that killer?"

"No," Jake said. "That's why we're here now."

Pete Burridge chuckled dourly.

"It's sure taking you folks a long time," he said. "I'd have figured you'd have given up by now. Haven't you got fresher cases to solve? People keep getting murdered every day, I hear."

Riley was a little startled by his attitude. Pete wasn't shocked, saddened, or dismayed at the reawakening of this long-ago tragedy—not like the other people they had interviewed. Pete simply didn't seem to care much one way or the other.

Riley pulled up the composite sketch on her tablet and showed it to him.

"We think the killer might look something like this now," she said. "Do you think you've seen him?"

"No, I'm pretty sure I haven't. In fact, you're the first strangers to come into the place in quite a while."

As Bill started asking Pete routine questions, Riley turned her attention to her surroundings.

Could she get any sense of the killer here?

She climbed onto a bar stool, imagining that she was him.

He was sitting next to Portia Quinn, a twenty-one-year-old local woman who worked at a local clothing store.

He was trying the same pickup line he'd used on Melody Yanovich back in Brinkley.

She smiled at him—an encouraging sign.

Does he plan to kill her? she wondered.

No. Riley sensed that he regretted what happened last time. He was haunted and troubled by it. He sincerely hoped that this tryst was going to go well.

Riley's eyes fell upon an ashtray full of matchbooks with the bar's logo.

It seemed eerie to see it here, after all these years.

Just as the killer had done on that fateful night, she picked up a matchbook and put it in her pocket.

But before she could get deeper into her reverie, she heard a man shout from a booth.

"Pete, who're you talking to?"

"None of your business," Pete called back.

Jake squinted toward the booth.

"Hey, is that Roger?" he asked Pete.

"Sure is."

"Wow," Jake said. "I never figured I'd see him again. Kind of surprised he's still around."

The bartender chuckled.

"Oh, there's no killing off old Roger. Although to hear him talk, the whole world's trying to do him in. The government especially."

The man in the booth yelled again at Pete.

"It's the Feds, ain't it? Isn't that old Jake what's-his-name? I thought I'd seen the last of that nosy government bastard long ago. Tell all of them to get the hell out of here. They give me too much trouble as it is without actually showing up in this joint."

"Just ignore him," Pete said.

Jake chuckled in agreement.

Riley vaguely recalled ...

Roger—where have I heard that name?

Then she remembered—the ex-sheriff in Greybull had mentioned someone named Roger Duffy.

Riley turned away from the others and started to walk toward the booth where the man was sitting.

"Hey, where are you going, Riley?" Jake said. "I remember that guy. He's certifiably crazy."

Maybe he is, Riley thought.

But she had a hunch that she ought to find out for herself.

As she neared the man, she saw a half-empty glass of beer and a row of empty shot glasses on the table in front of him. He looked very old and very ill, with fingers knotted up from rheumatism or gout or both.

Riley sat down across the table from him. She winced at the stench of alcohol and body odor. Aside from being drunk and crazy, it seemed that Roger seldom if ever bathed.

Riley showed him her badge.

"I'm Special Agent Riley Paige with the FBI," she said. "I take it that you're Roger Duffy."

"Leave me the hell alone," the man growled.

"Have you got something on your mind, Roger?" Riley asked in a pleasant voice.

Roger Duffy's voice broke out into a snarl.

"Maybe you should tell me. You Feds have been monitoring my thoughts for years. You folks probably know what I'm thinking better than I do."

"We can't read your mind, Roger," Riley said.

The man chuckled grimly and raised his glass of beer.

"No? Well, the booze must be working. That's why I keep on drinking—to keep my brainwaves from being too easy to read."

He pointed to his head.

"You've got no business inside here," he said. "Stay the hell out."

Riley studied the man's tortured face. She had no doubt that he was a full-blown paranoid schizophrenic. He might well be on medication, but it probably didn't do much good, not with all the alcohol in his system.

Riley studied his haggard face carefully.

She remembered what Jake had called him earlier:

"Only the least reliable witness in the whole history of law enforcement."

Jake had also said that his description of the killer had been "rather colorful."

Now that she sat face to face with him, Riley found herself curious about what he'd seen—or thought he had seen.

She said, "Roger, twenty-five years ago you said you saw the man who killed Portia Quinn."

"Tell me something I don't know."

"That's what I'm hoping you can do for me," Riley said.

Again she brought up the composite sketch of the dark-haired, dark-eyed suspect and pushed it across the table so Roger could see it.

"We think he might look something like this now," she said.

Roger shuddered and looked away.

"I don't want to see it," he said.

"Why not?"

"For one thing, he didn't really look like that. For another thing …"

Roger's voice trailed off. But Riley understood what he was leaving unsaid. The man had terrified him deeply.

"Tell me what you saw," Riley said.

"You know all that already," Roger said, still looking away.

As a matter of fact, Riley didn't know—at least not much. Roger's description seemed to have been deemed too bizarre to put into the official record.

"Tell me anyway," Riley said.

Roger turned slowly toward the bar and pointed.

"He was sitting over there, right where you were a minute ago, chatting up Portia. Then he walked right toward me. He looked at me. His eyes weren't human. Streaming blue light was coming out of them."

He sounds crazy, all right, Riley thought.

But she tried not to let her skepticism get the best of her.

She said, "The other witnesses said that his eyes were dark like his hair—hazel-colored."

"Yeah, well, they didn't see him like I did. He looked straight inside me. I couldn't look away. I know what I saw. Then he went into the restroom. I sat here too scared to move. Finally he came out and he looked at me again. This time his eyes were normal—dark like everybody said. Then he went back to the bar and picked up Portia."

Roger leaned across the table.

"Those dark eyes—it was just a disguise. I saw who he really was. And I'm telling you for a fact—he was not of this world."

He let out a grunt of cynical laughter.

"But why am I telling you this stuff? You know it all already. No, that's all I'm going to say to you."

He swallowed down some more of his beer.

At that moment, Riley heard Bill's voice.

"Come on, Riley. We think we're through here."

Bill and Jake were headed for the front door.

Riley hesitated, still trying to decide what to make of what Roger had said.

It was certainly crazy.

But it had also been completely sincere.

She took out her card and reached across the table with it.

"If you think of anything, I'd like you to—"

"Huh-uh," he interrupted, with an angry wave of his hand. "I've already been too cozy with you. You won't get another word from me. If you want to find out anything else from me, just keep using your damned radio waves. But I'll do everything I can to scramble the signal, believe me."

Riley knew there was nothing else she could do.

She got up from the table and followed Bill and Jake out the front door.

"That was a bust," Bill said. "The bartender meant well, but he didn't give us anything helpful. I guess it's time to head back to Quantico."

With a chuckle, Jake said to Riley, "I guess you got to know old Roger."

"Yeah," Riley said.

"Crazy story, huh?"

Riley didn't reply as they got into the car. The truth was, she had a weird hunch. She didn't understand why, but her gut told her that there was a germ of truth in what Roger Duffy had told her.

CHAPTER NINETEEN

It was dark by the time Riley drove up to her house, and she felt distinctly uneasy. She more than half wished she weren't getting the weekend off. With the spare time, she was sure to obsess about Shane Hatcher's riddle and she still had no idea what to make of the Shakespearean line he had texted her.

She probably wouldn't be able to solve the thing. That would be the worst of it.

I'd be better off working, she thought.

When she opened her front door and stepped inside, the first thing she saw was April rushing toward her, jumping up and down. Her daughter's eyes were wild with alarm.

"Mom! Oh my God! You're home! I thought you'd never get home!"

Riley was startled. Had there been some catastrophe since she'd been gone?

"What's the matter?" she asked.

"You're late!"

"Late for what?"

April yelled, waving her arms.

"Dinner!"

For a moment, Riley didn't know what her daughter was talking about. She knew that she was too late for dinner, but Gabriela would have already fed the girls. Riley had planned to just make herself a sandwich. She was looking forward to soaking in a hot tub and going to bed early.

Then certain words played back in her mind ...

"I'll pick you up at eight if that suits you," he'd said.

Blaine! Yesterday he had phoned and after chatting for a while, they decided to get together for dinner; not the family dinner they had talked about earlier, but just the two of them this time.

Riley looked at her watch. It was now 7:45.

"Oh, my God!" she said.

"Don't tell me you forgot," April said, pacing with agitation. "I've been texting you for a half hour now."

Riley had been tired and not expecting any essential calls.

"I was driving. My phone was off."

"So what are you going to do?"

She felt a flash of panic.

"I can't get ready in time," she said.

"Well, you can't cancel, either," April said. "Not at the last minute like this."

Riley took out her cell phone. She saw the thread of anxious texts that April had sent. Then she sent a text to Blaine.

So sorry. I just got home. Give me a half hour?

She waited for just a few seconds. Then she got a reply ...

OK.

April was peering around her, looking at the phone.

"He sounds mad," April said.

"He doesn't sound anything. He just said OK. It'll be all right."

April stepped back and looked her mother over, up and down.

"No, it won't be all right," April said. "You look awful. You look like you've been on the road all day."

"I *have* been on the road all day."

April grabbed her by the hand.

"Come on," she said. "Let's see if we can pull off some kind of a miracle. We've got to work fast."

As April dragged her toward the stairs, Riley noticed that Jilly was sitting in the living room.

"Hi, Jilly," Riley said. "How was your day?"

Jilly didn't reply. She just crossed her arms and glared at Riley.

On the way up the stairs, Riley whispered to April.

"I don't think Jilly's happy that I'm going on a date."

"Yeah, I know," April said. "I've been trying to tell her Blaine's a really good guy. But something else is bothering her too. She's tried calling Dad several times and he won't call back."

Riley felt a prickle of anger.

That bastard! she thought.

But she realized that she shouldn't be shocked. Ryan was just being his old self. She only wished she hadn't built up Jilly's hopes by trying to bring him back into their lives. April might be disappointed, but she was accustomed to her father fading in and out of their lives. Jilly, badly in need of a father figure, had attached herself to Ryan.

April ushered Riley into her bedroom.

"You get cleaned up," April said. "I'll find something for you to wear."

Riley went into the bathroom, took off her clothes, and got into the shower. The hot water reminded her that she was aching all over from so much traveling. The water felt good, but she couldn't take time to enjoy it.

She got out of the shower and turned a dryer onto her hair,

combing it to hang free around her face. She kept looking in the mirror, reminding herself of what April had said.

"You look like you've been on the road all day."

Was she going to be able fix that in less than half an hour?

Riley came out of the bathroom and saw that April had spread out three dresses on her bed. For a moment Riley wondered—when was the last time she'd worn a dress? Then she remembered that it had been at a funeral last month. Dresses simply weren't the best attire for chasing killers.

She frowned at the selection of attire. They all seemed a bit low-cut or short-skirted for tonight.

"I don't know," she said.

"Mo-om! You don't have time get all wishy-washy about this."

Riley ignored April and walked over to her closet. She took out a basic black dress with sleeves.

"How about this one?" she asked.

"Mom, that looks matronly. This is your first real date with him. You've got to look sexy."

"I don't want to look like a vamp."

"Well, you'd sure better not look boring."

Riley probed around in the closet some more. She knew that Blaine's restaurant was a nice place. Customers there wore clothing that ranged from casual to classy. Could she find something in that in-between area?

April pushed past her and rummaged around in the closet until she found another dress.

"This one's perfect," April said.

"It's red," Riley said.

"Well, dark red. It's not too flashy."

April handed the dress to Riley. She looked it over. It really wasn't bad. She figured that the sweetheart neckline wasn't too low. And she knew that the simple lines would look good on her.

"OK, we'll go with this," she said to April. "Now shoo. Get out of here. I can take things from here."

April looked at her watch.

"You've got fifteen minutes," she said. "Don't blow it."

"Shoo, I said!"

April left the bedroom. Riley put on the red dress and high heels. She looked at herself in the mirror, surprised at what she saw.

She really did look quite attractive.

For a second, it didn't quite feel real, as if she were wearing a costume.

Who would ever guess that she was an FBI agent?

Is this the real me? she asked herself.

She decided it was one version of the real her—a version she hadn't glimpsed in quite a while. Maybe it was time she got reacquainted with the woman she was looking at right now.

She walked out of her bedroom. April was waiting for her at the bottom of the stairs.

"Hurry!" April said. "Blaine just pulled up in the driveway."

April helped Riley into her nicest jacket. As Riley walked outside, Blaine got out of the car. Smiling, he walked around and opened the passenger door for Riley.

She wondered—how long had it been since a man had gotten out of a car to open a door for her?

A long time, she thought.

It was a weird feeling. She wondered if she could get used to it.

But as she got into the car, Hatcher's message went through her head again.

"Deny thy father and refuse thy name."

Riley sighed. She couldn't help but obsess about what the riddle meant. Was she going to be able to enjoy this date at all?

CHAPTER TWENTY

Over dinner with Riley, Blaine found it hard to ignore the images that kept flickering through his mind. Riley seemed to be enjoying herself, and he certainly liked being with her again.

But he was haunted by darker times.

He still felt pain in his ribs that were broken on that awful day back in January, when he'd tried to stop a brutal monster from killing Riley's daughter. Then he reminded himself of another terrible day, when Riley had rescued his daughter from the wrath of his ex-wife. Phoebe had come to his house drunk and dangerous when he wasn't home, but Riley had charged in and stopped Phoebe from attacking poor Crystal.

He thought that Riley seemed to attract danger, but she also handled it well. Better than he ever could, he was sure. And he'd never expected to date an FBI agent, especially someone as forceful as this. But he found both her strength and absolutely genuineness exciting. Of course, she was also very good-looking, and in that red dress she was stunning tonight.

He was glad to see that Riley seemed to be enjoying herself, smiling and cheerful, and saying all kinds of good things about her grilled salmon.

Blaine also remembered a bittersweet moment months ago when he and Riley had commiserated about the trials and tribulations of parenthood—and for a lovely few seconds, Riley had taken his hand and he had squeezed hers back. That one was a good memory.

More than once, there had been a spark between them. Events and family considerations had separated them, but might that spark still be there?

Was he going to find out this evening?

Right now they were just finishing dessert—raspberry cheesecake prepared in his own Blaine's Grill kitchen. Riley had been telling him all about the cold case she was working on. Despite his distracting memories, Blaine found it fascinating to hear how Riley was applying her mind to murders that had taken place a quarter of a century before.

Brilliance—that was another attribute that Blaine discovered he liked very much.

"How many cold cases have you worked on?" he asked.

"This is my first," Riley said.

"How does it feel? In comparison to other cases, I mean."

Riley seemed to mull over the question.

"It feels—strange. When we got started, I couldn't shake a feeling of futility. Everything about it seemed so far away, hard to get hold of. The evidence seemed stale somehow, like it didn't mean as much anymore. But before long ..."

Blaine noticed that Riley shuddered a little.

"It feels like it all happened yesterday. Like it's not a cold case at all. It's just as urgent and pressing as any new case."

She shrugged a little and added, "Justice is justice, I guess. And it's better late than never."

Blaine realized how much he'd missed having her as a neighbor.

Riley took another bite of her cheesecake and sighed with approval.

"This is the best cheesecake I've ever tasted. And raspberry— that's my favorite!"

Blaine stifled a chuckle.

Yes, I know, he wanted to say.

Maybe later on he'd tell her how he knew.

It depended on how things went from here.

When they both finished eating, Riley said, "Thanks so much, Blaine. I've had a lovely time."

"Oh, but the evening's not over yet," Blaine said.

Riley looked at him with a dubious expression.

Oh, no, he thought. *She thinks I'm making a pass at her right here and now.*

He'd made plans of a different sort.

And now he was feeling awfully nervous about how those plans would play out.

"Would you like to take a walk?" he asked.

What if she says no?

"I'd love that," Riley said.

He helped her into her jacket and they left the restaurant.

It was a cool March night with a pleasant promise of spring in the air. The area around Blaine's restaurant was charming, a restored cultural district. A few temporary booths had been set up, and materials were scattered about for many more to follow.

Blaine explained as they walked, "Tomorrow there's going to be a big arts and crafts fair here."

"Oh, yes, I read about that," Riley said. "It sounds like it's going to be marvelous."

"Yes, there will be lots of people and music. Come on, let me show you something."

As Blaine led Riley toward a particular building, he was glad to hear the music playing inside. He had expected that, so things were moving along just fine.

He escorted her inside, where a large hall had been decorated with colorful flowers and trees to welcome the spring. A band was on a platform rehearsing for tomorrow.

When the leader of the group saw Blaine and Riley, he grinned and nodded.

Blaine gave the bandleader a wink.

Then the band started playing an old song—"One More Night" by Phil Collins.

Riley gasped with delight.

"Why, that's my favorite song!" she said.

"I know," Blaine said. "I asked my friend Mickey to play it tonight."

Riley looked at him with surprise.

"You know? How?"

"The same way I knew that raspberry cheesecake was your favorite dessert."

Riley stared at him for a moment, trying to catch his meaning.

Then she rolled her eyes and laughed and said, "Oh, no!"

Blaine laughed.

She's figured it out, he thought.

That afternoon, April had called Blaine to make sure he knew everything he needed to know for his date with her mother. He'd asked April about Riley's favorite dessert and favorite song. April had been thrilled to give him that information and much more.

Still laughing, Riley said, "I'm going to give that girl a serious talking to the next chance I get."

"Don't be too hard on her," Blaine said. "She was just doing her job."

"Tattling about her mother's favorite things?"

"Precisely."

Riley just looked at him for a moment. Then with an impish glint in her eyes, she said, "May I have this dance?"

Blaine smiled and nodded, then led her through a pair of double doors that led outside into a dimly lit garden patio. The lovely music followed them into the cool night air.

They started to dance slowly and close.

After a few moments, Riley lifted her face up to his, and their lips met.

When the kiss came to an end, a strange and curious expression crossed Riley's face.

Blaine wondered—had the kiss been OK?

He suddenly felt terribly insecure.

Then Riley said in a quiet voice …

"O Romeo, Romeo, wherefore art thou Romeo?"

Blaine felt a smile rise up inside him.

What an amazingly romantic thing to say! he thought.

But then he realized that Riley wasn't looking at him at all. She was looking at a balcony that hung over the garden. A young woman was standing there staring into the night.

"Of course!" Riley murmured aloud. "Why didn't I figure it out before?"

Blaine couldn't help feeling a bit deflated.

Their romantic moment was definitely over.

"Has this got something to do with your cold case?"

"No," Riley said distractedly, still looking away from him. "I mean yes. Another cold case."

Then she looked at him and said, "Oh, Blaine, I'm so sorry, but I've got to go home right now. This has been wonderful. We'll do it again. I promise."

Blaine smiled a bit stiffly and led her to his car.

As he drove Riley home, Blaine told himself that the date had been as much of a success as he could have hoped for.

But he had to wonder what on earth she had meant when she'd said …

"O Romeo, Romeo, wherefore art thou Romeo?"

CHAPTER TWENTY ONE

Instead of responding to Blaine's occasional attempts at conversation, Riley was focused on a different set of words. She had very little to say as he drove her home. She was listening to the line that kept rattling through her head.

"Deny thy father and refuse thy name."

Of course! she thought. The meaning of Hatcher's message should have been obvious to her right away.

But she had been distracted by the thought that the message had something to do with her own troubled relationship with her father—that is, if it meant anything at all.

But now she knew—it was all about that name that came in the very next Shakespearian line.

Romeo, Romeo, Romeo ...

She remembered something else that Juliet had said in that same scene ...

"What's in a name?"

As things turned out, there was a lot of meaning in that name—Romeo.

That is, if Riley's new insight was right.

She knew she was being rude, but she couldn't help it. If her hunch was correct, she was on the verge of a discovery that was going to change her life forever. The thought had taken her breath away.

When Blaine pulled up in front of the townhouse and parked, Riley leaned over and gave him a swift, unromantic kiss—nothing at all like the lovely kiss they'd shared back in the garden.

"Oh, Blaine, I'm so sorry to bail on you like this but ..."

Blaine smiled rather weakly. Riley knew that the poor guy had no idea what her sudden mood change was all about.

And she couldn't tell him.

She couldn't tell anybody—at least not yet, and maybe never.

"It's OK, Riley," Blaine said.

"We'll do this again, I promise."

As soon as the words were out, she wondered if they were true.

If things in her life changed as much as she expected, would there still be a place for Blaine in it?

How could she know?

How could she make such a promise?

She told herself that she was being irrational. After all, what would it mean to finally bring her mother's killer to justice?

Surely it would make everything in her life better—including her relationships.

I'll make things right with Blaine, she told herself.

But doubt kept tugging at her.

Blaine smiled and silently squeezed her hand. Riley got out of the car and hurried into her townhouse. She went straight upstairs and plopped herself in front of her computer. She paused for a moment, mulling over her hunch.

She remembered that her father had served in the 11th Battalion of the 30th Marines infantry regiment.

But he'd never told her the actual name of the company he'd commanded.

He'd always seemed to be almost superstitious about saying the name aloud.

Riley knew that "Romeo" was the word the military used for the letter R—like "Alpha" for A or "Charlie" for C. She also knew that the Marines sometimes used those words to designate companies.

She went to the US Marines website and looked at a list of the companies in the 11th Battalion, 30th Marines.

She gasped a little when she saw that one of the companies was indeed called the Romeo Company.

Then she asked herself, *What years did Daddy serve?*

She remembered that he had been in Vietnam during the late 1960s.

She ran a search and quickly found the 1968 roster of the Romeo Company. And sure enough, she found her father's name:

Sweeney, Oliver J. CAPTAIN

This is it, Riley thought. *The unit Daddy commanded.*

She had found the trail that Hatcher had wanted her to find.

But how was she supposed to follow that trail?

It looked like there were more than two hundred names on this roster.

Was one of those the name of her mother's killer?

Riley had always been told that it was a guy who had come into the candy store to rob it and whoever happened to be there. A random act of robbery that turned into murder. The possibility that the murderer was somehow connected with her father had never occurred to her. He had been overseas at that time.

But that seemed to be exactly what Hatcher was suggesting with his cryptic clue.

And now, how was she going to find the killer among these names?

Riley didn't even know how many men on this list were still alive.

Riley dialed the phone number for Marine Corps Base Quantico. The switchboard connected her with a man in the general information department. Riley explained that she was a BAU agent, although she didn't mention that she wasn't officially working on the case.

She said, "I need all the information I can get about men who served in Romeo Company, Eleventh Battalion, Thirtieth Marines, in the late 1960s. I've got a roster for 1968 in front of me, but I need to know more. Is that kind of information available?"

"Certainly," the man said. "But I'm afraid not at this hour. You should call tomorrow between eight and five. Explain what you need to know to an administrative assistant. We'll be glad to help you then."

Discouraged, Riley thanked the man and ended the call.

Then she sat at her computer feeling stranded.

There wasn't a thing she could do right now.

But how was she going to get any sleep tonight?

All I can do is try, she thought.

She undressed and got into bed.

*

All was darkness, except for one spot of light directly in front of Riley.

Someone stepped into that light.

It was Blaine.

He stepped toward her with a friendly smile on his face. Without knowing why, Riley pushed him sharply aside.

Then Bill stepped into the light and approached her. She pushed him aside as well.

Behind Bill was Brent Meredith, and she pushed him too ...

... then Ryan ...

... then Gabriela ...

... then Jilly ...

... and even April.

She pushed away every single person in the world she cared about.

She didn't know why, except that she had a terrible feeling that they were all standing in her way.

Finally, she found herself facing a silhouette of a man. She couldn't see his face, but she knew who he was.

He was her mother's killer.

She had found him.

And now she was alone with him.

She could hear him snickering with satisfaction.

He thinks he's won, *Riley thought.* He thinks he's beaten me.

Then with dread she wondered ...

Is he right?

Riley awoke and sat bolt upright in bed. She was sweating and shaking all over.

Just a nightmare, she realized. But it was unlike any other nightmare she could remember having.

And for some reason, it was uniquely terrifying.

What did it mean?

Without knowing why, Riley dreaded the answer to that question. Just thinking about it only frightened her more.

It meant nothing, she decided. *Nothing at all.*

Riley lay back down and went to sleep again. She managed a dark dreamless sleep for the rest of the night.

*

Riley woke up early the next morning—too early to make that call to Marine Corps Base Quantico.

As she got out of bed and got dressed, she found herself thinking ...

No phone calls. Not today.

For one thing, she doubted that she could get all the information she needed over the phone. For another thing, she felt the need to *do* something, to get out of the house and deal with someone face to face.

Riley walked downstairs and found Gabriela already making elaborate preparations for tonight's dinner.

"Buenos días, Señora Riley!" she said with a bright smile. "I didn't hear you come in last night."

"Are the girls up yet?" Riley asked.

"No. They were wondering last night what you would want to

115

do with them today. I didn't know what to tell them."

Riley's heart sank. Of course, it was Saturday.

She hadn't considered that the girls might be looking forward to doing something together today. But she was completely preoccupied with the Romeo code. She would just have to make it up to them somehow.

"Gabriela, I've got to go out on some errands," she said. "I'll just grab a roll and go."

"When will you be back?"

Riley gulped.

"I don't know," she said. "It may take a while."

Gabriela gave her a silent, penetrating look that made Riley wince. She grabbed a breakfast roll and left the kitchen. She ate the roll quickly on her way to the car. As she pulled out of the parking area, that sinking feeling deepened, and she felt mysteriously sad.

Riley knew that it was only a short drive to Marine Corps Base Quantico.

Even so, she had the feeling that she was going a long way from home.

CHAPTER TWENTY TWO

As Riley neared Quantico, she hoped the trip was going to be worth it. It wasn't a visit she wanted to make. In fact, she felt a lump of dread in the pit of her stomach.

She checked in through the familiar front gate, but today she wasn't taking her usual route. She was headed into the main Marine Corps Base that took up most of the big eighty-six-square-mile property.

As she went by, she gazed at the statue that symbolized pride and honor. It was a smaller replica of the Iwo Jima Memorial at Arlington National Cemetery—the statue of six Marines raising an American flag.

The sight did not make her feel warm and welcome.

She had far too many unpleasant memories of military life from her childhood.

She hadn't been to this part of the base very often—which was odd, because she worked very close by. The FBI Academy and BAU were actually tenants on this property. But she never came here except when business demanded it.

She passed through additional security and stated her business. Then she was directed to the office of Dudley Carter, an administrative support assistant. The sight of so many people in uniform as she walked down the hall stirred her sense of dread. She could remember when her dad had dressed like that.

When she walked into Carter's modest office, she was relieved to see that the young man was a civilian—or at least wasn't wearing a uniform, and there wasn't anything the least bit military about his manner. He was a skinny guy with thick-lensed glasses and a small jaw.

She presented her badge and introduced herself and explained why she'd come.

"I take it this has to do with an FBI case," he said.

Riley felt her throat tighten as she said, "Yes."

How many lies was she going to have to tell this man?

She said, "I need information about men who served in Romeo Company under Captain Oliver Sweeney back in the late 1960s. It was a unit in the Eleventh Battalion, Thirtieth Marines."

Carter seemed a little skeptical.

"That kind of information is easy to get online," Carter said.

"I know, but I need to winnow them down. I need to find out

which men are still alive, and where they are now."

Carter looked at Riley for a moment.

Riley felt nervous.

Was he going to ask her about what kind of case she was working on?

Was he going to ask for the name of her superior at the BAU?

If so, what was she going to say?

Steady, she told herself. *It's not like you're asking for classified information.*

Finally Carter turned toward his computer and said, "Give me the years you're looking for."

Riley told him the years that her father had commanded Romeo Company.

Carter clacked away at the keyboard for a few moments.

He said, "I've got two hundred forty-three living men and their addresses here—but those are only the ones we have current records about. I'm sure that there are some who are still alive, but who we've lost track of. And some of the ones I've got here might have died since our info was updated."

Riley felt a pang of despair.

How could she possibly sort through that many names?

It would be one thing if she had BAU resources at her disposal.

But she was completely on her own.

"How many of those men are living in Virginia?" she asked.

Carter typed a bit more.

"I see twenty-five," he said.

That will have to do, Riley thought.

She asked Carter to print out the list of names and addresses. Then she made her way out of the building.

She breathed a little easier out in the open air, away from all the people in uniform and the oppressive military rigidity of the place. But she was still anxious. She got into her car and sat behind the wheel looking at the list that Carter had printed out for her.

She had twenty-five names and twenty-five addresses.

Was this information of any use at all?

How could she possibly know?

Whoever killed her mother must be alive—otherwise why had Hatcher given her the clue at all?

But was it one of the men on this list?

It might be any of the 243 names that Carter had started with— or none of them.

It was only a wild guess that the murderer even lived in

Virginia.

It wasn't even a hunch.

Her gut wasn't telling her anything at all.

She closed her eyes tight and tried to think it through.

A man who served with her father in the Marines had possibly—just possibly—murdered her mother.

She was still struggling to grasp that likelihood.

After all, she had spent her life thinking that the killer was just a random armed robber.

She thought the killing had been pointless, meaningless, stupid.

But now she realized …

It was personal.

At least that's what Hatcher's message implied. The killer must have been someone who held a bitter grudge against her family—probably against her father.

She groaned a little.

Someone who hated Daddy, she thought. *That hardly narrows it down!*

After all, her father had probably inspired some degree of dislike or even hatred among almost all the men who ever served under his command. He'd made enemies faster than any other human being she'd ever known.

He'd even made enemies out of both his own daughters.

She looked at the piece of paper in her hand.

That was all it was—a piece of paper. With names printed in neat lines, names followed by data that could well be completely useless.

Faces, she thought. *I need to look into people's faces.*

And they had to be people who hated her father.

Little by little, an idea occurred to her of where people like that could be found.

She was beginning to remember something that Daddy had said about being shut out.

She took out her tablet and started searching for the place she had in mind. As she did so, the knot of anxiety that had been growing inside her got larger.

People who hate my father, she thought with a shudder.

All her life, she'd known a man who hated him more than anyone else on earth.

And that was her father himself.

CHAPTER TWENTY THREE

By the early hours of that afternoon, Riley was driving west into the Appalachian Mountains. Her apprehension mounted with every passing mile. As the landscape climbed around her, she felt as if she were driving deep into the darkness of the past.

She remembered that her father used to hang out at a VFW post in Milladore, a little town not far from his cabin. During one of her rare visits to his cabin some years ago, he'd complained that he'd gotten kicked out and banned from the post.

"Why?" Riley had asked him.

"Why do you think?" he'd growled.

She could think of a thousand good reasons why he'd gotten himself kicked out. Still, she'd felt sorry for him. She knew that his membership in the Veterans of Foreign Wars had meant a lot to him.

He'd earned it, after all.

To join the VFW, one must have been decorated for foreign service in actual combat. She knew that her father had earned more than his share of medals, including a Combat Action Ribbon and an Expeditionary Medal. He'd proudly hung those medals on the wall of his cabin. They were still there—and they would probably stay there now that Riley wasn't going to sell the place. She wasn't likely to take them down, and she doubted that Shane Hatcher would either.

She didn't know exactly why her father had gotten kicked out of that post. But she might still find some of his enemies there—perhaps a whole nest of them.

She drove into Milladore and saw that it looked much like Denison—a rundown little town that had seen better days. Businesses were boarded up, and many houses looked as though they were no longer inhabited.

As she parked in front of the VFW post, the building reminded her of the Waveland Pub—so dilapidated that for a moment she wondered if it was still open. But there were a few old cars and bikes in the weedy parking lot, and she saw some grizzled old men coming and going through the front door.

When she got out of the car, she heard an old country western song playing inside the post.

She suddenly wondered …

Are they even going to let me in?

She realized she should have thought of that before.

She wasn't a veteran herself, of course.

A large man with chewing tobacco stuffed in his cheek stood just inside the doorway. Judging from his considerable brawn, Riley took him to be a bouncer.

"Ain't seen you here before, little lady," he said. "What kind of action you seen?"

Riley was about to pull out her badge when another man called out from inside.

"Let her in, Chester. I like the looks of her."

Well, I guess that's one way to get in here, she thought.

Perhaps this was even a lucky break. Things might go better if she didn't have to identify herself as an FBI agent. For the time being, she'd just let the men wonder what the hell she was doing here.

As she continued on inside, she saw that the place was every bit as rundown inside as it was outside. There were a number of men there—some playing pool, others sitting at restaurant tables, and a handful sitting at the bar.

At a glance, Riley didn't see a single young man in the lot, much less any women of any age. There were surely no veterans here of Afghanistan or Iraq. This wasn't a town where young people were likely to settle down and spend their lives. Probably a good many of these guys had served Vietnam, some in the Korean War, and maybe even a few in World War II.

A man sitting at the bar was waving her in, his lecherous smile revealing a couple of missing teeth. Riley guessed that he was the guy who'd called out to vouch for her a moment before.

"Sit down here, honey," he said, patting the stool next to him.

Riley fought down the urge to say she wasn't his "honey" and to fuck the hell off.

Now isn't the time, she thought.

She sat down on the bar stool next to him.

Still leering, the man asked her, "What'll you have to drink, cutie? I'm buying."

Riley almost refused the offer. But she figured it was best to keep everyone here more or less happy to see her.

Besides, she thought wryly, *it's not like I'm on duty.*

She said, "I'll have a double bourbon, straight up."

The bartender chuckled, and the buyer's smile faded a little. Riley guessed that he'd expected her to order something more "ladylike." Now he seemed to be a little bit intimidated.

121

The bartender poured her the bourbon and she took a sip.

She planned to drink slowly, probably not even finish it. Right now the drink was something of a prop, just her way of fitting in.

The bartender asked, "Where're you from?"

"Fredericksburg," Riley said.

The bartender snorted with surprise.

"What brings you all the way out here to these boondocks?"

"Curiosity," Riley said. "Do any of you fellows happen to remember a retired officer who used to come in here? His name was Oliver Sweeney."

The bartender chuckled darkly.

"Yeah, I reckon pretty much everybody here remembers ol' Psycho Sweeney. We kicked him out of here years ago. How's he doing these days?"

"He's dead," Riley said.

The bartender chuckled again and shook his head.

"Is he now? Well, I'm all broken up to hear tell of it. What's he to you and you to him?"

Riley was about to say something vague before the man sitting next to her let out a peal of sharp laughter.

"Holy shit!" he said. "You're Psycho Sweeney's little girl, ain't you?"

Riley wasn't pleased at being identified. But there was no point in denying it.

"How do you know?" she asked.

With another laugh, the man said, "Hell, do you ever look in the mirror? It's written all over your face, girl. You look just like him."

Riley felt her face redden—whether from embarrassment or anger, she wasn't sure. But the man was right. Sometimes when she looked in a mirror, she could see her father looking back at her.

And she hated that.

"Why was he banned from this place?" she asked.

The bartender shook his head.

"It got to the point where there was no putting up with him," he said. "After he'd had just a couple of drinks, you couldn't even look at him without him punching you out."

The man on the barstool added, "How do you think I lost these teeth? I reckon half the guys in this joint were on the receiving end of that fist of his at one time or another. And they couldn't even tell you why."

The bartender squinted at Riley with interest.

"But why are you here?" he asked. "What do you want?"

Riley struggled with an answer for a moment.

But then she realized …

I might as well tell the truth.

"I'm looking for the man who killed my mother."

She noticed a change in the expression of the man sitting next to her. He wasn't leering anymore. He looked genuinely sympathetic.

"Girl, that's some ancient history you're talking about there," he said. "How long has it been since poor Karen got shot down in that candy store?"

"Thirty-four years," Riley said.

"Oliver never got over it," the man said. "It's part of what made him so mean, I guess. But do you really think you'll find the man who killed her in this joint?"

The bartender said, "Guess I can see your logic. This place is full of men who had reason to hate him. But there ain't nobody here who hurt her in any way, that's certain."

Riley had a sinking feeling that the bartender was right.

Was she here on a fool's errand?

Before she could think it through, she heard a rough voice behind her.

"Oliver Sweeney's daughter, are you?"

Riley turned and saw an enormous hulk of a man looming over her. He was obviously drunk and he had a sneer on his face.

He pointed to his crooked nose and said, "See this nose? Oliver broke it for me. And I've been waiting years to get my own back."

He drew back his fist, and Riley knew that a sucker punch was on his way. Fortunately, the man's reflexes were slow from however much alcohol he had consumed. Riley easily ducked the blow, and the swing of his arm threw him off balance. She hurled herself out of her chair headfirst into his stomach, and they both fell to the ground.

Riley wound up straddling the man. Before he could move, she raised her fist, ready to slam it into his face if necessary. She could tell by the man's stunned expression that he wasn't going to put up any resistance.

But then she looked up and saw four other men standing in a menacing semicircle around her.

This isn't going to be easy, she thought.

For a fleeting instant, she thought of drawing her weapon.

But then she heard the bartender's voice from behind the bar.

"Back off, boys," he said.

She turned around and saw that the bartender had picked up a shotgun and was pointing it at the group.

The man sitting on the barstool let out a whoop of laughter.

"Hell, the apple don't fall too far from the tree, does it? You're a lot like your daddy in more ways than one."

With his shotgun still raised, the bartender gazed at Riley with an admiring smile.

"Lady, I like your style. But I hope you'll understand that I've just got to ask you to leave. Nothing personal."

Riley wavered for a moment.

Should she take out her badge and show them that she was an FBI agent? She couldn't imagine that it would do any good.

Besides, the bartender was right. If any one of the men here was her mother's killer, Daddy would have killed him years ago.

She climbed off the prostrate man and walked silently away.

As she reached the door, she heard a man's voice.

"Lady …"

She turned and saw that it was the bouncer she had met when she first arrived. His expression was kindly now.

He said, "Your daddy warn't always a bad man, not deep down. And he sure enough served his country. It was just life and 'Nam and Karen's death that messed him all up inside. That's how he got all mean."

Riley was too touched to know what to say.

The bouncer smiled.

"You're not exactly a civilian yourself, are you?"

Riley smiled back at him and produced her badge.

"I'm Special Agent Riley Paige with the FBI," she said.

"I'm not surprised," the bouncer said. "You really are a regular chip off the old block. So are you here in an official capacity?"

"No," Riley said. "This is personal. All I want is to find my mother's killer."

The man looked away for a moment, as if thinking about something.

"Lady, I don't want to tell you how to do your business. But I wonder if maybe you're going about this the wrong way."

"How so?" Riley asked.

"Well, if you're looking for a man who hated your daddy, you're casting a pretty wide net. Maybe you should be looking for somebody *he* hated. Mean as he was, he didn't actually hate all that many folks in particular. It was more like he had it in for human beings in general. But …"

The bouncer paused.

"I can think of one man he really hated," he said.

"Who?" Riley asked.

"That would be Byron Chaney. Served with Oliver in 'Nam. Byron was wounded, and he got an honorable discharge. They were close friends for years until something went wrong between them. I never did know what it was. But your daddy hated him something fierce. Byron stopped coming in here ages ago."

Riley caught her breath.

"Where can I find this man?" she asked.

"Don't rightly know. Byron fell on bad times, they say. His life fell apart, and so did he. Got really messed up. Last anybody here heard about him, he was working up north of here at the Forsyth Ski Resort. I reckon he's still there."

Riley was almost too excited to speak.

"Thank you," she said. "Thank you."

The man nodded and smiled.

Riley walked out to her car with a feeling of renewed hope.

CHAPTER TWENTY FOUR

Reeling with excitement about this new information, Riley sat in her car in the weedy parking lot of the VFW post. Her hands fumbled nervously as she unfolded the long list of living men who had served with her father.

Sure enough, there the name was:

Chaney, Byron SGT

After all these years, was she closing in on her mother's killer?

She also kept thinking about what the bouncer had said.

"Your daddy warn't always a bad man, not deep down."

It had seemed like a startling insight to Riley. She herself had long since given up thinking of her father as ever having been a good man.

Had she misjudged him?

She certainly hadn't ever spent much time thinking about what kind of man he must have been before the war, and before his wife's death.

Should she have shown him more understanding in life?

Maybe, she thought.

But all she had to go on was the way he'd behaved while she was growing up. He had been consistently cruel to her, to her sister, to anyone she saw him with.

How could she have understood whatever was driving him?

The bouncer had also said ...

"Mean as he was, he didn't actually hate all that many folks in particular."

Now that Riley thought about it, she realized that this was true.

Her father had railed against the world and human nature.

But how often could she remember him singling out an individual for his ire?

Seldom—if ever.

So if he'd really hated this man named Byron Chaney, it must truly mean something.

Riley had heard of the Forsyth Ski resort, and knew that it was somewhere farther north. She checked her car's GPS service for directions. Then, just as she was about to start driving, her cell phone buzzed.

She felt a wave of guilt as she saw that it was a text from April.

In her mind, Riley saw again the sharp, silent look Gabriela had given her this morning when she'd told her that she was leaving without spending time with the girls.

The message from April read …

Where are U?

Riley typed back …

I'm in Milladore.

April's reply came quickly …

Working on a case?

Riley sighed, her guilt rising.

She typed evasively …

I have 2 c some people 2day.

After a few seconds, April replied.

Will u b home for dinner?

Riley felt her throat tighten.

It was up to her to decide, right now.

She could drive straight home and spend the rest of the day with Jilly and April.

She could forget about Byron Chaney, at least for today.

After all, what was her hurry? Everything he might be involved with had happened a long time ago.

Surely she could pay her visit to him some other time.

She wanted to type *Yes, I'll b home in time.*

But her fingers simply wouldn't do it.

If Byron Chaney was truly her mother's killer, she couldn't let another day pass without bringing him to justice.

She didn't know what kind of justice that might be, but it couldn't wait.

She typed …

I don't think so. See U later tonite.

She sat staring at the phone for most of a minute.

April didn't reply at all.

Riley's eyes filled with tears and she stifled a sob.

She tried to rationalize her decision, telling herself that there would be other Saturdays, and besides, someday April would be grateful that Riley had found justice for her grandmother's death. But of course that was nonsense. April had never known her grandmother. Why should she be grateful?

Riley knew that there was simply no escaping the truth.

Her motives were completely selfish.

But she couldn't bring herself to do otherwise.

She began to drive north, following the spoken GPS directions.

127

For the next hour and a half, Riley drove steadily northward on the interstate that ran through the Shenandoah Valley. The Forsyth Ski Resort was on the slopes of the Appalachian Mountains, almost at the West Virginia state line.

When she arrived on the grounds, she saw that it was the kind of winter resort that relied on artificial snow to fill out the season. She noticed a vacant golf course as she drove along. Doubtless the place offered other recreational activities for tourists and vacationers.

Right now it appeared to be in between seasons.

Would Byron Chaney be working here even so?

She desperately hoped that this wasn't going to be a wasted trip.

She walked into the spacious front lobby of the main building. A kindly-looking middle-aged woman was at the front desk. Riley quickly decided that things might go better if she appeared to be here in an official capacity. So she pulled out her badge and introduced herself to the woman.

Riley said, "I'm looking for a former Marine, a veteran who might be working here. His name is Byron Chaney."

The woman looked a little worried.

"Is he in some kind of trouble?" she asked.

Riley had no idea how to answer that question.

Instead she said, "I need to talk to him about a case I'm following up on."

The woman seemed slightly puzzled.

"Are you sure you've got the right person?" she asked.

"Is he here?"

"Yes, I'm sure he is. Byron lives right here on the grounds. He's sort of our handyman—odd jobs, cleaning up, repairs, working on the grounds, that kind of thing. But he hasn't been off this property for years. I don't understand how he could help you."

Riley was starting to realize that the woman felt protective of Byron Chaney. She wondered why.

"It's an old case," Riley said.

The woman said nothing for a moment. She seemed very reluctant.

Finally she pointed outside.

"You'll most likely find him in his room. It's over there in the maintenance building—a little door around on the far side next to our equipment storage area."

Riley thanked the woman and walked across well-kept grounds to the maintenance building. She went around the structure and found big garage-type doors on the back. A smaller door had a sign on it that read "EMPLOYEES ONLY."

She knocked on the door.

She got no answer, then knocked again.

A scratchy, rough voice called out from inside.

"Who is it? What do you want?"

A shudder ran through Riley's body.

She remembered the man in the candy store saying to her mother …

"Give me your money."

Was this the same voice, weathered with age?

She didn't yet know.

CHAPTER TWENTY FIVE

Riley felt dizzy with apprehension. Was her mother's killer on the other side of that door?

"Who is it?" the voice called again.

Riley wavered.

How should she introduce herself?

Should she say right away that she was an FBI agent?

Finally she called out, "I just want to talk to you."

"Like the sign says, 'employees only.'"

Not knowing what else to say, Riley simply replied, "Please."

A silence followed.

"Come on in," the man finally said.

Riley opened the door onto a large, damp space filled with equipment and storage of one kind or another—lawn machinery, garden tools, piles of boxes on pallets. She didn't see anybody at first.

"In here," the voice said.

Riley turned and saw an open door that led into a small room. She went to the doorway.

The man was sitting on a cot wearing jeans and a flannel shirt. He looked old—probably older than he really was, Riley guessed. He was bulky and muscular, but looked oddly frail and fragile somehow. His hair was cut in much the same military-style buzz cut that her father's had always been. His heavily lined face had a dull, grayish cast to it.

The room was dimly lit, with no windows. Everything was extremely neat, and very sparse. A handful of books on a small table stood tidily between two bookends. A small throw rug on the floor was placed squarely next to the cot.

Riley immediately noticed the absence of any pictures or photographs.

The man was staring at an old black-and-white TV that was sitting on a wooden bench at the end of the cot. A soccer game was playing, but the sound was off.

"What do you want?" the man asked without looking at Riley. His voice was hoarse and scratchy. She stepped inside.

"Are you Byron Chaney?"

"Who's asking?"

Riley decided that he wasn't going to talk to her unless she gave him an official reason. She took out her badge.

"I'm Special Agent Riley Paige with the FBI," she said.

The man turned his head and looked at her. His eyes were deep set and dead looking. His expression showed just a hint of worried surprise.

Riley took another step forward and sat down on a stool near his cot

"You've got the wrong guy," he said.

"You don't know what I'm here about," Riley said.

"Whatever it is, you've got the wrong guy. Those days are long behind me."

Those days? Riley wondered.

What did he mean by "those days"?

She folded her hands to keep them from shaking. They felt damp and clammy. As the moments passed, it seemed more and more certain to Riley that this man was her mother's killer.

The man said, "Look, I've been straight for years. I've worked hard to turn things around, my life and all. And these people here at the Forsyth, they're kind to me, they take care of me. What you see in this room—this is all I've got in the whole wide world. I'm asking you, please don't take it all away."

Riley didn't speak for a moment.

Then she asked, "Did you serve in the Marines? Romeo Company, Eleventh Battalion, Thirtieth regiment?"

Byron Chaney nodded silently.

"Did you serve with Captain Oliver Sweeney?"

A strange, stricken look crossed Byron's face.

"He was my commander. He was my ..."

His voice faded and he looked away. Riley sensed that he was about to say "friend." But for some reason, he couldn't say the word aloud.

She wondered why.

Then he said in a low voice, "Wait a minute."

He turned his head slowly toward her.

"Riley? You said your name's Riley?"

Riley nodded.

A hint of a smile flickered on his face.

"Oh, I should have recognized you right away. But I guess you don't remember me. No, of course not, you were too little. You used to call me 'uncle.'"

Suddenly, a tumble of events played out in Riley's mind.

She was very young, playing games with a man who had a merry, contagious laugh.

He'd taken her to a circus. Her mother had been there too. And her sister.

Riley gasped.

"Uncle By," she said aloud.

The sudden memories were strong, but they were hard to believe. This man who was now so ravaged had once been charming and handsome. He'd been in their lives for such a short time … she'd been so young … she hadn't thought about him for all these years.

His smile spread wide.

Yes, she could glimpse him in that smile, the man he had once been.

"An FBI agent!" he said in an awed whisper. "Oh, your daddy must be so proud!"

Riley felt a hard lump form in her throat.

"Byron, Daddy died. He had cancer."

Byron face sagged with shock.

"When?" he asked.

"Last November."

He lowered his head.

"I hope he's finally at peace," he said.

Riley felt as though her whole world was whirling around her, changing by the second.

Nothing in her life seemed real.

Was it really possible that this man had killed her mother?

Now she couldn't imagine that it was true.

And yet, she sensed that he was harboring some kind of dark secret.

She spoke slowly and carefully.

"Byron, I didn't come here on a case. This isn't an official visit. It's personal."

Byron looked up at her again with a curious expression.

Riley said, "I'm trying to find out who killed my mother."

Byron looked like he'd been jolted by an electric shock. Tears started to form in his eyes.

"Oh, Lord, Lord, Lord," he said.

His voice sounded thick and heavy with guilt.

"Was it you?" Riley asked, her own voice quavering. "Did you shoot her?"

Byron was stammering between sobs.

"It was … I can't … I don't …"

Riley couldn't breathe at all now.

132

She knew she was about to find out something she might really not want to know.

And she knew that once she learned the truth, she wouldn't be able to drive it from her mind.

She'd have to live with it for the rest of her life.

She wanted to get up from the stool and run out of the room. But she felt completely paralyzed.

"Tell me," she said.

Byron wiped his nose and eyes with his sleeve. He tried to pull himself together.

"Riley, your daddy was a good man. But he was a hard man too. He couldn't help it, 'Nam made him that way. He was in command there. He had to give all kinds of awful orders. And sometimes he had to decide who lived and who died—even among his own men. Soldiers hated him for it, except me. I guess I was the only one who understood. I was his only real friend."

Byron groaned.

"I got a bad leg wound, and I got an honorable discharge and came home. When your daddy came back from his tour, he and I stayed close. I got to know Karen, and your big sister, and you. I got to be like one of the family. But ..."

He stopped.

"Please try to tell me," Riley said.

Byron cleared his throat noisily.

"I could see what the war had done to him. He was drinking a lot in those days. And I saw how he was treating your sister, hitting her for no reason at all. He treated your mother badly too. Oh, it broke my heart."

Byron shook his head.

"Then Oliver got called back for duty, this time in Lebanon. And when he went away—well, I guess your mother and I realized that we'd fallen in love without even knowing it. We got romantically involved."

Riley's mouth dropped open in shock.

She'd never in her wildest dreams imagined that such a thing had happened.

Byron continued, "I wanted to make everything right. I wanted her to leave Oliver. I wanted to marry her. I loved Oliver like a brother, but he was bad for her, and I was sure I could be good for her. And your sister, Wendy—oh, she was a wild one, but I had a good way with her. I knew I could be a good father to both of you."

He fell silent for a moment.

133

"Karen thought about it—I think she thought about it hard. But in the end ... she couldn't do it. She couldn't let him down that way. She couldn't turn her back on him. And she ended it between us. And then ..."

He choked back a gasp.

He said, "I can't help thinking ... I got her killed."

Riley shivered all over.

"What do you mean?" she asked.

"He found out when he was overseas—about me and Karen. I don't know how. I guess one of his buddies around town wrote to him about it. He didn't pull the trigger. He wasn't even in the country. But I've always wondered ... did he arrange it? Did he make it happen?"

At that moment, Riley felt something far beyond mere horror. A tingling blackness rose up inside her. She realized that she was on the verge of fainting.

She struggled to stay conscious. She had to hear this story out to the end.

Byron said, "When he came back from Lebanon, I thought maybe he'd kill me too, and I half hoped that he would. Instead he just pushed me away, never spoke to me again. That was worse. My life went to pieces after that. I drank, fought, stole, did time in jail. It took years and years before I got straight again. And now ... here I am."

His voice trailed off, and he gazed off into space, as if lost in the past.

As Riley stared at him, his face seemed different to her now.

It was as if the years dropped away, and this ravaged old man became the charming, generous, good-hearted young veteran he once was—the man her mother had fallen in love with.

The man that Mother might have married, she realized.

What would life have been like if that had happened?

Wendy might not have left.

And Wendy and Riley might both have called this man "Daddy."

It staggered her imagination.

Just then someone called from outside the door. Riley recognized the voice of the woman who had greeted her in the lobby.

"Byron, we've got a plumbing problem. Could you come and help us out?"

Byron called back, "Yeah, I'll be right there."

He got up from his cot and walked toward the door.

Suddenly, it was as if Riley weren't even there.

"Byron ..." Riley said.

He shook his head.

"Forget about this," he said without looking at her. "Forget everything I said."

Riley held out her card.

"Take this," she said. "Call me if you remember anything."

He took the card without a word. Then he left the room and walked away.

Riley sat on the stool for a whole minute in a state of shock. Then she managed to collect her wits, leave that building, and go back to her car.

As she started to drive, she kept hearing Byron's voice.

"Forget everything I said."

Riley wished she could. But that was never, ever going to happen.

CHAPTER TWENTY SIX

Darkness closed in around Riley as she drove toward Fredericksburg. It was a clear night with stars and a bright moon. But even so, Riley felt as if it were the blackest night she'd ever known.

She clutched the steering wheel to steady herself.

Home, she kept thinking. *I've got to get home.*

But she had a weird and terrible feeling that she had no home to go back to. It seemed like everything she'd known about her life was a lie.

Her head was flooded with images and memories of her childhood.

But were any of them real?

She almost lost control of her car and veered off the road. She knew she couldn't keep driving like this.

Besides, it suddenly occurred to her that she was hungry. She hadn't eaten anything since early that morning, and only a roll then.

I've got to stop somewhere, she thought. *I've got to get control of myself.*

Riley pulled off the highway into a truck stop. She got out of the car and walked unsteadily inside, sitting in the first booth she came to. She ordered a sandwich and coffee, forgoing the beer she really wanted.

Waiting for her food, she tried to assess all that had happened.

She simply couldn't wrap her mind around it.

How had she even gotten started down this desperate road in search of her mother's killer?

Then she remembered Hatcher's message.

"Deny thy father and refuse thy name."

That's where it had all begun. And now that she had a moment to put the pieces of the puzzle all together, she realized that Hatcher had known all along exactly where his clue would take her—into ever deeper doubts and uncertainties.

She shuddered at the thought.

But why? she wondered.

Why had he led her into this purgatorial state of doubt about everything in her world?

He must have had some reason.

After all, Shane Hatcher styled himself as her mentor—both as a detective and as a human being.

He must have intended all this as some kind of lesson.

Riley's food arrived. As she sipped her coffee and nibbled listlessly on her sandwich, she kept wondering.

Maybe Hatcher wanted her to learn that not all riddles have answers. If so, he'd taught her that lesson much too well.

She felt herself sinking deeper and deeper into despair.

Even as Riley shook her head and told herself to snap out of it, she knew that this was too much to handle on her own. She had to talk about it with somebody. But who?

The girls were out of the question. April was dealing with too much as it was, and Jilly wasn't ready to delve deep into the history of her new family. Obviously Ryan wasn't an option, and Riley didn't yet know Blaine well enough. It was too much of a burden to put on Gabriela. And how could she talk with Bill about it, when she was working on a case with him and wasn't supposed to be trying to solve this mystery at all?

But one person came to mind.

She had known a DC forensic psychiatrist named Mike Nevins for many years. He sometimes consulted on BAU cases, and Riley had found him a valuable resource. He was also a close friend who had helped her recover from PTSD after an especially traumatic case.

She took out her phone and started to dial his office. But then she remembered—Mike wouldn't be in his office at this time on a Saturday night. He'd surely be at home.

She had his emergency number. But did this qualify as an emergency?

Riley quickly assessed her own state of mind.

She was shaking all over, on the verge of tears.

She sincerely didn't think she could get through the night without someone's help.

It's an emergency, she decided.

She dialed the number, and Mike answered in his smooth, pleasant voice.

"Riley? What's wrong?"

Riley struggled to keep from crying again.

"Mike, I'm in bad shape. Something has happened, and I really can't deal with it. Could you just talk to me for a little while?"

"I'd be glad to. But don't you think it would be better to talk face to face?"

Riley found herself unable to speak.

"Where are you?" Mike asked.

"I'm—on the road. In a truck stop."

"How long would it take to get to my office?"

Riley mentally struggled with the question. She could barely remember exactly where she was.

Finally she said, "Maybe an hour and a half."

"Do you think you'll be OK driving?"

For a moment, Riley wasn't sure. But the sound of Mike's voice had already calmed her down somewhat.

"I think so," she said.

"Good. I'll meet you at the office. I'll be there waiting for you."

They ended the call. Riley abandoned her sandwich and coffee, went out to her car, and started to drive.

*

It was late by the time Riley arrived at Mike's office building. She parked and looked at her cell phone. She saw the last exchange of texts she'd had with April.

April had typed …

Will u b home for dinner?

And Riley had replied …

I don't think so. See U later tonite.

She'd sent that last message many long hours ago. April had never replied. Was she angry, disappointed, bitter?

Maybe all three, Riley thought.

And why shouldn't she be?

She'd spent the whole day away from home. Her work often kept her away from home. Even when she was in the house, she was often far from home, at least in her mind.

Anyway, April was probably asleep now, and so were Jilly and Gabriela.

Whenever Riley got home, she'd walk into a still, quiet house with no one to greet her, no one to give her a hug and ask how her day had been.

She'd be alone.

And Riley couldn't help but think she deserved it.

The office building was locked up, but a button beside the door was labeled "After Hours Appointments." As soon as she pushed the button, a buzzer released the door.

She went inside and found Mike waiting for her in his office doorway. She was surprised to see him looking as neat and dapper as usual, wearing an expensive shirt with a vest.

Riley couldn't help but smile.

To look at Mike, one wouldn't guess that it was late at night and long after office hours. He looked like he was in the middle of a typical workday.

They both sat down in his comfortable, softly lit office.

"Tell me what's going on," he said, looking very concerned.

Riley's throat hurt with anxiety. She gulped hard.

"I've been trying to solve my mother's murder," she said.

Mike's eyes widened. They had talked about the trauma of her mother's death many times.

"Cases don't get much colder than that," he said.

"I know, Mike. You see, I got this weird clue from a special source, and I didn't understand it at first, but—"

Mike interrupted her.

"Riley, hold it for a moment."

Riley stopped, wondering what was the matter.

Mike said, "You know that I'm a stickler for doctor-patient confidentiality. But be careful what you tell me. If you're breaking the law, or might break the law in the near future, I'm compelled to intervene. Confidentiality ceases to apply. Do you understand what I'm telling you?"

Mike was looking intently into her eyes. That gaze told her exactly what he meant.

He had guessed in an instant that Shane Hatcher had been the source of her information. Riley knew that it had been easy for him to guess. After all, Mike had put her in touch with Hatcher to begin with—back when Hatcher was still a prisoner in Sing Sing. Mike had told Riley that Hatcher's expertise would be a great help on a case she was then trying to solve.

Of course, everything was different now that Hatcher was on the lam. Riley's whole relationship with him was illegal. If Riley so much as mentioned that she'd been in touch with Hatcher, Mike would have no choice but to tell her superiors, probably Brent Meredith.

"I understand," Riley said.

"Good," Mike said. "Now tell me whatever you can."

Riley suddenly had to fight back her tears.

"I found out something terrible, Mike," she said. "My mother had an affair shortly before she died. I found the man she was involved with. I talked to him. His name is Byron. He told me all about it. He said he wanted her to divorce Daddy and marry him, but she wouldn't."

"That must have been a terrible shock," Mike said.

Riley held her breath for a moment, then said, "I think maybe Daddy—did something awful."

Mike's brow wrinkled with surprise.

"Do you mean he might have been the killer?"

"No, he was overseas when it happened, but he found out about the affair, and Byron thinks ... and now I think maybe ..."

Her voice trailed off.

Mike said, "Take a moment and try to remember. Maybe when you were little, you knew that something was going on that you didn't understand. Do you remember anything at all? Just close your eyes, relax. If there's anything, it will just come to you. When it does, tell me about it."

Riley closed her eyes and breathed slowly.

She began to remember a scene that had puzzled her all her life.

CHAPTER TWENTY SEVEN

It made no sense to Riley that the scene she was remembering had haunted her for so long. Nothing had actually happened. It was just a conversation that had replayed itself in her mind many times.

The whole thing came back to her again as she sat with her eyes closed in Mike Nevins's office. She still had no idea what it meant.

Mike said, "Tell me what you're remembering."

With her eyes still closed, Riley described the memory to Mike.

"I was maybe five years old. I walked into the kitchen, and Mommy and my sister, Wendy, were talking. Wendy was about fifteen years old. Mommy was crying. Wendy kept saying, 'Mother, please do it.' She was crying too. 'You'll be much happier. I'll be much happier. So will Riley. We'll all be happy.' But Mommy kept sobbing. 'I can't,' she said. 'I talked to the chaplain. He told me why. I just can't.'"

That was all there was to it. Why had this stayed with her for so long?

Suddenly, it was as if a light turned on inside Riley's mind. She opened her eyes and looked up at Mike.

He said, "Now you understand what was going on, don't you?"

Riley nodded. "They were talking about Byron. Mother told Wendy that Byron wanted her to divorce my father and marry him. Wendy wanted her to do it. She begged her to do it. But my mother couldn't. It had something to do with something a chaplain had told her."

In a very gentle voice, Mike said, "It was a different time, Riley. Wives were expected to stay with their husbands. And if she asked a military chaplain what to do, he'd have told her that she couldn't leave him. He'd have said it could be a matter of life or death. Her husband was serving overseas in a combat zone. Getting news like that might get him killed. It sometimes happened. 'Dear John' letters were all too often followed by death on the battlefront."

A tide of sadness swept over Riley—sadness for her mother, her sister, and herself.

"Wendy ran away not long after that," Riley said. "I think Mother blamed herself for that. She kept thinking that everything was her fault, even everything that was wrong with Daddy, the way he treated her and everybody else. She denied herself her one chance at happiness, but she blamed herself even so. She blamed herself right up until the day she died."

Riley was sobbing now. She opened her eyes and Mike handed her a handkerchief.

"She could have been happy," Riley said. "When I think about what might have been …"

She couldn't imagine it, much less put it into words—the life she might have lived if her mother had divorced her father and married Byron.

Now there was something else she needed to say.

"I had a nightmare last night, Mike," she said. "I was pushing people away, everyone I loved and cared about—just shoving them aside, because I thought they were standing in my way. Finally there was no one left except *him*—the man who killed my mother."

"What do you think your dream meant?" Mike asked.

Riley paused. She hadn't let herself really think about it until now.

"There might be a terrible price to pay for what I learn. I could wind up all alone …"

Her voice trailed off again, and Mike said exactly what she was thinking.

"With only the demons of your past to keep you company."

Riley nodded.

"Riley, there's one thing I've learned as a therapist. The past is gone, the past is absent. You've got to live in the present. We all do. The here and now is as scary as hell, for all of us, all the time. It's the hardest thing in the world to deal with—much harder than making peace with the past. Think about your mother, consumed with guilt, dying with that burden on her shoulders. Learn from her example. You don't want to wind up like her."

Everything Mike was saying made perfect sense to Riley.

And of course, that was exactly why Riley had come to him for help.

Riley wiped her eyes and drew a deep breath. She felt her body relax.

"What are you planning to do next?" Mike asked.

Riley shrugged. "I don't think there's anything more I can do— to find my mother's killer, I mean. I'll just have to live with the possibility that my father had something to do with her death. I'll never really know."

"What have you got going on tomorrow? Are you supposed to work on the Matchbook Killer case?"

"No, I won't get back to that until Monday."

"Then spend tomorrow with your kids."

Riley could hardly believe how simple that sounded.

Could she really do that?

What was stopping her?

"Thanks, Mike," she said. "Thanks so much."

Mike smiled warmly.

"I'm glad to help. Now go on home. It's time for both of us to get some sleep."

*

When Riley woke up the next morning, bright sunlight was pouring in through her bedroom window. She looked at the clock and saw that it was almost ten o'clock.

Yesterday had left her so exhausted that she had woken up much later than usual.

Alarmed, she almost jumped out of bed to get ready for work.

But then she remembered that it was Sunday—and not like many other Sundays in her life. No case was pressing. She didn't have to work today.

It was a strange feeling. She wondered if she could get used to it. She had slept hard, without any dreams she could remember. Now she closed her eyes and drifted off again. In what seemed like no time at all, she was awakened by a wonderful smell.

Bacon, she realized. *Coffee.*

She heard a knock at the door and April's voice.

"Mom, are you going to sleep all day?"

Riley sat up in bed, fully awake. April came in through the door with a smile on her face and a tray full of food. April carried the tray over to her, walking carefully not to spill anything.

Then Jilly appeared in the doorway, smiling as well.

"Good morning, Mom," she said.

Riley felt overwhelmed with gratitude.

"Thanks so much!" she told both girls.

"Oh, don't thank us," Jilly said. "Gabriela did the cooking."

"But it was Jilly's idea," April added.

Riley could hardly believe her ears. It was such a sweet gesture from all three of them—Gabriela, April, and Jilly. She remembered how sad, guilty, and alone she'd felt yesterday—and how terribly far away from home.

It was as if her little family knew that she needed something to make her feel better.

Riley propped the pillows behind her and started to eat. The girls sat down on the edge of her bed.

"So," Riley asked, "what does everybody want to do today?"

April's eyes widened.

"You mean you're taking the day off?" April asked.

"I don't see why not," Riley said. "So—any ideas?"

April and Jilly looked at each other, then at Riley.

"There's a street fair in Old Town," April said. "How about that?"

Riley remembered her curtailed date with Blaine Friday night, and how she'd seen booths and displays being prepared—all promising lots of arts and crafts and music.

"I thought that was yesterday," Riley said.

"It opened yesterday," April said. "It runs through today."

"That sounds wonderful," Riley said. "Let's go as soon as everybody finishes eating."

April and Jilly laughed.

April said, "Everybody else has eaten except you."

"You'd better catch up with the rest of us!" Jilly said.

The girls scampered out of the room and Riley hastened to finish her breakfast.

*

Awhile later, Riley and Gabriela wandered among the artists' displays while the girls dashed from booth to booth.

"Look at the *bolsos*!" Gabriela exclaimed, pointing.

Riley followed Gabriela to a booth displaying handmade handbags. Riley saw right away why they had caught Gabriela's attention. They were colorfully woven in what resembled a Guatemalan style.

"Would you like me to buy you one?" Riley asked.

"Oh, I have one already," Gabriela said.

"But it's getting old."

While Gabriela hesitated, Riley waved to the woman running the booth, claimed the bag, and paid for it. Gabriela smiled and said *gracias* two or three times. The girls came running toward them.

"Listen! Music!" April said.

Gabriela and Riley followed the girls into the large hall that Riley and Blaine had visited Friday night. Sure enough, the same band was there, playing a lively tune. The place was thoroughly decorated now, and people were dancing on the wide floor.

Just then the bandleader noticed Riley. He smiled at her, waved, and cut the song short. Then he led the band in "One More Night."

Riley stood there smiling and blushing.

"What's that all about?" April asked. "Who's that guy?"

"Just a friend of Blaine's," Riley said.

April looked at her impishly, obviously trying to figure out what her mother was blushing about. Jilly interrupted before April could ask a lot of nosy questions.

"Hey, isn't everybody else hungry? I sure am."

Riley chuckled to herself. No, she wasn't hungry. She'd had breakfast much later than the others, after all. But it only seemed fair to join the rest of them for something to eat.

They all continued walking, looking for a place to eat, and they ended up passing by Blaine's Grill. The place was bustling with business, and Blaine had set tables out on the sidewalk. Riley felt self-conscious to be here; she hadn't intended it.

She was relieved to see anyway that it didn't look as though they could possibly get a table.

Riley saw Blaine's daughter, Crystal, wandering among the tables, apparently helping out with the extra business. She suddenly spotted them.

"April!" Crystal cried excitedly.

Crystal ran from the restaurant as April ran for her, and the two hugged as if they were long-lost friends.

"What are you doing here!?" Crystal asked.

"Just walking around," April said.

"Oh my god, you have to come sit down and eat here! I will be so offended if you don't!"

Without waiting for an answer, Crystal turned and waved to a group of busboys, and like magic, an extra table was set up outside. The other waiting patrons looked at Riley and her group jealously as they were ushered past the long line and seated.

Riley, Gabriela, and the girls sat down.

"I'll be right back!" Crystal said.

A moment later she rushed off into the busy restaurant, and suddenly a waiter appeared. They were clearly all getting the VIP treatment. Was it because of Crystal and April? Riley wondered. *Or because of me?*

"Can I take your order?" the waiter asked.

Gabriela was looking at the menu indecisively, and the girls started playfully arguing about what they wanted.

Riley remembered the delicious raspberry cheesecake she'd had on Friday.

"Just surprise us all with something sweet," she said.

Riley noticed that Blaine himself was taking an order elsewhere. She felt a pang of sadness at how she'd left things with him on Friday. She wondered if he was still on speaking terms with her.

But then Crystal went over to him and said something in his ear, and Blaine glanced their way and waved and smiled warmly at Riley.

Maybe he'll give me another chance, she thought.

But then something else caught Riley's eye. A man about her father's age was sitting at a table with his family—a wife, grown children, and grandchildren. All of them were laughing and having a wonderful time.

For a moment, the man looked just like Byron Chaney—or at least how Byron would have looked if his life had unfolded very differently. There was a woman at the table—the man's daughter, Riley guessed—who looked much like Riley. She was smiling and teasing her father.

Riley felt a deep pang of sadness. There it was, only a few feet away—the life she might have lived.

From where she was sitting, it looked perfect—not riddled with mistakes and regrets and failures like the life she'd actually lived.

Riley looked all around. Suddenly, she felt terribly out of place here among these happy people.

It was a feeling that she knew all too well.

Tomorrow she'd be back in her own element, doing what she was meant to do—hunting down monsters and bringing them to justice.

It was a sad thought, but Riley managed to smile as Crystal brought dessert to their table.

Riley kept on smiling, but her mind was really back on the job.

Would she, Bill, and Jake finally get a break in the Matchbook Killer case?

CHAPTER TWENTY EIGHT

Riley arrived at the BAU early the next morning, feeling more than ready to get back to work. On her way to her office, she was greeted by Bill and Jake walking toward her in the hallway.

"It looks like maybe we've got a break in the case," Bill told Riley with a grin.

"What do you mean?" Riley asked.

Jake said, "Woody Grinnell gave me a call this morning. He'd put out those fliers with the composite sketch, and it may have paid off. A guy came into Woody's Diner this morning and said he might have actually seen the killer."

Riley's head buzzed with excitement.

"Did he recognize the face in the sketch?" she asked.

"Not exactly," Jake said. "It sounds like he saw the killer on the night of the murder."

Riley felt a spasm of disappointment.

"That long ago?" she asked. "Surely he told the police about it at the time."

"Apparently not," Jake said. "Woody says we should check it out, talk to the guy in person. I told him we'd meet him at his diner in Greybull ASAP."

"Then let's go," Riley said.

The three of them headed straight out of the building and got into the BAU vehicle they had used on Friday. As Riley started driving, Jake and Bill chatted about the weekend they'd had. They'd spent a lot of it together, starting with Bill's son's swim meet on Saturday. Yesterday evening they'd watched a basketball game at a sports bar.

As Bill and Jake relived the game highlights, Riley felt glad that they were bonding so well. They were two of her favorite people in the world, and she'd known that they would have a lot in common.

Finally Bill asked, "How about you, Riley? How was your weekend?"

Riley gulped.

"Oh, just a little of this and that," she said.

She was grateful that Bill and Jake resumed their conversation and didn't ask her for details. But as she drove, bits of her own weekend replayed in her mind.

She was still haunted by Byron Chaney's story—and by his

guilt-stricken outcry.

"I can't help thinking ... I got her killed."

Riley shuddered at the memory. She wished she had never succumbed to Hatcher's tempting offer. What possible good had it done her?

The more she thought about it, the more she doubted that she'd ever truly solve the mystery of her mother's death.

The whole thing seemed so futile—which made her feel all the more glad to have another case to work on today.

Maybe we're going to get the break we need, she thought.

*

About an hour and a half later, Riley parked in front of Woody's Diner.

Woody greeted Riley, Bill, and Jake as they came inside.

"Perfect timing!" Woody said. "Tony just finished his morning route and got here a few minutes ago."

Woody led them straight to a large booth away from other customers. A perfectly ordinary-looking man wearing a US Postal Service uniform was sitting there. Riley guessed that he was in his thirties.

Woody invited the group to sit down, then ordered coffee all around.

"This is Tony Veach," Woody said to Riley and her companions. "He's the guy I told you about. He came in this morning and said he might have seen something the night of the murder. Tell them what you told me, Tony."

Tony looked a bit reluctant.

"I don't know if it will help much," he said. "It was a long time ago. The truth is, I hadn't even thought about it for years. But then I saw that flier yesterday, and I went home and memories came back and I had nightmares ..."

His voice trailed off.

Riley said, "Just try to remember as well as you can."

Tony took a sip of coffee.

"I guess I was about seven years old," he said. "My parents didn't keep me on a very tight leash, and I went out exploring a lot. I especially liked going out in the woods on clear, bright nights."

Tony paused for a moment, looking thoughtful.

"One night I was poking around through the woods—I found out later it was right near where Tilda Steen was buried. I heard someone moving around, and I got scared and ducked behind a tree to hide. I peeked from behind the tree and—"

Tony winced a little.

"Look, I was just a kid. I'm grown up now and I know better. But at the time, I was sure it was a ghost."

Riley was startled. She noticed that Bill and Jake were exchanging doubtful glances.

Tony continued, "I ran home as fast as I could. I didn't tell anybody right away. But a few days later, they found Tilda's body in the woods. So I told my dad that I'd seen a ghost that night, right there where it happened. He didn't believe me. Why would he? He told me there's no such thing as ghosts and I should forget all about it."

Tony shrugged uneasily.

"Which is pretty much what I did. Until now."

Riley got ready to ask Tony more questions, to try to parse out what he'd really seen—if he'd seen anything at all.

But then she was hit by a different impulse.

She said, "Let's all go over there. Right now."

"Go where?" Woody asked.

"Where Tilda's body was found."

Woody squinted skeptically.

"There's not much to see—not anymore."

"Let's go anyway."

Bill and Jake looked surprised, but Riley insisted, and the group left the diner. Woody and Tony got into a separate car, and the agents followed them in their own vehicle.

"This doesn't sound good to me," Jake said.

"Not to me either," Bill said. "It reminds me too much of that crazy guy in Denison—the one who said the killer was from outer space. This guy doesn't seem crazy. But he was a kid at the time, and kids have got wild imaginations."

Jake said, "Maybe he didn't see anything at all. Maybe he wasn't even there that night. Maybe his memory is playing tricks on him. We all know how that sometimes happens."

Riley kept driving behind the other vehicle without commenting.

She understood how Bill and Jake felt, but her gut was telling her something different.

She had now talked to two witnesses who thought they'd seen something bizarre—one said it was a space alien and the other thought it was a ghost. That alone seemed like a strange coincidence, if it really was just a coincidence.

Riley had a hunch that maybe it wasn't.

But her heart sank as they arrived at their destination and the two cars parked alongside the road. The woods where the body had been found were being cleared for a housing development. Bulldozers and other heavy machinery were noisily at work.

Riley remembered what Woody had just said.

"There's not much to see—not anymore."

She now saw that he really meant it. Was there any possibility of finding clues to a murder that had happened twenty-five years ago in a place like this?

Everybody got out of their cars. They followed Tony to the edge of a patch of woods. He pointed among the trees.

"I saw what I saw right over there."

"Take us there," Riley said.

As they walked into the trees, Riley realized that this patch of woods wasn't going to be here much longer. Any day now it would get leveled by the rumbling, lumbering bulldozers. If they had let the case go cold any longer, whatever they might still find here would be gone.

If it isn't gone already, Riley thought.

A short distance into the trees, Tony turned all around, getting his bearings. Then he walked over to a large oak tree.

"I'm pretty sure this is the tree I hid behind," he said. "I'll never forget it. See this crooked knob in it? Looks like a face. It's bigger than it was back then."

Riley looked and indeed saw the distinct growth in the tree.

Then, pointing, he added, "I saw him coming from over there."

"Tell us exactly what you saw," Riley said.

Tony squinted as he tried to retrieve the memory.

"The first thing I saw … well, it was crazy, but I thought it was just a disembodied head floating in midair. And hands, hanging open so I could see all the fingers. The face and the hands were so bright, they seemed to be glowing. His mouth was moving—I think he was muttering to himself, but I couldn't hear him over the crickets. Then I saw that he actually was all there—it was just so dark that his arms and legs and torso blended into the background at first. It was his eyes that really freaked me out. They were such a bright blue. They didn't look natural."

Riley recalled what Roger Duffy had said about the suspect's eyes.

"Streaming blue light was coming out of them."

Now she almost wondered if maybe Duffy hadn't been as crazy as he'd seemed.

"What about his hair?" Riley asked.

Tony looked a bit puzzled.

"I ... didn't notice, I guess."

Riley was sure that the memory was still there. She just had to nudge it along.

"Was it glowing like his face and hands?" she asked.

Tony tilted his head thoughtfully.

"No," he said. "His hair was dark, like the rest of his body, and it almost seemed to disappear into the background."

Riley was getting an image in her mind of a weirdly mask-like face and glove-like hands moving through this area. No wonder the poor kid had been scared. No wonder his father had told him he was talking nonsense.

"And you're sure he wasn't carrying anything?" she asked.

"No, his hands were empty."

Riley thought for a moment, then asked, "What happened next?"

Pointing again, Tony said, "He continued along that way and disappeared from sight. I'd been frozen in my tracks the whole time I watched him. I came to my senses and ran straight out toward the road. Just then a car came speeding by. Maybe it was him, but I didn't get a look at the driver."

Bill and Jake were listening with extreme interest.

"What kind of car was it?" Bill asked.

Tony shook his head.

"I didn't notice. What I *did* notice ... well, I told Dad about that too, and he said I was just imagining it."

"What was it?" Riley asked.

Tony let out a chuckle of self-doubt.

"Maybe I'd seen too many Godzilla movies. I was sure that the top of the car had been ripped by some gigantic prehistoric monster."

Riley wondered if he'd maybe imagined that part. After seeing what looked like some kind of a phantom moving through the forest, surely his imagination must have been running away with him. Still, she knew that she needed to keep this detail in mind.

Riley asked Woody, "Where was the body buried?"

Woody pointed.

"Right over there, not more than twenty feet away from here. I'll take you there."

"No," Riley said. "I'll go there by myself."

Woody looked a little puzzled.

"She knows what she's doing," Jake said.

Woody shrugged.

Tony asked, "Is there anything else I can tell you?"

"I don't think so," Riley said.

Tony shuffled his feet a little.

"In that case, I need to get back to my afternoon route," Tony said.

"And the lunch rush is just starting at my diner," Woody added.

"You guys go on ahead," Riley said. "You've been a great help."

Woody and Tony headed back to their car.

Riley, Bill, and Jake stood in the wooded area looking at each other.

"Do you want my help?" Jake asked Riley.

Riley knew that he was thinking about how he'd prompted her along at the Baylord Inn back in Brinkley. But this time things felt different to her.

"I think I'd better do this on my own," Riley said.

Jake nodded. "Bill and I will wait for you in the car."

In a few moments, Riley was standing alone in the patch of woods.

She took slow, deep breaths as she prepared herself to enter a dark, terrible place—the mind of the killer.

CHAPTER TWENTY NINE

Riley turned around slowly. In a setting like this, was she going to be able to get in touch with the mind of a murderer at all?

She was surrounded by trees, but bright noon sunlight filtered through their branches. Heavy machinery rumbled and clanged nearby.

Was she really going to be able to block the sunlight and the sounds? Could she imagine being in this place on a still, moonlit night?

First things first, she thought.

She took out her tablet computer and brought up the case files, then found crime scene photos that had been taken here twenty-five years ago. She needed them to get her exact bearings.

Then she walked in the direction where Woody had pointed. It was easy to find the spot she was looking for. Except for a fallen log, the placement of the trees was still much the same as it was in the photos.

She looked through the pictures, which showed Tilda Steen's freshly uncovered body from various angles. Unlike the two victims before her, she was fully clothed when she'd been buried. She looked grotesque in the photos—with dirt all over her, and with signs of decomposition already apparent.

As Riley scanned the scene, she realized that one thing hadn't changed over the years. Then as now, the highway was visible from this spot. The killer had buried the girl close to the road—so close that the smell had been noticed a few days later by a passing bicyclist.

The murderer had surely known that this body would be found, just as the others had.

She tucked the tablet away. She wouldn't need it now.

In spite of the distractions, she found herself slipping into his mind quite easily.

In just a few moments, it seemed to be a moonlit night. The sounds of heavy machinery gave way to the constant drone of crickets in the moonlight.

Riley gasped. She was inside him now, seeing things through his eyes.

And there Tilda lay at his feet, in the shallow grave he had just dug.

She looked asleep rather than dead.

What was he thinking?

How small and light she is, Riley thought.

He could have carried her farther into the woods—much farther.

But he wanted someone to find her.

Maybe if someone found her, they'd find him, and stop him.

Now Riley could feel his arms getting back to work again, shoveling dirt onto the body.

But not too much dirt, Riley thought.

He didn't want to cover the body too thoroughly.

He didn't bother to replace all the dirt he had dug up to make the grave.

Instead, he threw rocks, twigs, moss, and leaves over her—just enough so that he couldn't see any part of her.

Then it was done.

He felt no relief, only mounting self-hatred.

He felt sick at heart about what he had done. There was a sharp bitter taste in his mouth. He wished he could turn back the clock to just a little while ago, when she had still been alive.

In fact, he wished he could turn back the clock several months, before he'd killed the other two girls.

They hadn't deserved to die—not on account of his failed lust.

But one way or the other, he was going to have to live with this horrible deed—and the other dead girls as well.

"I'm an evil man in an evil world," Riley imagined him thinking.

But what was done was done.

It was time to get away from this place.

He gripped his shovel in his hand and turned to walk back to his car—

Wait a minute, Riley thought.

Something was wrong with that image.

She remembered how Tony had described those glowing hands. They'd been *"hanging open so I could see all the fingers."*

He'd been walking away from the grave when Tony had seen him.

But he hadn't been carrying the shovel. Tony had been sure the man hadn't been carrying anything.

Riley took herself back into the killer's mind at the moment when he'd finished covering the body.

She felt his whole body quivering with rage and disgust.

He looked at the shovel in his hand.

"Never again," he murmured aloud.

Riley could feel the tension in his arm and shoulders as he swung the shovel back, then the release as he threw it away from him.

Suddenly, Riley snapped out of her trancelike state.

The shovel!

Remembering the precise imagined sensation of throwing it, she walked in that direction. Her footsteps took her straight to the fallen log she had noticed earlier. She knelt down and frantically probed the mulch under it.

She felt a sharp pain in her fingers as they hit something hard. She tugged and pulled until it came out from under the log.

Sure enough, it was the blade of the shovel. The metal was rusted almost through, and the wooden handle was so rotted that it crumbled to pieces in her hand. It had been pinned there ever since the tree had fallen.

Riley felt a sickening wave of despair.

The shovel could have served as a valuable piece of evidence— if it had been found at the time.

But in its current state of deterioration, it was of no use at all.

And yet a possibility was forming in her mind.

He threw away the shovel, she thought.

He'd wanted to be rid of everything that had anything to do with the murders.

She walked back toward the car, where Bill and Jake stood waiting.

She had a new idea of where the search should lead next.

CHAPTER THIRTY

When Riley emerged from among the trees, she saw that Bill and Jake were standing by the car looking at her expectantly.

"Did you get anything?" Jake asked.

Riley held up the shovel blade.

"The killer threw it aside after he finished covering the body," she said. "Fallen leaves and underbrush are thick out there, so this could have easily gotten covered up in the days before the body was found. The cops on the scene must have missed it."

Jake shook his head.

"Damn," Jake said. "I wanted to comb this crime scene with my own people. But I got yanked off the case before I got a chance. And like I said earlier—Woody's a hell of a nice guy, but never was much of a cop."

"So where does this leave us?" Bill asked.

"With the car," Riley said. "We might be able to trace it."

Jake grunted with disapproval.

"Fat chance," he said. "Tony couldn't even remember its make."

Riley said, "Yeah, but do you remember what he did say about it?"

Bill said, "He said it looked like some monster had ripped it up on top."

Riley nodded.

"I know it sounds crazy, but I think there's something to it. Other parts of Tony's story are starting to make sense."

Then Jake let out a chuckle.

"Son of a gun," he said. "I think I get it. Do you remember how they used to make cars with vinyl roofs back in the seventies and eighties? They'd gone out of fashion about the time of these murders. But some of those cars were still out on the road."

Bill said, "Sure, I remember. Those vinyl roofs were a pain in the ass. They got damaged much too easily. Even the weather wore them out."

Jake added, "And do you remember how they sometimes looked after they got damaged?"

Bill nodded.

"They tore in long strips—like they'd been ripped by giant claws," he said. "And a car with such visible damage would be easy to identify. The killer must have wanted to get rid of it."

Riley added, "He wanted to get rid of everything related to the murders."

Jake scratched his chin thoughtfully.

"That narrows our search at least some," he said. "We're talking about a car that was probably old in 1992, one of the makes that might have had a vinyl roof. We can put our BAU techies to work searching records. They can go through owner-to-owner sales that took place in this area just after the last murder. That is if the killer didn't just abandon the car."

But Riley was thinking along different lines. A hunch had been growing in her head since she'd probed the killer's thoughts back among the trees. She remembered the sheer revulsion he must have felt when he threw the shovel away.

"I don't think he just abandoned the car," she said. "I don't think he even simply sold it. He was through with killing. The car's very existence sickened him. He wanted it gone—completely gone."

Jake's eyes widened with understanding.

"He wanted to have it destroyed," Jake said.

Bill yanked out his cell phone.

"We need to look for local scrapyards," he said.

Riley and Jake watched while Bill searched.

"I think I've found a place to start," Bill finally said. "The junkyard closest to Greybull is the Codner Scrapyard. Their ad says it's been in business since 1960."

Riley snapped her fingers.

"Bingo," she said. "Let's start right there."

*

It was a short drive from Greybull to the scrapyard. As Riley and her companions got out of the car, she was surprised at the place's appearance. She'd never visited a scrapyard before, so she'd expected this one to be the very picture of chaos.

Instead, everything was neatly arranged around a wide open area. The ground was bare dirt, but clean and orderly. On one side was a metal building and next to that was an array of parked whole cars in various states of dilapidation. At the far end was an open shed full of shelves covered with spare parts. On the other side was a sheer, solid wall of crushed metal.

A middle-aged man wearing jeans and a safety helmet climbed out of the cab of a massive yellow material handler.

"What can I do for you folks?" the man asked.

Riley and Bill took out their badges and introduced themselves and Jake.

"I guess you'd want to talk to the owner," the man said. He pointed to the main building. "You'll find her over in the office."

When Riley, Bill, and Jake walked into the office building, they were greeted by an elderly woman wearing coveralls and heavy shoes. She was sturdily built with leathery skin, and she was smoking a cigarette.

"What's your business?" she asked.

Riley and her companions introduced themselves again.

The woman squinted.

"FBI?" she said. "That don't sound good. Should I fetch me a lawyer?"

Judging from how she talked without removing the cigarette in her mouth, Riley guessed that she was a dawn-to-dusk chain smoker.

"No," Riley said. "We're here investigating a cold murder case, and we're just looking for some help."

The woman shrugged.

"Murder, eh? Well, I don't guess you'll find any dead bodies around this place. But you're free to look around, maybe I've overlooked a corpse or two."

She let out a burst of raspy laughter and offered Riley her hand.

"By the way, I'm Audrey Codner. I've been here forever."

Riley shook her hand.

"Then maybe you can help us," she said. "We're looking for a suspect, and we think he may have junked a car here twenty-five years ago."

The woman rolled the cigarette between her lips.

"That's quite some time ago—before we got this damn fool thing."

She thumped an archaic computer with her hand.

"Still trying to figure out how it works. Back then my husband Caleb kept the records, did it all on paper. He croaked in 1998—God rest his ornery soul."

As tough as the words sounded, Riley detected genuine affection in Audrey's voice.

"Come on, I'll show you," Audrey said.

She led Riley and her companions through into a room filled with shelves laden with cardboard boxes.

She said, "If the car came through here, there's a record of it here somewhere."

Riley felt daunted by the sheer quantity of files that must be here.

"What kind of records do you have?" she asked. "License plates?"

"Naw, the license plates would have been returned to the DMV by the owner. But we do have to get proof of ownership before we take a car. Usually that means we have the title. Sometimes we take a copy of the registration card instead. And a copy of the owner's driver's license."

This sounds promising, Riley thought.

She exchanged looks with Bill and Jake and sensed that they were thinking the same thing.

The woman climbed a stepladder to one of the shelves.

"What year are you looking for exactly?" she asked.

"Nineteen ninety-two," Bill said.

The woman pulled a heavy box off the shelf, lugged it down the ladder, and plopped it onto a worktable.

"I've got three boxes from that year," she said. "This one should get you started. But tell me more about this car you're talking about."

Riley said, "We don't know the make, but we think it had a badly damaged vinyl top. We think the suspect wanted to have it destroyed."

Audrey puffed at her cigarette.

"Say, that kind of rings a bell. Caleb was here working one day when I was away visiting my folks. When I got back he told me about some guy who'd come in with a car. It was in good shape except for the vinyl roof, which was pretty beat up. Caleb said the guy looked real strange and gave him the creeps. Something about his eyes, Caleb said. He never told me exactly what it was."

Riley's pulse quickened.

We're on the right track, she thought.

Audrey thought for a moment, then said, "Yeah, Caleb was really puzzled by that one. Perfectly good vehicle, just needed some repair. But the guy was as anxious as hell to get rid of it. He didn't want any money for the car, but he didn't want Caleb to resell it or even sell parts from it. He wanted to see it crushed. He insisted on watching while Caleb and the crew did it. Caleb said it was the damnedest thing. He couldn't understand it."

Riley had to catch her breath.

"Did your husband mention the man's name?" she asked.

"I'm afraid not," Audrey said.

"What about the make of the car?" Bill asked.

Audrey scratched her head.

"No, except that it was kind of old but still in pretty good shape. Except for the vinyl."

Jake asked, "What happens to cars after they're crushed?"

Audrey let out a short chuckle.

"Did you see that mountain of metal when you came in? That's what the cars get to be. Then the shreds are sold for their scrap value. Even if a car was still under there somewhere, good luck trying to find it."

Audrey patted the box.

"Help yourselves to whatever you can find." Then pointing the shelves, she added, "If you need more stuff from 1992, you'll find it over where this came from. Let me know if there's anything else I can do."

As Audrey wandered back to her office, Jake pulled the lid off the cardboard box and immediately began to rummage through its contents.

His face dropped with disappointment.

"What a mess," he said. "The late Caleb Codner wasn't exactly a crack records keeper."

Bill and Riley peered into the box. Right away, Riley saw the problem.

The box was stuffed with records from 1992, but in no particular order—certainly not by date. It looked as though Caleb had simply shoved the folders into the box haphazardly whenever he got them.

Bill said, "I guess we'd better get those other boxes she mentioned."

Riley and Jake pulled down the other two boxes from 1992 and hauled them over to the table. On his cell phone, Jake started searching for car makes of that era that might have had vinyl tops.

Jake said, "I'm getting a lot of possibilities—Consuls, Capris, T-Birds, Cortinas, Volvos ..."

Bill started pulling files out of the first box.

"Jot down a list, Jake," he said. "This could take a while."

In a matter of minutes, the table was strewn with files full of documents. Riley found it hard to stay focused. What was she looking for exactly, aside from one of the car brands that might have had a vinyl top? Their search seemed so vague, she worried that she could easily miss it. She was sure that Bill and Jake felt the same way.

*

After what seemed like a long while, Jake let out a yelp of glee and held up one of the folders.

"I think maybe I've got it," he said.

Riley and Bill huddled next to Jake.

The folder he'd found was labeled "NO RESALE."

Jake showed Riley and Bill the papers in the file.

Jake said, "This car was a 1982 Ford Granada, which had exactly the kind of vinyl roof we're looking for. The instructions were to destroy it immediately."

Jake pushed a yellowed piece of paper toward Bill and Riley.

"Here's a copy of the registration card and a driver's license."

The images on the paper had faded, and it didn't look like it had been a good photocopy to begin with. The registration card seemed to have been crumpled up, then spread out again before it was copied. The face on the driver's license was especially bad. Was it the spectral character described by Roger Duffy and Tony Veach? Possibly, but Riley couldn't tell for sure.

Bill grumbled, "I guess Caleb wasn't a stickler for what kind of documentation he'd accept."

Jake said, "Well, I'm not sure I blame him. Caleb wasn't paying for the car, but he wasn't going to be able to sell it or even the parts. Why bother with details? He had no way of knowing he was dealing with a murderer."

Riley peered closely at the license.

"The name is smudged and impossible to read," she said. "So are most of the numbers."

Jake waved another piece of paper.

"Maybe this will help," he said.

It was the receipt—and sure enough, it was legible.

Riley's heart pounded as she read.

The man's name was Reed J. Tillerman, and the address was 345 Bolingbroke Road in Greybull.

"Do you think that's his real name?" Jake asked Riley.

Riley didn't reply, but she had her doubts. The smudged name on the driver's license didn't look that long.

Bill was running a search on his cell phone.

"It's a real address, anyway," Bill said. "It's not actually in Greybull. It's in a rural area just a short drive from here."

"What are we waiting for?" Jake said. "Let's go!"

They walked back into the office and thanked Audrey Codner for her help.

"Any time," Audrey said. "By the way, what did this suspect of yours do exactly?"

"He killed three women," Riley said.

Audrey growled and shook her head.

"Oh, yeah. The Matchbook Killer. I sure do remember that poor girl over in Greybull. I hope you catch the bastard. Come back if there's anything else I can do."

Riley and her companions headed out of the building got back into the car, and Riley started to drive. As excited as she was, a long-ago voice kept pushing its way into her mind.

"Give me your money."

It was the voice of her mother's killer—and it sounded startlingly clear, as if she'd heard it just yesterday.

Riley stifled a sigh.

She had work to do, and didn't want to be distracted—especially by something she couldn't do anything about, perhaps not ever.

Maybe solving the Matchbook Killer case would drive that old torment out of her mind.

Riley started to dare to hope.

CHAPTER THIRTY ONE

Riley felt puzzled when she arrived at the address that she, Bill, and Jake were looking for. It certainly didn't look like the lair of a serial killer. A sign in front of the property read ...

Shaffer Family Farm
pony rides
baby animals
organic produce

Riley pulled the car into a large parking area to one side of an attractive, three-story farmhouse. Everything around them looked so incredibly picturesque that she could hardly believe it was real. It was spring in rural Virginia, and the landscape was astonishingly green and fresh. This seemed like another world and an earlier, more innocent time.

When she and her companions got out of the car, a baby goat came dancing toward her. She drew her hand back when the animal tried to nibble her fingers.

She heard a child's voice say, "Lucky won't hurt you. He's just looking for treats."

The boy was about eight or nine years old. He was surrounded by several other baby goats.

A woman came out of the house. She looked a little younger than Riley, and her complexion was ruddy and healthy.

She said, "Fritz, take these goats back to the barn."

The boy led the little goat named Lucky away, and the other goats followed them.

The woman smiled broadly at the new arrivals.

"Welcome to the Shaffer Family Farm," she said. "I'm Sheila Shaffer. You're just in time for fresh strawberries."

Riley and her colleagues introduced themselves.

At the sight of their FBI badges, Sheila Shaffer's eyes widened with surprise.

Riley said, "We're looking for a man who may have lived here twenty-five years ago. His name might have been Reed J. Tillerman."

The woman looked mildly puzzled.

"You must have the wrong place," she said. "We Shaffers have lived here for generations. I've never heard of anybody by that name."

Riley brought up the old composite sketch on her tablet and showed it to Sheila.

"No, I don't recognize him," Sheila said. "Sorry."

Riley, Bill, and Jake looked at each other. Riley felt disappointed, and saw her disappointment mirrored in the eyes of her companions. Had the address on the receipt been faked, and the name as well?

We shouldn't have gotten our hopes up, Riley thought.

Before they could ask any further questions, a man came along leading a small Shetland pony. He was about Sheila's age and looked as hearty and healthy as she did. Like Sheila and the boy, he had freckles and red hair.

"Anybody for pony rides?" the man asked. "Just thought I'd ask before I put Jimbo back in his stall."

The woman said to Riley and her companions, "This is Frank Shaffer, my husband. He's lived here longer than me—all his life." Then she said to Frank, "Honey, these folks are FBI. They say they're looking for someone who may have lived here twenty-five years ago."

Turning toward Riley, Sheila asked, "What did you say his name was?"

Riley showed the sketch to Frank. She said, "He might have been calling himself Reed J. Tillerman."

"I was just a kid back then," Frank said. "I don't remember the name Tillerman, but there's something about that first name, Reed …"

His voice trailed off.

Then he said, "Dad might have been able to tell you, but he passed away years ago. Let's go talk to Aunt Maddie. She was my dad's sister. She's the only one still around who might remember something."

Riley, Bill, and Jake followed Frank and Sheila to a fenced-in yard full of chickens. An older woman in a plain cotton dress was scattering grain to the hens. Riley was amazed.

Does anybody really do this by hand anymore?

Frank said, "Aunt Maddie, these FBI folks are looking for somebody named Reed J. Tillerman who might have been here twenty-five years ago."

Still spreading chicken feed, the woman chuckled.

"Twenty-five years is a long time," she said. "If he was ever here, he's long gone."

Frank said, "But I think I remember something about a guy with that first name, Reed. Didn't Dad once rent out our cottage to some stranger?"

The woman stopped feeding the hens and looked up.

"Oh, my," she said. "I haven't thought about him for a long time. My brother Luther sure wasn't happy about that character."

She pointed across a pasture.

"The family's old first house is over yonder—just a little place. Nobody has lived there for years. Luther once thought it might be nice to rent it to folks. But he only rented it to one man. Yes, I think his name *was* Reed something."

"Yeah, now I remember," Frank said. "Dad really didn't like him."

Aunt Maddie shook her head.

"No, he surely did not. That man was a peculiar fellow, kept to himself the whole time he was here. I never saw him except at a distance, and even then only after dark. Did you ever get a good look at him, Frank?"

Frank shrugged. "Not that I can remember," he said.

"Something about his looks gave Luther the creeps," Aunt Maddie said. "Luther wouldn't say what it was about him, except he didn't like his eyes. One night Reed Whatever-His-Name-Was just up and left without saying a word and we never saw him again. 'Good riddance,' Luther said. He never rented the house out to anybody else."

Riley felt a tingle of excitement.

She asked Aunt Maddie, "Do you think your brother kept any records of that rental? Receipts or anything like that?"

"Oh, I doubt it," Aunt Maddie said. "He wanted to forget all about it. And if he did, well, I sure wouldn't know where to begin looking for it."

"Could you show me this house?" Riley asked.

"Certainly," Aunt Maddie said.

The older woman led the group across the pasture, and the small cottage appeared as soon as they walked over a rise. It was in a hopeless state of disrepair, with vines growing all over it. Several cows were lying in the tall grass in front of the house.

Frank explained, "We've been using it for feed storage for years. But it's getting too rundown even for that. Downright dangerous. We plan to tear it down soon and build a decent shed."

The place didn't look at all promising, and Riley doubted that the killer had left any belongings inside. Even so, the house

165

intrigued her.

"Could I have a look inside?" she asked.

Frank said, "Sure, but watch your step. The floor's in bad shape, and the whole place is liable to cave in one of these days if we don't tear it down first."

Frank led Riley among the cows and up the sagging steps onto the front porch. A screen door hung broken on its hinges. Frank pushed the front door open and invited Riley to enter.

The light was dim inside, but Riley could see that the living room was stacked full of hay bales. There wasn't a stick of furniture in sight.

Frank explained, "Our cattle are pasture-raised dairy cows. In winter we like to have some high-quality hay on hand. That's what we store here."

He showed Riley a door that opened into another room. It was full of salt blocks and big metal garbage cans.

"Those cans are full of grain," Frank said. "Grain boosts our cattle's milk production."

Riley turned slowly around, taking the place in. Then she looked into a couple of doors where she saw a bathroom and a kitchen, both of which had been stripped of fixtures and appliances.

"Not much to see, I guess," Frank said.

That was true—but even so, Riley picked up a mysterious vibe from the place. It wasn't hard to imagine it full of quaint antique furniture.

"Could you leave me alone a moment, please?" Riley asked Frank.

Frank tilted his head uncertainly.

"It's not very safe in here," he said.

Riley almost gestured to her weapon to indicate that she was in no danger. Then she reminded herself ...

That's not what he means.

"I'll be fine," Riley said with a smile.

Frank nodded.

"OK, but be real careful."

Frank walked out onto the porch. Riley could hear him talking to the others outside.

The vibe grew stronger. She could slowly start to feel the killer's presence.

Riley breathed slowly as she let the specter of the killer expand inside her.

It was a familiar presence now—familiar from the motel room

in Brinkley and from just a short while ago in the wooded area where she'd found the shovel. Once again, she sensed that he was helpless and terrified, ashamed and guilty.

And now Riley knew that she was sensing his feelings from the very last time he had set foot in this place. She could see and feel it vividly. It was late at night, and he had just finished killing and burying Tilda Steen. He'd driven back here. He could feel the grit of dirt on his hands.

Riley followed his footsteps into the bathroom.

It was easy to imagine the simple porcelain fixtures that once were here.

Retracing his movements, she went through the motions of washing her hands, watching the vestiges of dirt whirl down the drain.

But it wasn't enough.

He didn't feel clean.

Even a long hot bath wouldn't be enough to make him feel clean again.

Riley could hear his thoughts echoing through her brain.

"I've got to get rid of it. All of it."

Getting rid of the shovel hadn't been enough. Not nearly enough. He had to get rid of *everything.*

He even had to get rid of himself—or at least the man he'd been since he came to live here just a few weeks ago.

He'd been staying in this house since it started—since he'd killed the college student in Brinkley, then the other girl in Denison, and just then Tilda Steen in Greybull.

And now she could hear him think …

"I've got to get out of this house."

He had some pathetic notion that if he got rid of everything around him, he'd somehow be different inside.

She could feel his desperation as he went through the house gathering his belongings—so few that they must have fit easily into a small suitcase.

She traced his footsteps toward the front door.

Then she stepped outside into the afternoon sunlight.

But still she felt the darkness of that ugly night—the darkness he would never be able to shake off.

He imagined that this was the beginning of the rest of his life—a better life.

But Riley knew deep down in her gut …

He never became a good man.

Perhaps he'd never murdered anyone else during all the years since.

Perhaps he'd never committed any sort of crime.

But in his heart and soul, he was still the man who murdered those women.

He had no goodness in him.

As much as he might have wanted to, he'd never learned to be a kind, caring human being.

And now, Riley thought, the time was long overdue for him to be brought to justice.

Riley's reverie was interrupted by a voice.

"Reed! Now I remember!"

The voice yanked Riley back to the present moment. She was standing on the rickety porch with a group of people standing in front of her, not only Bill and Jake, but also the Shaffers—Sheila, Frank, and Aunt Maddie. Aunt Maddie's expression was eager and excited.

"His name *was* Reed. But that wasn't his first name. It was his last name."

"What was his first name?" Riley asked breathlessly.

Aunt Maddie nodded.

"James. I'm sure that's what Luther told me. His name was James Reed."

Riley saw her colleagues' mouths drop open. She shared their excitement, but cautioned herself not to get her hopes up again.

She said to Aunt Maddie, "Please try to remember, ma'am. Did your brother say anything else about him that we should know?"

The woman shook her head.

"Nothing much—except that he really didn't like him. He actually didn't like him so much that he didn't want to talk about him at all."

Riley handed Aunt Maddie her card.

"Please, all of you—if you remember anything else, I want you to get in touch with me right away."

Riley and her colleagues thanked the family for their help. Then they made their way back to their vehicle. They stood next to the car discussing this new bit of information.

"So do you think we've got his real name?" Bill asked.

"I don't know," Riley said. "For all we know, James Reed was a made-up name, and his real name is Reed J. Tillerman. But I know who we should ask for help."

She got on the phone and called up Sam Flores, the BAU's

head lab technician. She put him on speakerphone so Bill and Jake could be in on the conversation.

"Sam, we need some help here," she said. "We're over near Greybull working on the old Matchbook Killer case."

"Oh, yeah," Sam said. "The one I aged the composite sketch for. How's that one going?"

"That depends," Bill said.

"Maybe you can help us," Jake said.

"Name it," Sam said.

Riley thought for a moment.

Finally she said, "We've got two possible suspect names—Reed J. Tillerman and James Reed. One name might be made up, the other might be real. What can you give me on those names?"

Riley could hear Sam's fingers dancing on his keyboard.

Finally he said, "Well, I've got good news and I've got bad news. I'm going to give you the good news first. You can eliminate Reed J. Tillerman. It sounds like it ought to be a common name. But I can't find a single Reed Tillerman anywhere, alive or dead or indifferent."

"OK," Riley said. "What's the bad news?"

"Well, there are several thousand guys named James Reed across the country."

Riley, Bill, and Jake exchanged glances.

"Can you narrow that down to a more specific area?" Jake asked.

"How specific do you want?" Sam asked.

Riley and her colleagues thought for a moment.

Finally Riley said, "How about within the general area of the three towns where the murders took place? Brinkley, Denison, and Greybull?"

"I can do it," Sam said. "But it might take a while. Is tomorrow OK?"

Riley felt a reflexive impulse to tell him the situation was urgent.

After all, the situation usually *was* urgent.

But not this time—not on a cold case.

With an almost silent sigh, Riley said, "Tomorrow will be fine. Thanks."

She ended the call, and she, Bill, and Jake stood looking at one another.

"So—what now?" Jake asked.

Bill shrugged. "That's all we can do right now. We might as

well head back to Quantico. I'll drive this time."

Riley was relieved to get a break from driving. She climbed into the back seat while Bill and Jake sat in the front.

Just as Bill got the car moving, Riley's phone buzzed. She didn't recognize the number, so she just let it ring. The caller left a message, and when Riley listened to it, she heard a familiar quavering, elderly voice.

"This is Byron Chaney. I've got to talk to you."

CHAPTER THIRTY TWO

Riley's hand shook as she held the phone. She could hardly believe her ears. She'd felt sure that she had heard the last of Byron Chaney.

She listened to the message again.

It's him, she thought. *It's definitely him.*

She started to return the call right then. But she had to stop herself.

Jake and Bill were both sitting right in front of her, with Bill driving and Jake in the passenger seat. Neither of her old friends knew anything about her search for her mother's killer. She couldn't tell them. So whatever it was Byron wanted to talk about, Riley couldn't talk about it in their presence.

She'd have to wait.

They were headed back to Quantico, but she wasn't sure she could stand the suspense until then.

To Riley's great relief, Bill soon announced that they needed to stop for gas.

As soon as they pulled into a gas station, Riley said that she needed to use the restroom. She scrambled out of the car, hurried into the convenience store, and locked herself in the little restroom.

Before she took out her phone, she looked in the mirror.

Is this really me? she asked herself.

Was she really sneaking away from her best friends to make a phone call?

How had she gotten to be so furtive, so untrusting, so secretive?

She fought down a sense of shame and dialed Byron's number.

When his familiar tired, hoarse, scratchy voice answered, she said, "It's me. What did you call about?"

"I've been thinking since you came here. I haven't been able to stop thinking. I haven't been able to sleep much. It's been making me crazy."

For a moment Riley wondered—had Byron really called her with new information?

Or did he only want to commiserate, to wallow some more in the guilt he felt about her mother's death? That was the last thing Riley wanted to hear right now.

She forced herself to keep quiet and listen.

Then Byron said, "Your daddy and I had a buddy in 'Nam,

name of Floyd Britson—he was Sergeant Floyd Britson back in the day. Floyd tracked me down and gave me a call a couple of years ago. For no real reason, just to reconnect, talk about old times. I hadn't heard from him in years. We got to talking about your daddy, and what a good man he was, but how tough he was, and how easy he made enemies."

Byron fell silent for a moment.

"Tell me," Riley said anxiously.

"He mentioned your daddy getting into a fight once with another Marine—not a man I knew personally. Of course, your daddy was in lots of fights. But Floyd said this time was especially nasty. Your daddy did a lot more than just beat the guy senseless. He humiliated him in front of his buddies, made him look like a total fool, made everybody laugh at him, destroyed his self-respect. The guy didn't get over it. From that day on, he told everybody that he was going to get back at your daddy one way or the other."

Byron paused again.

Then he said, "I didn't think much of it while Floyd and I were talking, or even afterward. But now, the more I think about it ..."

Byron's voice trailed off.

Riley's heart was pounding now.

"What was the man's name?" Riley asked. "The man my father fought with?"

"I don't know. I'm not sure Floyd even told me. If he did, I can't remember. I've been racking my brain all day, but I just can't remember anything else. I don't think he said anything more than what I just told you. He didn't even say where the fight happened or when."

Riley struggled to keep her voice from shaking.

"I've got to get in touch with Floyd Britson. How can I reach him?"

"Well, I'm hoping he's still alive," Byron said. "He didn't sound so good when I talked to him. He said he'd just been put in a nursing home, and he wasn't too happy about it. It's in a little town called Innis."

The name registered with Riley instantly. Innis wasn't more than fifty miles from Quantico.

"Do you know the name of the nursing home?" Riley asked.

"Sorry, no."

Riley couldn't think of any further questions to ask.

"Byron, thanks," she said. "This really means a lot to me."

Riley ended the phone call and paced in the small restroom.

Then she used her cell phone to get the list of vets of the Romeo Company who still lived in Virginia.

Sure enough, there the name was:

Britson, Floyd T SGT

And if Byron was right, she'd be able to find him in a nursing home in Innis.

Riley knew that Innis was a small town, and it ought to be easy to locate a nursing home there. She did a search on her cell phone. Sure enough, there was only one nursing home in Innis—Eldon Gardens Assisted Living.

Of course, she wanted to go there right away.

But that was impossible.

She pulled herself together and walked out toward the car. She saw that Bill had finished filling the tank, probably several minutes ago. She hoped that he and Jake wouldn't ask her why she had taken so long.

When she got into the car, she was relieved to realize that Bill and Jake had been engaged in idle small talk. They didn't seem to have noticed her absence.

Bill started the car, and they continued on their way to Quantico.

*

When they all got out of the vehicle in the BAU parking lot, Jake called out to Riley as she walked away toward her own car.

"Hey, Riley. Bill and I are headed out for a drink. Why don't you join us?"

Riley winced a little. Bill and Jake were spending a lot of time together. Surely they must have felt as though she were avoiding them.

She simply shook her head no.

She could see the disappointment in Jake's face.

He said, "Come on, Riley. It's not like I'm going to be in town forever."

His words stung Riley.

It was true. After so many years apart, Riley wished she could spend more time with her mentor and old friend.

But she couldn't do that. Not right now.

Riley tried uneasily to think of an excuse.

Then Bill said, "Leave her alone, Jake. She just wants to spend time with her kids. She's got the right priorities."

Riley felt a crushing spasm of guilt.

As usual, Bill was judging Riley in the best possible light.

And he was absolutely wrong.

But she didn't contradict Bill, and he and Jake headed away toward Bill's car.

Riley looked at her watch as she walked to her own car. If she went home right now, she'd be there in time for dinner. She wavered. She told herself that she could go talk to Floyd Britson some other time.

But when? she wondered.

She had no idea how much time she was still going to have to spend working on the Matchbook Killer case.

She also had a strange, irrational feeling that this visit couldn't wait.

She got into her car, took out her cell phone, and typed a quick text message to April.

Plz tell Gabriela I'll be late for dinner.

She sent the message and sat staring at her cell phone for a moment, then typed.

Not very late I hope.

Then she typed …

I'm sorry.

She started her car and drove out of the parking lot.

CHAPTER THIRTY THREE

By the time Riley pulled into the town of Innis, she was in the grip of powerful and confusing expectations.

What might she learn from Floyd Britson?

Would it help put her mind at ease?

Or would she be better off not learning it at all?

She saw that Innis was a pleasant little town littered with historical markers and other vestiges of its colonial past. The building that housed Eldon Gardens Assisted Living looked startlingly modern in the midst of older structures. It also looked more like a nice hotel than Riley had expected.

Riley parked and walked into a spacious lobby, which was decorated here and there with flower arrangements.

She approached the female receptionist and said, "I'd like to talk to a resident of yours. His name is Floyd Britson."

The woman gave Riley a quizzical look.

"I don't believe you're a member of the family," she said.

Riley wondered how she could seem so certain.

She also wondered what to say.

Should she try to bluff her way in by claiming to be a distant relative?

Riley swallowed a sigh of despair. One way or the other, she was going to have to be deceptive.

It was getting to be too much of a habit.

She took our badge and showed it to the woman.

"I'm Special Agent Riley Paige, FBI. I'm working on a case. I'd like to talk to Floyd Britson. I think he might be able to help with my investigation."

The woman looked genuinely puzzled now.

"Mr. Britson? Are you sure?"

Riley nodded.

"I can't imagine how he could be any help, but ..."

The woman paused, then said, "Well, since it's official business, I'll take you to him."

As the woman led Riley through the building, Riley found the place strangely unsettling.

It wasn't disagreeable—far from it. Everything was almost breathtakingly pleasant, immaculately tidy and neat, all in restful pastel colors. And the seniors she walked by looked perfectly happy, and their voices were hushed and gentle.

So what was it that bothered her here?

She quickly realized—it was because she knew she would be perfectly miserable here. So much order, so much neatness, would be a nightmare for her. She'd probably lose her mind if she ever had to live in a place like this.

She thought back to Byron Chaney in his spare little room.

What little he had left in life, at least it was his own.

Riley half hoped that she'd wind up more like Byron than the elderly people who lived here.

The woman led Riley through an open door into a large, well-lit, comfortable room that looked like a modest hotel suite.

An elderly man was sitting upright in a hospital bed, and a woman about Riley's age was sitting in a chair beside him. Both were African-American. Riley breathed a small sigh of relief that she hadn't tried to pass herself off as a blood relative.

The man was staring off into space. The woman was quietly reading to him from the Bible.

"Excuse me, Ms. Stafford," the receptionist said to the woman who was reading. "This is Agent Riley Paige with the FBI. She was hoping she could talk a bit with your father." Then the receptionist said to Riley, "This is Floyd Britson and his daughter Elaine Stafford."

The receptionist left the room.

"I don't understand," Elaine said, putting the Bible aside.

"I know," Riley said. "But if I could talk to your father …"

Elaine shook her head.

"You can try," she said. "But Daddy has Alzheimer's disease. He's not likely to be able to tell you anything you want to know."

Riley felt a shiver of dismayed surprise as Elaine offered her a chair.

Riley sat down, and Elaine patiently and slowly began to speak to her father.

"Daddy, this woman is an FBI agent. I don't know what she wants to ask you, but I'm sure it's important. Could you listen to her? Could you try to help her?"

The man nodded as if he vaguely understood.

"Mr. Britson, you were a Marine sergeant years ago, weren't you?"

"I was," Floyd said with what sounded like a note of pride.

"And you served under Captain Oliver Sweeney in the Romeo Company, right?"

Floyd chuckled a little.

In an oddly distant voice he said, "Ollie the Ox. Ollie Ollie Oxen Free."

Riley guessed that Floyd was slipping into some old memory of her father—a nickname and a well-worn joke on that nickname.

"I'm his daughter," Riley said.

Floyd smiled and looked straight at her.

"Little Riley! Goodness, how you've grown!"

He remembers me, Riley thought.

Riley tried to remember Floyd from her childhood. But whatever memories she might have once had of him seemed to be long gone.

She asked, "Do you remember when my mother was killed? Daddy's ... Captain Sweeney's wife?"

Floyd looked vaguely alarmed.

"Karen? Killed? When did that happen?"

But then his face settled into an expression of sad realization.

"Oh, yeah. The shooting. A little while back. Lovely woman. Awful."

Riley was starting to feel encouraged. Floyd didn't seem to have any sense of time or chronology, but bits of memory did seem to be resurfacing.

"Do you have any idea who did it? Shot her, I mean."

Floyd shook his head.

"No idea. No idea at all."

Riley thought hard. What was the best way to nudge the truth out of this man?

"Mr. Britson—"

"Please, call me Floyd."

"Floyd, you have an old Marine friend named Byron Chaney. You got in touch with him a couple of years back. You talked to him by phone."

Floyd laughed softly.

"I guess I did if you say I did. My memory's not what it used to be. Folks tell me it's not going to get any better."

"Do you remember Byron Chaney?" Riley asked.

"Sure, I remember old By."

Riley took a deep breath.

She said, "When you talked to Byron on the phone, you mentioned a fight Captain Sweeney got into."

Floyd chuckled again.

"Old Ollie the Ox. Got in lots of fights. Never lost a single one of 'em."

"This one was especially bad," Riley said. "He really humiliated somebody."

Floyd squinted, trying to remember.

"If you say so," he said.

Riley stifled a sigh. She sensed that Floyd's concentration was slipping.

"You talked to Byron about it," she said. "You said the man swore revenge against my father ... Captain Sweeney."

"Maybe he did," Floyd said, sounding more vague by the second.

"Do you remember that man's name?"

Floyd fell silent. For a moment, Riley thought he'd dropped completely out of the conversation.

Then he began to hum a tune—a hymn, Riley felt pretty sure.

I've really lost him, Riley thought.

But finally he seemed to return to Riley's question.

"No, I do not," he said.

Riley's heart sank.

"Please, please, try to remember," she said.

Floyd's brow knitted in deep concentration.

"Luster," he finally said.

Riley felt a tingle of excitement.

"Is that his name?" she asked.

Floyd was quiet for a moment, then said again, "Luster."

"Is that his name?" Riley asked again.

But Floyd's head drooped forward, and his eyes completely glazed over.

Riley desperately wanted to hear more. It took all her self-control not to shake him and try to bring him out of his trance.

Elaine touched Riley on the shoulder.

She said, "Ma'am, I'm sorry. But this is too much for him. Leave him be."

Riley sat there staring at Floyd for a moment.

Then she handed her card to Elaine.

"I really need to know that name," she said. "Please contact me if he remembers anything else."

Taking the card, Elaine said, "I will, ma'am. But an hour from now, I doubt that he'll remember he even talked to you. I'm really sorry."

Riley knew that there was nothing more to say or do here. She thanked Elaine and left the building. She got into her car and drove on home.

*

Later that night after the girls and Gabriela had gone to bed, Riley went to her office to mull over what she'd learned today—if she'd learned anything meaningful at all.

She brought up the list of twenty-five vets on her computer.

She already knew that Byron Chaney was there, and also Floyd Britson.

But she scanned the names and saw no one named Luster.

She was swept by a wave of confusion. Had she heard it right?

Yes, she was sure that was the name that Floyd had said. She'd heard him say it twice.

Then she remembered what Byron had told her on the phone earlier.

"He mentioned your daddy getting into a fight once with another Marine ..."

Then Byron had added ...

"... not a man I knew personally."

Riley groaned aloud.

Now the hole seemed glaringly obvious.

The Marine named Luster had never been in the Romeo Company at all.

So how on earth was Riley going to begin looking for him?

Would she have to search through all the Marines living in Virginia who had served during those years, trying to find a man named Luster?

Perhaps she could do that, but right now the prospect was too much for her to think about. And of course, Luster could be just a nickname.

Besides, why was she going to all this trouble? If there was anyone in the world who knew the truth already, she knew who it was.

It was Shane Hatcher.

Again, she looked at the bracelet on her wrist with its tiny inscription ...

"face8ecaf"

It was time for Hatcher to stop playing games.

It was time for her to demand the truth from him.

She opened up her video chat program and typed in the characters. She let the call ring for a whole minute.

Nobody answered.

179

Riley's blood was boiling with anger. She had to restrain herself from picking up her computer and throwing it to the floor.

That bastard, she thought.

Why had she ever made her pact with that devil?

And where was he right now? And what was he doing?

Probably in Daddy's cabin, she thought. *Probably laughing at me.*

She choked down her rage, walked downstairs, and poured herself a drink.

Tomorrow would be another day—and she'd be back at work on the Matchbook Killer case. She prayed that she, Bill, and Jake would get a break.

She didn't know how much more discouragement she could stand.

CHAPTER THIRTY FOUR

Early the next morning, Riley was enjoying breakfast with her family when her phone rang. She still felt guilty for missing dinner the night before, and they all ate in awkward silence.

Her heart jumped when she saw that the call was from Bill. Leaving April, Jilly, and Gabriela clustered around the kitchen table, Riley answered the phone as she got up and stepped out of the kitchen.

"I hope you've got some good news," she said.

"I might," Bill said. "I got to the BAU bright and early. Remember that drinking glass in the evidence locker?"

"Yeah—the one the killer handled."

"Well, Sam's team did get some good DNA off it. And they also got DNA off the plastic flower container we found at the cemetery. Those two samples definitely match."

Riley's head buzzed with excitement. The killer had put flowers on Tilda Steen's grave. He was still alive and very possibly still living in the area where he had murdered three women.

But she remembered something Jake had told her. His incompetent partner had smeared up the fingerprints on the glass years ago.

"What about prints on the plastic container?" Riley asked.

"Sam's people found some good ones. But they couldn't match either the prints or the DNA with anything in FBI records."

Riley clicked away possibilities in her mind.

"That doesn't have to be a problem," she said. "Not if we can locate an actual suspect. If the prints and the DNA match, we'll have our killer. Was Sam able to narrow down the list of names?"

Bill chuckled.

"That's more good news," he said. "Sam ran James Reed and the reverse, Reed James. There are lots of guys by those names, but he only found three about the right age who have lived in that area. One of them is dead, so he's not our guy. And we can pretty safely eliminate one of the others."

"Why?" Riley asked.

"I'll send you photos of the men right now."

Riley waited for a moment until an email arrived with a photo attachment. The photos were both from recent driver's licenses. Riley immediately saw what Bill had meant. One of the men was African American. And as weird as some of the witness descriptions had been, they'd been consistent on one detail.

The killer had pale skin.

The other photo showed a pale man with dark hair and dark eyes.

But did he look like the aged composite sketch Sam had given them?

Not exactly, but close enough to get her attention.

She asked, "Where does the lighter-skinned James Reed live?"

"Right in Brinkley, the college town where Melody Yanovich was killed."

Riley was thrilled.

"I'll be at the BAU as soon as I can get there," she said.

"No need," Bill said. "Jake and I will pick you up. Then we can drive straight to Brinkley."

"OK," Riley said. "Just give me a few minutes to get ready."

Riley went back into the kitchen and kissed Jilly and April on the forehead.

"Gotta go," she said breathlessly.

"Are you catching a bad guy today?" April asked with a smile.

"Maybe," Riley said, smiling back at her. "Just maybe."

Riley hurried off to her bedroom to get dressed.

*

The three agents were all in good spirits as they headed toward Brinkley. None of them had said outright that they'd found the man they were looking for, but Riley knew they were all excited at the possibility.

Bill was driving so she got out her tablet computer and searched for the James Reed who lived in Brinkley. She found a few local news items about him.

She read from the tablet, "James Mill Reed is an English professor at Brinkley College."

"How long has he been teaching there?" Jake asked.

Riley skimmed an article.

"For twenty-eight years," she said.

"Wow," Bill said. "Since three years before the murders happened. He might have been one of Melody Yanovich's teachers."

Riley didn't say anything. She let that possibility sink in for a moment.

She knew that Brinkley College used to be a women's school.

What kind of predator might James Reed have been all these years?

Were the deaths of those three women the only sins in his past?

She skimmed through more online information. She didn't see anything about accusations of sexual harassment or any other such transgressions. Instead, she saw that he'd been honored with praise and awards during his many years at the college.

But Riley knew that a list of tributes didn't mean he was innocent. It might only mean that he was exceptionally cunning, cruel, and manipulative.

She struggled to hold her anticipation in check as Bill drove them back to the pretty little college town.

*

When they got to Brinkley, Bill parked the car in front of James Reed's house. It was an attractive old brick house a short distance from the campus. Riley thought it looked very suitable for a highly honored academic.

They were greeted at the door by a slim, elegant woman with a charming smile. She appeared to be in her fifties.

"May I help you?" she asked.

Riley and Bill produced their badges and introduced themselves, then introduced Jake.

"Is this the residence of James Mill Reed?" Riley asked.

The woman looked puzzled.

"Yes," she said slowly. "I'm his wife, Shanna."

"Is your husband at home?" Riley asked.

"Yes. May I ask what this is all about?"

"We'd like to talk to him, please," Riley said.

Shanna Reed called up the stairs.

"Jim, there are people here to see you. I'm afraid it's rather … urgent."

A few moments later, a dapper man walked briskly down the stairs. Riley quickly tried to assess whether he resembled the aged composite sketch. The man's brown hair was streaked with gray, and he had brown eyes. His skin was fair, but not startlingly so.

He didn't look *unlike* the sketch.

When they all introduced themselves, Riley saw that James Reed's face suddenly grew a full shade paler.

He said to his wife, "Honey, could you give us a few minutes alone?"

Shanna looked worried now.

"What's going on?" she asked.

"Please," James Reed said.

Shanna nodded and went up the stairs. James invited the agents into his living room, where they all sat down. James eyes darted guiltily among the three visitors.

"What's this all about?" he asked.

His face looked positively ashen now.

"Mr. Reed ..." Bill began.

Riley knew that Bill was about to ask him specifically about the murders twenty-five years ago. But on a gut impulse, she decided to take a different approach. With a subtle hand gesture, she signaled Bill to let her start the questioning.

Then she asked, "Perhaps you should tell *us,* Mr. Reed."

James Reed hung his head and slumped forward miserably.

"Maybe I should get a lawyer," he said.

Riley spoke gently and carefully.

"You could do that. But I think you really want to tell us."

Reed sat in silence for a moment.

Then he said, "I know this is ... an appalling thing to say ..."

Riley's senses quickened, hanging on his next words.

Then he said, "I thought ... the statute of limitations ..."

His voice faded off.

Bill apparently couldn't keep quiet any longer.

"Statute of limitations?" Bill said. "There's no statute of limitations on murder."

The man looked up.

"But it *wasn't* murder. Not really."

Riley exchanged puzzled looks with Bill and Jake.

James Reed made an imploring gesture.

"It happened so long ago. I thought I'd put it all behind me. I've got a family now. A wife, grown children, grandchildren. I've tried to live a good life."

Riley stared hard into his eyes, trying to grasp what she was hearing.

It didn't make sense.

In her experience, the kind of monster who killed three women wouldn't show such open remorse. He might feel it, but he'd keep it buried deep inside. He'd never admit it to a living soul.

Something's wrong, she thought.

Then he said in a choked voice, "I was giving a lecture at St. John's College in Annapolis. I had drinks with students and faculty afterwards. I got pretty drunk. I could have stayed in a hotel that night, but I decided to drive the whole way home. It was stupid. Like I said, I was …"

His voice trailed off again.

"She—the girl—was riding her bicycle alongside of the road. I saw her clearly. But I just didn't have full control of my car, and I swerved into her, and she went down in the ditch. I stopped and got out of the car and ran over to her body but she was already—"

A sob rose up in his throat.

"I didn't contact the police. I drove on home. I didn't tell anyone, not even my wife. I read about it in the papers the next day."

Then, with tears in his eyes, he looked around at Riley, Jake, and Bill.

"But according to Maryland law … I mean, I looked it up … I really thought …"

Jake let out a low growl.

"Yeah," Jake said. "Maryland has a three-year statute of limitations on vehicular manslaughter or even homicide."

Riley could see that Bill and Jake looked as stunned as she felt.

Like her, they didn't know whether to believe his story.

Might it be just a ruse to distract them from the murders he'd actually committed?

Finally Bill said, "Mr. Reed, we want you to voluntarily give us your fingerprints and a DNA sample."

The man's mouth dropped open with shock.

"Why?" he said. "I just confessed. Why do you need evidence?"

Riley knew that Bill was getting ready to ask him specifically about the Matchbook Killer's murders.

But at that moment, her eyes locked with Reed's.

And she knew …

He's not the killer.

Before Bill could say anything, Riley said, "Mr. Reed, we'll leave now."

She rose from her chair and saw expressions of perplexed protest in her colleagues' eyes.

"Come on," she said to Bill and Jake. "Let's go."

As soon as she, Bill, and Jake stepped out the front door and started walking toward the car, Bill started complaining.

"Are you out of your mind, Riley? He might have been playing us back there."

"Bill's right," Jake said. "It would be one hell of a clever trick, making up an act of vehicular manslaughter as an alibi. But the kind of man we're looking for might just pull such a stunt. We've got to check out his story. We've got to ask more questions. We've got to get DNA and prints."

Riley opened the car door and got inside.

"He has his share of guilt but he's not our man, guys," she said. "Let's go."

"How do you know?" Bill asked.

Riley shook her head.

"Because of his eyes," she said. "I could tell by his eyes."

CHAPTER THIRTY FIVE

A few minutes later, Riley, Bill, and Jake were sitting in a café arguing about her decision.

"Let me get this straight," Bill said to Riley. "He's not our man because you don't like his *eyes*?"

Riley took a sip of coffee.

"They don't fit the witness descriptions," she said.

Jake let out a snort of disapproval.

"Witness? Which witnesses do you mean? Crazy Roger Duffy, who saw light shooting out of the killer's eyes? Or that postman who thought he saw a ghost when he was a kid?"

"Yeah," Riley said. "Those witnesses."

Bill and Jake sat staring at her for a moment. Riley felt a wave of impatience with them.

"Listen to me, both of you," she said. "Has my gut ever been wrong about something like this? Ever?"

Riley could see their expressions softening.

They know I'm right, she thought.

"OK, so where does this leave us?" Bill asked, breaking the silence.

Riley thought for a moment. Then an idea started forming in her mind.

"I'm going to call Sam Flores," she said.

She took out her cell phone and got Flores on the line, putting him on speakerphone.

She said, "Sam, we need help. Those names you gave Bill didn't pan out. But I think we should give it another try."

"How?" Flores asked.

Riley thought for a moment.

"Sam, you're good at thinking outside the box. I think the killer's name is a variation on the names we've got—James Reed and Reed J. Tillerman. Run another search. Try every possible variation you can get on those names."

Riley thought a bit more.

Then she said, "Widen the search area. And give us images."

"OK," Flores said. "How soon do you need results?"

Riley almost repeated what she'd told him yesterday:

"Tomorrow will be fine."

But no. It was time to solve this case once and for all. Justice had been delayed for twenty-five years. They mustn't waste another minute.

"Right now," she told Flores.

She ended the call. They all waited in silence, sipping their coffee and eating their sweet rolls.

Riley found herself thinking about the irony of what had just happened.

They had found a guilty man.

James Reed just wasn't guilty of the crime they'd suspected him of.

And Reed was right—the statute of limitations on his crime had run out many years ago.

Reed would never be brought to justice now, except in his own guilty heart.

But maybe that was justice enough.

Is anybody innocent anymore? Riley wondered.

Then she shuddered a little as she thought about herself—her forbidden pact with Shane Hatcher, her moments of vengeful violence, and a host of other crimes and sins. She especially remembered how she'd once killed a psychopath who had held her and April prisoner. She had savagely smashed his head with a rock, time and time again.

James Reed has got nothing on me, Riley thought bitterly.

Then her phone buzzed. The call was from Sam Flores.

"Have you got something for us?" Riley asked.

"Maybe. Just maybe. I ran across a certain R. James Tiller who lives in Cabot. I checked more carefully and found out that the R stands for Reed."

"What about images?" Riley asked.

Sam brought up a year-old newspaper article with the headline, "Valedictorian Receives Societal Club Scholarship."

In a black-and-white photograph, two men were handing a certificate to a proud teenager wearing a graduation gown. According to the caption, the girl's name was Sylvia Capp. The man on her right was the club president. On her left was R. James Tiller, the head of the club's Service Committee.

Riley couldn't tell much about Tiller's eyes, but his face seemed remarkably pale. He also looked a little like the aged composite sketch, except that his hair looked white rather than gray. But of course some men's hair whitened at an early age.

Riley asked Flores for Tiller's address and ended the call.

"It sounds like a long shot," Jake said.

"It's all we've got," she said. "Let's go."

*

Cabot was a suburb on the east side of Richmond. The drive took them around the city, quite some distance from where the crimes had been committed. But this didn't raise any special doubts in Riley's mind. She'd known all along that the killer had possibly moved away from the area. If Reed James Tiller really was their killer, at least he hadn't moved out of state.

Maybe we're lucky this time, she thought.

When Bill pulled the car up to the address Flores had given them, the house looked so perfectly ordinary that Riley checked the information again.

It was a small, brick ranch house placed at the far side of a wide, well-trimmed lawn. It looked a lot like other houses they had passed as they followed a network of streets that ran through a neighborhood near the James River.

It was the right address, but it looked like the last place in the world where one might expect a murderer to live.

Riley, Bill, and Jake walked across the lawn and rang the doorbell.

A short, chubby middle-aged woman answered the door. Riley detected that she had once been fairly pretty. But what struck Riley most was how extremely ordinary she looked—just like the house and the neighborhood.

"Can I help you?" the woman asked with a smile.

Riley, Bill, and Jake introduced themselves. The woman seemed surprised but hardly alarmed.

Riley asked if J. Reed Tiller lived here.

"Why, yes," she said. "I'm his wife, Celia."

"We'd like to talk to Mr. Tiller, if that's possible," Bill said.

"You should be able to do that any time now," Celia said, still smiling. "He's on his way home from work. He works in Richmond."

Looking a little confused, she added, "Has there been ... some sort of trouble?"

Riley didn't want to alarm the woman.

"No," she said. "We just want to ask him a few questions about someone he might have known a long time ago."

The woman relaxed a little.

"I'm sure James will be glad to help," she said.

"We'll wait in our car," Riley said.

"Oh, no, that wouldn't be comfortable," Celia said. "Come on in."

She led Riley, Bill, and Jake into a cozy, neat, blandly decorated living room.

"Let me call James and let him know you're here," she said.

She picked up a phone and told her husband about his official visitors.

She hung up and said, "James says he'll be glad to help however he can. Could I get you anything? Tea, coffee, soda?"

"We're fine, thanks," Riley said.

Celia sat down, and so did Bill and Jake. Riley stayed on her feet, looking around at the almost uncannily ordinary living room.

She heard Bill ask, "How long have you been married?"

Celia said, "Twenty-two years. We have one child—a daughter, Lena. She's away in college. It's her third year at Bon Secours College right over in Richmond."

"Oh, a nursing school," Bill said in a friendly voice. "I take it she wants to go into medicine."

Riley knew that Bill was launching into their familiar drill—keeping small talk going while Riley took in their surroundings.

She looked carefully at framed family pictures on the wall. They showed the Tillers over the years, from when their daughter was a toddler to her high school graduation.

Right away, she was struck by James Tiller's appearance in all the pictures.

The white hair she'd noticed in the newspaper photo had nothing to do with age.

His hair had looked that way since he was much younger.

But what most startled Riley about him was his eyes.

They were a piercing light shade of blue.

He's an albino, Riley realized.

It all began to make sense in her mind.

He'd been described by witnesses as brown-haired with hazel eyes.

He'd dyed his hair, of course—perhaps to disguise himself, but possibly out of simple youthful vanity.

But what about those eyes?

She remembered what Roger Duffy had told her about seeing the killer in the Waveland Tap in Denison.

"He looked at me. His eyes weren't human. Streaming blue light was coming out of them."

Riley got it now. To a schizophrenic like Roger, a man with

those eyes must have come from another world.

She remembered something else that Roger had said.

"Then he went into the restroom. I sat here too scared to move. Finally he came out and he looked at me again. This time his eyes were normal—dark like everybody said."

Of course! Riley realized.

The killer had been wearing colored contact lenses. Probably they had irritated his eyes when he was at the bar, and he had taken them out for a while. He'd gone to the restroom to put them back in.

Just as Riley was putting these thoughts together, the front door opened and someone came in.

Riley saw that it was Tiller himself—eerily pale, with white hair and cold blue eyes.

He came into the living room.

"Celia tells me you're from the FBI," he said with a smile. "What can I do to help you?"

"We just have a few questions," Riley said, still standing.

Tiller sat down near his wife.

"Celia, get these good people some coffee," he said.

"They told me they didn't want any," Celia said shyly.

"I insist," Tiller said.

Tiller then asked his guests whether they wanted cream or sugar.

"Go bring it, dear," Tiller said to Celia.

"Of course, James," Celia said in a rather timid voice. Then she disappeared into the kitchen.

This little exchange spoke volumes to Riley.

It was clear that Celia had always been a docile, obedient wife—the only kind of woman that a man with such deep sexual insecurities could possibly stay married to.

Celia quickly came back with the coffee, serving everybody like a perfect hostess.

With a chill Riley realized that Celia's docility was very likely the only reason he hadn't murdered her. She posed no threat to him. He'd even been able to perform sexually with her—at least enough to have produced one child, and Celia hadn't demanded anything more of him.

For many years now, he'd lived his ideal life with his ideal mate.

He thought he'd put his crimes behind him.

Until now.

What surprised Riley most at the moment was his extreme self-possession.

From having probed his mind several times, Riley knew that part of him was eaten up with guilt and shame.

But over the years, he'd learned to mask those feelings from everyone he knew.

She spoke slowly and deliberately.

"Mr. Tiller, I see that you only had one child. Why is that? Didn't you want to have more?"

His white eyebrows pulled together.

"I don't understand the question," he said.

Now there was a note of defensiveness in his voice. Riley felt sure that she was pushing the right buttons now. She was subtly questioning his virility—and he couldn't take that.

Not if she kept pushing him.

It's time to tear that mask away, Riley thought.

CHAPTER THIRTY SIX

Sitting in the living room with his wife and the three FBI agents, James Tiller felt a sharp stab of fury at the woman's question.

The bitch, he thought.

She had a lot of nerve, asking a question like that—about how many children he had.

Her smile exasperated him still further.

Then she said, "And you only had a daughter—no sons. Such a shame. Surely you wanted sons. If you'd only had more children, maybe one would have been a son. But you didn't. I wonder why."

James felt his face twitch.

He'd spent his whole life pushing women like this one away.

When he was young he'd even killed two of them—that bossy college student in Brinkley, and that slut in Denison.

As for the third girl ...

He still didn't know quite why he'd done it.

He remembered when they'd walked into the motel room and she'd quietly told him she was a virgin.

Something happened.

His heart had softened toward her.

He didn't want to hurt her.

But he'd killed her anyway.

Somehow, it had felt like an act of mercy.

It was as if by killing her he'd be saving her from ...

... what?

From life, he guessed.

It was the only reason he could think of after all these years.

But he mustn't get lost in his memories now.

He also couldn't let this cop bitch get the best of him. He hadn't survived all these years by being weak or stupid.

"Could you please tell me what's your business today?" he asked, straining to sound polite.

Still with that insufferable smile, the woman said, "We were wondering if you ever lived at 345 Bolingbroke Road near Greybull. It's a lovely little farm."

It was all he could do not to shudder with alarm.

Of course he recognized the address. He'd lived there during the time he committed the murders.

Why had the law caught up with him now, after all this time?

It wasn't fair. He'd been living a decent life.

Was there some way to thwart these agents?

Surely not.

They probably had all the proof they needed already.

So why was the woman asking all these questions?

The answer was obviously to humiliate him. She was playing with him, toying with him.

How much more of this could he be expected to take?

It wasn't reasonable.

*

Riley could see that she was getting to him. He was rubbing one hand against the other. Due to his pallor, his face looked unnaturally red.

Just a little more, Riley thought.

She thought that he was actually shaking a little.

"Mr. Tiller, are you familiar with the so-called Matchbook Killer? He murdered three women twenty-five years ago."

Tiller gripped the arms of his chair.

"It doesn't sound familiar," he said. "But twenty-five years was a long time ago."

"Yes, that's true, isn't it?" she sat.

Riley noticed the change in Celia's expression. She was looking more and more confused—and more and more frightened.

She never imagined this, Riley thought. *She still doesn't understand.*

Riley sat smiling at Tiller silently for a moment.

Then she said, "Mr. Tiller, I guess we should get right to the point. The FBI has reopened the Matchbook Killer case. And we're eliminating suspects. I assure you, this interview is just routine. All we want to do is cross you off our list. And it will be easy to do."

She held his gaze until he blinked.

He got up from his chair and stepped away from the others.

Then Riley said, "You see, we have the actual killer's DNA. We got it from a drinking glass that he handled many years ago. And he's been leaving flowers on one of the victims' graves for years, so we were able to get both prints and DNA from the flower container. Now all we need from you are your fingerprints and a DNA sample. I'm sure you understand."

"I understand," he said.

He was standing beside a desk now, opening a drawer.

Riley's reflexes quickened. Her hand moved toward her weapon.

But Tiller moved with astonishing speed.

In an instant, he was standing behind his wife's chair, holding a hunting knife to her throat.

Celia let out a hoarse cry of sheer terror.

Riley was on her feet now, and so were Bill and Jake. None of them had had time to draw their weapons.

Celia managed to gasp out the words, "What are you doing?"

"Shut up!" Tiller said. He pushed the tip of the blade into her soft skin.

She twitched slightly as a few drops of blood trickled down her neck.

"Keep still!" Tiller demanded.

The woman seemed stunned. She made neither movement nor sound.

He moved the tip of his blade to her carotid artery.

Riley knew that he could sever the artery in a fraction of a second.

Would they be able to save the poor woman then?

Riley doubted it.

Tiller snapped at Riley, Bill, and Jake.

"Put your guns on the sofa. Your phones too."

All three of the agents did as they were told. They had no choice.

"Easy, easy," Bill was saying in a soft voice. "You don't want to do this."

"Don't tell me what I want," Tiller said.

"What are you going to do?" Jake asked.

Tiller didn't reply immediately. He looked dazed for a few seconds.

"You're all going to the basement," he finally said. "You'll stay there until …"

His voice trailed off. Riley knew that he had no idea what to do next.

He motioned with his head toward a door to his right.

"The basement's right there," he said. "Go. Get down there."

Bill obediently walked toward the door, with Jake and Riley behind him. Bill opened the door and started down the stairs. Jake followed behind him.

Riley's mind raced, desperately searching for options.

She could see that the latch on that door was set to lock when it closed behind them. They wouldn't be able to get out of the basement—at least not quickly or quietly. Then what would happen to Celia? Would Tiller kill her instantly or take her hostage?

Riley couldn't allow either of those things to happen.

Bill and Jake were on their way down the stairs. Just as she approached the doorway, Riley whirled around and launched herself at the killer.

With her attention focused on his hand with the knife, she dove across the intervening space and slammed into him. The weapon flew out of his hand.

But Riley's momentum carried her into the frightened wife, and they both crashed to the floor. As Riley struggled to untangle herself from Celia and regain her footing, she heard the basement door slam shut. Then a blow to her own head disoriented her.

She knew the man had her by the hair, pulling her head back.

She thought she heard a crashing sound. She didn't know what that was.

She struggled to get a grip on the hands that held her from behind with surprising strength.

Then she felt the point of the knife at her throat.

She heard his words: "Die, bitch."

CHAPTER THIRTY SEVEN

As James Tiller gripped her from behind, Riley felt like a trapped animal.

The knife was sharp against her throat.

It'll come any second now, she realized.

Her dazed mind wondered how it would feel to die. Then she heard another familiar voice.

"You don't want to do that, pal."

It was Jake's voice. Or was she just imagining it?

"I'd love to pull the trigger," she heard Jake say. "Just love to."

Riley felt Tiller's grip loosen, and the knife dropped from his hand.

She scrambled away from him and looked around.

Jake was standing there holding a small pistol to Tiller's head.

Tiller looked terrified.

"Hands behind your back," Jake said.

Tiller complied, and Jake cuffed him, reciting his rights as he did so.

Poor Celia was crouching on the floor, sobbing uncontrollably and shaking convulsively. A little blood was still trickling down her neck but Riley could see that the wound wasn't dangerous. She knew the woman's emotional wounds would be harder for her to deal with.

Bill was standing nearby talking on his cell phone.

"I need assistance," he was saying. "Send a wagon to pick up a suspect. Whoever is closest. Local cops would be fine." He hesitated a moment and looked at the crying wife. "And send an ambulance. I have a wounded victim here. Not life-threatening."

Riley tried to get to her feet, but staggered. She felt Bill's firm hand on one arm, steadying her.

"Hold it," he said. "Sit down over here."

He steered her to the sofa. Riley plopped down next to the guns and phones still scattered there, right where they'd put them.

Bill said, "You got a pretty bad blow to the head."

"I think he kicked me," Riley said. "But everything is clearing up now. How did you—"

"We smashed the door open."

Now she realized what had caused the crashing sound she'd heard when she was nearly unconscious. Bill and Jake must have both thrown themselves against the door to break through it.

Bill crouched down beside Celia to calm her down. He said, "I've called for an ambulance. They'll take care of you."

He looked up at Riley and added, "And I want that medic to look at you."

"I'm fine," Riley said.

Bill smiled.

"No you're not," he said.

Riley reached up and touched her forehead and found that it was bleeding.

"Just stay right there," Bill said. "We'll take care of everything."

For once, Riley did as she was told.

Jake had Tiller lying face down on the floor with his hands cuffed behind him. The man didn't look like he would ever put up any more resistance.

Riley asked Jake, "Where did you get that gun?"

Jake grinned. "Come on, Riley. This is Jake you're talking to."

He tugged on his pants leg to show an ankle holster.

Riley smiled back at him.

How could she have forgotten that Jake always carried an extra weapon? She had even done that herself on some occasions.

As they all waited for help to arrive, Riley realized that she felt a little more stable.

She felt good enough to do something she'd scarcely ever hoped to do.

She picked up her cell phone and dialed the number for Paula Steen, Tilda Steen's mother.

"Riley!" Paula said. "How lovely to hear from you! How are you?"

"I'm fine," Riley said, her voice croaking a little after all the stress and exertion.

"Are you sure, dear?" Paula asked with concern. "You sound a little ... off."

Riley chuckled a little.

"Really. I'm fine. And I've got good news."

"What news?"

Riley took a long, slow breath. She remembered what Paula had said to her at least once every year.

"My daughter's killer will never be brought to justice."

How sweet it was to be able to tell her she was wrong.

"We've got him," Riley said. "My partners and I. We're arresting him right now."

"Got who? You're arresting who?"

"Him," Riley said.

Riley paused to let the truth sink in. Then she heard Paula gasp.

"Oh, my heavens," Paula said.

Riley thought she heard a sob.

"Are you OK?" Riley asked.

"Yes," Paula said in a choked voice. "Oh, yes. And thank you. But how? How did it happen?"

"That's a long story," Riley said. "I'll tell you soon."

Paula was definitely crying now.

"Where is he?" she asked. "Is he alive?"

"We're taking him into custody right now. The local cops will pick him up any minute now. I'm sure he'll be held in the Cabot police station for the time being."

"Cabot? You're in Cabot? Why, that's not far from here at all."

For a moment Riley was surprised. But then she remembered—although she'd never met Paula Steen, she knew that she lived close to Richmond.

"I'm coming there," Paula said. "To the police station."

Riley suddenly felt a little uneasy.

"Paula, are you sure that's a good idea? You won't be able to talk to him."

"I don't care," Paula said. "I just want to see him in custody."

Riley understood. The woman certainly deserved that small satisfaction after all these years.

"OK," Riley said. "I'll meet you there in a little while."

Riley heard sirens approaching. At the moment, it seemed like an oddly cheerful sound.

CHAPTER THIRTY EIGHT

Awhile later, Riley stood in the police station looking through the two-way mirror into the interview room at James Reed Tiller. He was chained to the heavy, battleship-gray table, staring at the tabletop. He looked strangely catatonic, almost like a figure of wax.

But Riley sensed that there was a lot boiling inside him.

His murderous self, so long suppressed but always lurking deep inside, had finally risen again.

And now he was going to pay the consequences.

Riley heard footsteps to her left, then a woman's voice.

"Riley? Are you Riley?"

Riley smiled. She recognized that voice at once. It was Paula Steen. She turned and saw her. Paula was every bit the sweet little grandmotherly figure Riley had always imagined when talking to her on the phone.

"They told me I'd find you here," Paula said, walking toward her, smiling.

Then she touched the bandage on Riley's head.

"But you've been hurt!" she said.

"It's nothing."

"It doesn't look like nothing."

Riley laughed.

"I've had worse, Paula. Believe me, it's nothing."

It was true. The medic had checked her back at Tiller's house, and she had no apparent concussion. Her head was going to ache for a good while, though. She didn't want to start taking the prescribed painkillers yet. She still had too much to think about.

Riley and Paula rather shyly hugged each other.

Then Paula looked through the window.

"Is that him?" she asked.

"Yes," Riley said.

"Has he confessed?"

"No, but we've got plenty to convict him. And Virginia has the death penalty. If he's sentenced to death, he'll get a choice between electrocution and lethal injection."

Paula just stared at him for a moment.

Then she stammered, "He doesn't look ... I guess I expected ..."

Her voice trailed off, but Riley understood. To family members of murder victims, the killer always looks strangely ordinary. That was true even of James Tiller, with his strange pale appearance.

Paula turned toward Riley and asked, "Can I ... talk to him?"

Riley had been expecting this. And it worried her.

But how could she say no?

She looked at the guard standing next to the door. He'd heard their whole conversation. He nodded at Riley, then quietly opened the door.

"Stay in the doorway," Riley told Paula. "Don't go all the way into the room."

Paula obediently stepped into the doorframe, and Riley stood right behind her.

In a quavering voice, Paula told him, "I'm Tilda Steen's mother."

The man looked up at her with a strangely blank expression.

Paula drew herself up, gathering quiet determination.

"Every year ... on the day she died ... I left flowers on her grave."

A tiny smirk crossed Tiller's face.

"So did I," he said.

Paula recoiled a little. Riley realized that she'd never known about this.

But then Paula's nerves seemed to settle.

She said, "If I'm still here, still alive ... after you're gone ... I'll leave flowers on your grave too."

The man looked shocked. Riley felt the same way. She could hardly believe her ears.

But then Paula added with a fierce hiss.

"Dead ones. Dead flowers."

Paula turned around and said to the guard, "I'm through."

The guard closed the door, and Paula collapsed in tears into Riley's arms.

"It's over, isn't it?" Paula murmured between sobs.

"It's over," Riley said.

"Thanks to you," Paula said.

Riley felt a flash of guilt. She wished she'd reopened this cold case a long time ago and finished it for Paula.

Paula kissed Riley on the cheek and left the building.

*

When Bill was driving Riley and Jake back to Quantico, they didn't say much during the drive. Riley felt exhausted, and she knew that Jake and Bill did as well. But the feeling of satisfaction among them was palpable.

Finally Riley asked Jake, "Do you feel ready to retire now?"

Jake chuckled a little.

"I dunno," he said. "I don't feel like I did that much on this case really."

Riley smiled. She understood how he felt. It was a common feeling after wrapping up a case—a feeling of not having done much of anything at all.

But it certainly wasn't true of Jake. It had been wonderful to have him back just this one final time as a partner and also a mentor. As skilled as Riley had always been at entering the mind of a killer, on this case Jake had inspired her to go farther and deeper than she ever had. And of course, there was something else.

"You saved my life," Riley said.

Jake laughed again.

"Yeah, there's that. A pretty good life's work, I guess. Sure, I'm ready to retire. But only from the field. I'll always have lots of work to do."

Riley knew what he meant. Jake would always be able to do his armchair work on cold cases, just like he'd been doing for many years now. Riley hoped that he'd be able to do that right up until he died.

*

By the time Riley got home, Jilly and April were already home from school. When she walked into the house, Gabriela and the girls all fussed over her bandaged head, demanding to know if she was OK. As if she were an invalid, they guided her toward the couch and sat her down.

"I'm fine," Riley told them. "Really, fine."

"Did you catch the bad guy?" Jilly asked.

"*I* didn't," Riley said. "*All* of us did. Me, Bill, Jake, and others too, like Sam Flores, our chief technician."

Jilly was hopping up and down with excitement.

"Tell us! Tell us the whole story!"

Riley sighed deeply.

"Not right now," she said. "Give me just a little time to catch my breath."

The girls noisily objected, but Gabriela calmed them down.

"Give *Señora* Riley some time to herself," she said.

Riley thanked Gabriela and went up to her office. As soon as she sat down at her desk, something strange happened.

All the satisfaction she'd felt at solving the Matchbook Killer case evaporated in mere seconds.

Replacing that satisfaction was anxiety and frustration.

She'd left another cold case unsolved.

The case of her own mother's murder.

CHAPTER THIRTY NINE

As Riley sat at her desk, a renewed feeling of hopelessness swept over her.

She remembered her visit to Floyd Britson at the rest home.

She remembered the single word he'd said in answer to all her questions:

"Luster."

She'd followed Hatcher's trail to a senile old man who couldn't possibly tell her what she wanted to know.

It seemed like a sick joke.

And the joke was on Riley.

Riley's hopelessness was morphing into anger.

This was all Hatcher's doing.

It was time to have it out with him.

She looked again at the inscription on her bracelet.

"face8ecaf"

The last time she'd tried calling Hatcher by that video address, she'd gotten no answer.

If she tried it now, would he answer this time?

He's got to, Riley thought. *He's just got to.*

She opened up her video chat program and typed in the characters.

The call rang three times.

And then ... there he was, sitting in front of an anonymous gray background.

An expression of pleasure crossed his dusky features.

"Hello, Riley," he said. "I believe congratulations are in order. You've brought the Matchbook Killer to justice."

Riley fleetingly wondered how he'd gotten the news so fast.

But she knew better than to be surprised.

Hatcher was a man of means with an uncanny reach. He had tendrils everywhere, detecting everything he wanted to know about anybody who mattered to him.

And Riley knew that she mattered to him intensely.

"You son of a bitch," Riley said in low snarl.

Hatcher's expression changed to one of mock hurt.

"You sound angry with me. I wonder why."

Riley couldn't control herself for a single second longer.

"You played me!" she snapped. "You sent me on a fool's errand—and you've done all this just so you could get my father's cabin. Well, I'm not going to let you get away with it. I'm going to come up there and throw you out—if I don't kill you first."

She suddenly realized she'd been shouting.

Her voice had surely carried all through the house.

Control yourself, she thought. *Don't let him do this to you.*

Hatcher said, "I don't understand what's wrong, Riley. I think I've been most helpful. I steered you onto the trail toward your mother's killer. I honestly don't see why you haven't found him by now. Did you locate Floyd Britson?"

"Yes," Riley said quietly.

"Did you talk to him?"

"Yes."

"And he told you something, didn't he? A single word."

Riley didn't reply. But it was obvious that Hatcher already knew about Floyd's mysterious utterance …

"Luster."

He must have talked to Floyd himself.

He must have heard Floyd say the exact same thing.

"You're almost there, Riley," Hatcher said. "You just need one more little nudge. I'll be glad to give you that nudge here and now. But I want a little favor first. I think you know what that favor is."

Again Riley didn't reply. She knew what he wanted all too well.

He relished hearing the darkest secrets of her life.

His power over her was so strong that she'd told him ugly things about herself—things she would never tell another human soul.

Just then there was a knock at the door. She heard April's voice.

"Mom, are you OK? We heard you shouting."

"I'm fine," Riley called back.

"Are you sure?"

"I'm sure. I just got mad at somebody on the phone. It's OK now."

She heard April walking away down the hallway.

Then she said to Hatcher, "I've got nothing to tell you."

"No?" Hatcher said. "What about Murray Rossum's death?"

Riley shuddered.

He'd hit upon a raw and recent memory.

Murray Rossum had been a pathetic specimen—a self-hating creature who killed young women by hanging.

When Riley had cornered him at last, he had hanged himself.

205

She'd done nothing to stop him.

She said, "I watched him die."

"And you enjoyed it."

"No," Riley said. "But I was ... fascinated."

"And a thought went through your mind as you watched him die. What was that thought, Riley?"

Riley was almost in tears now.

Hatcher had bored down to the awful truth.

She remembered a question that Hatcher sometimes asked her.

"Are you already, or are you becoming?"

He had answered that question himself once.

"You're becoming. *You're becoming what you've always been deep down. Call it a monster or whatever you want. And it won't be long before you* are *that person."*

Now she remembered standing there watching Murray die, his movements slowing, his body slackening, his eyes closing.

"Tell me what you were thinking," Hatcher said.

Riley spoke slowly in a choked voice.

"I thought ... I realized ... that I was *becoming*."

Hatcher let out a deeply satisfied chuckle. She understood why he felt such gratification.

Riley had just admitted to him the awful truth.

She was becoming just like him.

Almost as though she was becoming part of him.

After a silent moment, Hatcher said, "Now, about your mother's killer—well, he seems to be a mysterious creature, eh? Almost magical. A phantom, a ghost, a demon ..."

Then with a tone of great significance, he added:

"A *troll*."

Then his face disappeared.

He had ended the call.

Riley was shaking all over. She took long slow breaths to calm herself.

A troll, she thought. *Mommy was killed by a troll.*

That word, "troll"—she knew that it had become part of contemporary slang, especially to describe malicious people on the Internet.

But she felt sure that wasn't the kind of troll Hatcher meant.

Riley went onto the Internet and searched for information about trolls.

Some of it she already knew—that a troll was a legendary supernatural creature, like a gnome, an ogre, a goblin.

But then she ran across a phrase that jumped out at her ...

"Storybook trolls live under bridges ..."

Riley's heart started pounding.

The truth was coming together in her mind, so fast and hard that she could barely comprehend it.

She decided to run another search—this time for a location on a map.

She typed in the name *Luster.*

Then, in a strangely automatic way, she added: *Bridge.*

There it was, on a map right in front of her.

There was a Luster Street Bridge in Vickery, Virginia—an overpass in an urban area.

Riley didn't give herself time to think things through.

She leaped up from her chair, rushed out of her room, and headed downstairs.

She was about to go out the front door when she heard April's voice.

"Mom, where are you going?"

Riley turned and saw April's worried expression. She reached out to April and held her by the shoulders.

Riley couldn't help but cry now.

"I've got to go somewhere, honey," she said. "I might be gone for quite a while. But I'll be back. And when I come back ..."

She wanted to say ...

"I'll be back for good."

But the words wouldn't come.

Tears were welling up in April's eyes now.

"Mom, you're scaring me."

"I know," Riley said with a sob. "But everything's going to be all right. I promise."

Without another word, she ran out of the house, got into her car, and started to drive.

CHAPTER FORTY

It was a long drive to Vickery, Virginia. Night closed in around Riley as she drove toward the mountains, and it started to rain. Riley felt swept by wave upon wave of fatigue.

She could barely believe all that had happened that day.

She, Bill, and Jake had tracked down a killer and brought him to justice.

She'd even been slightly injured in the process.

But here she was, pursuing the darkest mystery of her life.

What mattered most at the moment was staying awake.

Finally she arrived in a manufacturing district on the outskirts of Vickery. It was an area with big metal buildings and warehouses, and large lighted parking. She knew that during the day, those lots would be full of trucks and cars. Tonight most of it looked deserted.

She pulled up to the end of the Luster Street Bridge. It was raining and dark, so she got an umbrella and a flashlight before getting out of the car.

Shining the light in front of her, she carefully made her way down the rough, wet hillside along the bridge. The bridge stretched over a dry ravine, not a riverbed. Even so, Riley felt sure that the ravine must flood when the rain was really heavy.

In the beam of her flashlight, she saw a few scattered belongings just beneath the overpass. There were definitely people under there in the shadows. It looked as though Luster Bridge had been a homeless haven for many years.

She shined her light around on several sleeping men, some of whom groaned with dismay at the glare. Then her flashlight fell upon one man who was sitting up on a surface of cardboard covered with plastic. He was gripping a half-empty bottle of rubbing alcohol, and his face was ravaged from a long and terrible life.

"Who's there?" the man asked.

That voice—it was unmistakable.

It had echoed through Riley's mind all her life.

The last time she had heard that voice, it had said to her mother

…

"Give me your money."

Riley suddenly felt paralyzed. She couldn't think of what to say.

"Show me your face," the man said.

Riley shined the flashlight in her own face. She thought she heard the man gasp.

Then there came a long, horrible silence, so long, she wasn't sure it would ever end.

"Dear God," the man said. "The last time I saw you ..."

Riley knew what he was about to say.

"... you were a little girl in a candy store."

He started to cry softly.

"I always knew you'd find me," he said.

Riley knelt beside him.

"What's your name?" she asked.

"Wade Bowman."

Riley gulped hard, then said:

"Tell me what happened—that day."

He shook his head, sobbing.

He sobbed so long, she didn't think he would ever speak, and she wondered how, if ever, she'd get it out of him.

But then suddenly, to her surprise, he spoke.

"I hated your daddy," he said. "He hated me. He made my life hell. I deserved it, I guess. I was a poor excuse for a man, especially for a soldier. But he ... humiliated me, ruined me, took away what little self-respect I had. I lost everything, went broke, and I—"

He paused a moment.

"I wanted to kill him. I went looking for him. Someone told me they saw him on the way to that candy store. So I went there to kill him. But when I went in, he wasn't there. Instead, I only saw your mother. I didn't know if I'd work up the nerve to come kill him again. And in that moment, I thought—what better way to hurt him? I can kill her instead...."

He choked on a sob.

"I don't know why I pulled the trigger. I did it to hurt him, I guess. But then I saw your face ... and I hated myself more than ever. I regretted it before I even finished pulling it. Your mother ... she was a beautiful person."

He was sobbing helplessly now.

Riley found it easy to guess the rest of his story.

Wade Bowman had lost himself forever in an agony of guilt and shame. He'd probably been homeless for years—perhaps ever since he'd killed her mother.

Bowman calmed a little and wiped his face and eyes with his sleeve.

Then he reached under a blanket.

He took out a tarnished snub-nosed revolver and held it out to

209

Riley.

"Here," he said. "I've wanted to give it to you for a long time."

Riley took the revolver. It felt startlingly heavy in her hand. She knew that she was holding the very weapon that had killed her mother.

"It's loaded," the man said. "Kill me if you want to."

Riley shuddered.

It would be easy to do.

But did she want to kill him? What *did* she want really, after all these years?

Justice, she thought.

And now justice was well within her reach There was no statute of limitations on murder. She could arrest him. She could bring him to trial. She could send him to prison, surely enough.

She thought of Shane, of what she was becoming. And she realized that she could stop becoming. If she killed this man, it would be too late.

But if she walked away, she could save herself.

She could arrest him, of course. But she looked around, at the squalor in which he lived, and she realized that a life here, under this bridge, was far worse than anything prison could offer.

Why send him to prison when he'd already passed a lifetime in hell? Through some mysterious agency, justice had been done a long time ago.

She turned around and walked away. She heard the man's sobs echoing under the bridge. She got back into her car and started to drive. She remembered crossing a river not far back. She found the bridge over the river and parked again.

She walked out onto the bridge and looked into the water.

She remembered something that some philosopher had once said—something about how one who fights with monsters should be careful not to become a monster.

She couldn't remember the words exactly, except for the last few words:

"And if you gaze long into an abyss, the abyss also gazes into you."

She looked down into the filthy river full of industrial pollution.

She thought …

The abyss and I now know each other very well.

She threw the gun into the water, got into her car, and started on the long drive home.

She sobbed the entire way.
It was over.
Finally, after all these years, it was over.

CHAPTER FORTY ONE

Riley got home very late that night. She slept long and hard, almost until noon, and when she finally woke up, she was surprised to realize that she actually felt good. She got dressed and went downstairs.

She heard Gabriela singing in the kitchen, which made the day seem even better. When Riley went in for coffee, Gabriela was happily working at what looked like a very special meal.

"Hello, Gabriela," she said.

Gabriela turned toward her and smiled.

"Buenos días, Señora Riley," she said. "You are very late, but that is good. Could I fix you some breakfast?"

"No, don't trouble yourself," Riley said. "It looks like you're fixing something special."

"Sí, did you forget? *Señor* Blaine and his daughter are coming to dinner tonight."

Riley smiled. Yes, she had forgotten. But it gave her something to look forward to.

She poured herself some coffee and got a sweet roll. She went to the living room and turned on a movie channel. It was showing an old movie that she'd seen but couldn't remember the name of. She didn't much care at the moment.

As she sipped her coffee and ate her snack, she remembered her experience yesterday with the abyss—and how the abyss had looked back into her.

The abyss was still there in the back of her mind.

It would probably never go away.

But it seemed to have receded.

She could distance herself from it, at least for now.

Life goes on, she told herself.

And she was ready for a break. Now that she, Bill, and Jake had solved the Matchbook Killer case, she wouldn't be expected at the BAU for a while. Since she had also suffered a bash to the head, she might not have to go in for a couple of weeks.

She finished watching the movie, read a few magazine articles, then watched the end of another movie. She had almost dozed off again when she was awakened by a flurry of activity.

The girls had gotten home from school.

April looked at Riley with concern.

"How are you doing, Mom?" she asked.

Riley remembered—the last time April had seen her, she was tearing out of the house on a mysterious errand.

She smiled, hoping that April wouldn't ask questions.

"I'm fine," Riley said.

Fortunately, both girls' minds were on other things.

"Mom, Blaine and Crystal are coming to dinner!" Jilly said.

"You've got to get dressed!" April said.

Riley looked down at her slacks.

"I am dressed," she said.

April and Jilly rolled their eyes at each other.

"OK," Riley said with a sigh. "I'll go change."

But before Riley could get up from the couch, the doorbell rang.

Jilly answered the door and simply stared at whoever was outside. Then Jilly turned and walked away, leaving the door open.

Ryan came inside.

Jilly left the room, and April crossed her arms.

Ryan looked shocked.

"This isn't a very pleasant greeting," he said.

"What do you expect?" April asked.

Ryan looked at Riley, as if appealing for her to intercede.

She had no intention of doing anything to make him feel comfortable.

She said, "I guess you're here to pick up the stuff you left in my room and the bathroom. I've packed it all up. You'll find it upstairs next to the bedroom door."

Ryan's mouth dropped open a little.

Then he went upstairs.

Jilly came back and the girls immediately made themselves look busy doing homework. When Ryan came back downstairs with his things, they paid no attention to him at all.

"I'll check back with you," Ryan said to Riley.

Riley simply nodded. She half-wanted to make some snide remark, but decided it wasn't worth the effort.

Ryan's coming and going was getting to be boring and routine—especially his going. She hoped that he'd be gone for a good long while.

When Ryan left the house, April jumped up.

"Your slacks, Mom! Change your slacks! Something casual but interesting. Put on those new palazzo pants."

Riley went upstairs, found the slacks April had mentioned, put them on, and looked in the mirror. They were soft and flowing, and

Riley liked the way they looked on her. Then she put on a knit top that accentuated her curves.

She was putting on sandals when her phone rang.

When she answered, she heard a young and eager voice say, "Agent Paige, my name is Agent Jennifer Roston. I hope this is an OK time to call."

Riley smiled.

"Of course it is," she said.

She'd heard of Jennifer. She was new at the BAU, but word had gotten around that she was full of promise—much like Lucy Vargas. Her scores at the academy were said to be off the charts. She'd already been on an assignment in Los Angeles and received commendations for her work there.

"Hello, Jennifer," Riley said. "Welcome to the BAU. I'm looking forward to our work together."

Jennifer laughed a little nervously.

"Well, Agent Meredith already put me on a little assignment. I think he put up a message about it in your BAU account."

"I haven't checked my computer yet," Riley said.

"I'm supposed to do some research on an old adversary of yours—Shane Hatcher."

Riley stifled a gasp.

"Good," she said, trying to sound pleased. "I'm glad to know someone's on that case."

"Right now I'm at Quantico going through files. I can't access some of the ones I need."

Riley knew that those files were her own research on Hatcher.

She said, "Well, since you're on the case, I'll be glad to give you access."

"That would be great. I'd like to start going through those files tonight. I want to figure out how he's supporting himself on the lam. He must have contacts. Or money."

"I'm sure he has both," Riley said. "I'll log on in a few minutes and open things up for you."

Jennifer thanked her and told Riley her ID code. Riley welcomed her to the BAU again, and they ended the call.

Riley immediately logged on to her BAU account. There was, indeed, a message from Meredith explaining that Jennifer was assigned to work on the Hatcher case.

"Please help her however you can," Meredith wrote.

Then Riley went to her own files about Hatcher. She went through them one by one, changing the access to include the new agent. She knew that some of them contained the kind of financial information Jennifer might be looking for.

When she got to the last file, she hesitated.

It was titled "THOUGHTS."

In it was a collection of personal thoughts and observations— also including financial information that would surely lead right to Hatcher.

Riley hadn't followed up on that information.

All along she'd told herself that she was too busy.

But now she realized—she hadn't wanted to follow up. She hadn't wanted to destroy Hatcher's access to resources that protected him.

Whatever she may think of him, however much she might even think she hated him, he'd been a great help to her.

And there was something in him that she respected.

He was hard and, in his own way, honorable.

Like my father, Riley thought.

She found that she was rather relieved that Jennifer Roston would be taking over the case. It wouldn't be on Riley's shoulders as much as it had been. Maybe she wouldn't have to lie anymore. Maybe she wouldn't feel guilty for not arresting him herself.

But here was a file that could end everything for Hatcher—and given the personal nature of what it contained, for Riley herself.

She debated a long time, feeling herself about to cross a line that could change her career forever.

Then she made a decision.

She selected the file and entered a code.

A message came up on the screen:

Delete file THOUGHTS?

She clicked yes. The file disappeared.

Riley shuddered.

She knew that she had just committed a criminal act. To protect an escaped criminal, she had broken her vows as an FBI agent.

It was a profoundly unsettling thought.

She and the abyss were staring at each other again.

And she had a sinking feeling that it wouldn't be the last time.

ONCE STALKED
(A Riley Paige Mystery—Book 9)

"A masterpiece of thriller and mystery! The author did a magnificent job developing characters with a psychological side that is so well described that we feel inside their minds, follow their fears and cheer for their success. The plot is very intelligent and will keep you entertained throughout the book. Full of twists, this book will keep you awake until the turn of the last page."
--Books and Movie Reviews, Roberto Mattos (re Once Gone)

ONCE STALKED is book #9 in the bestselling Riley Paige mystery series, which begins with the #1 bestseller ONCE GONE (Book #1).

When two soldiers are found dead on a huge military base in California, apparently killed by gunshot, military investigators are stumped. Who is killing its soldiers, inside the secure confines of its own base?

And why?

The FBI is called in, and Riley Paige is summoned to take the lead. As Riley finds herself immersed in the military culture, she is amazed to realize that serial killers can strike even here, in the midst of the most secure location on earth.

She finds herself in a frantic cat and mouse chase, racing to decode the killer's psychology. Yet she soon discovers she is up against a highly-trained killer, one that may, even for her, be too deadly an opponent.

A dark psychological thriller with heart-pounding suspense, ONCE STALKED is book #9 in a riveting new series—with a beloved new character—that will leave you turning pages late into the night.

Book #10 in the Riley Paige series will be available soon.

Blake Pierce

Blake Pierce is author of the bestselling RILEY PAGE mystery series, which includes eight books (and counting). Blake Pierce is also the author of the MACKENZIE WHITE mystery series, comprising five books (and counting); of the AVERY BLACK mystery series, comprising four books (and counting); and of the new KERI LOCKE mystery series.

An avid reader and lifelong fan of the mystery and thriller genres, Blake loves to hear from you, so please feel free to visit www.blakepierceauthor.com to learn more and stay in touch.

BOOKS BY BLAKE PIERCE

RILEY PAIGE MYSTERY SERIES
ONCE GONE (Book #1)
ONCE TAKEN (Book #2)
ONCE CRAVED (Book #3)
ONCE LURED (Book #4)
ONCE HUNTED (Book #5)
ONCE PINED (Book #6)
ONCE FORSAKEN (Book #7)
ONCE COLD (Book #8)
ONCE STALKED (Book #9)

MACKENZIE WHITE MYSTERY SERIES
BEFORE HE KILLS (Book #1)
BEFORE HE SEES (Book #2)
BEFORE HE COVETS (Book #3)
BEFORE HE TAKES (Book #4)
BEFORE HE NEEDS (Book #5)
BEFORE HE FEELS (Book #6)

AVERY BLACK MYSTERY SERIES
CAUSE TO KILL (Book #1)
CAUSE TO RUN (Book #2)
CAUSE TO HIDE (Book #3)
CAUSE TO FEAR (Book #4)

KERI LOCKE MYSTERY SERIES
A TRACE OF DEATH (Book #1)
A TRACE OF MUDER (Book #2)
A TRACE OF VICE (Book #3)

Collingwood Public Library
COLLINGWOOD PUBLIC LIBRARY
06 NOV 02 04:39pm
THIS IS YOUR DATE DUE REMINDER

Patron id: GREEN, Kalli

Way out west : on the trail of an
30075001281308   Due: 27 NOV 02 *

The opening of the Canadian West.
30075000320982   Due: 27 NOV 02 *

Battle for the West : fur traders
30075000122438   Due: 27 NOV 02 *

CALL 445-1571 TO RENEW ITEMS